PUDDIN' ON THE BLITZ

PUDDIN' ON THE BLITZ

Tamar Myers

This first world edition published 2019
in Great Britain and the USA by
SEVERN HOUSE PUBLISHERS LTD of
Eardley House, 4 Uxbridge Street, London W8 7SY.
Trade paperback edition first published
in Great Britain and the USA 2020 by
SEVERN HOUSE PUBLISHERS LTD.

British Library Cataloguing in Publication Data
A CIP catalogue record for this title is available from the British Library.

ISBN-13: 978-0-7278-8915-7 (cased)
ISBN-13: 978-1-78029-642-5 (trade paper)
ISBN-13: 978-1-4483-0341-0 (e-book)

All Severn House titles are printed on acid-free paper.

Severn House Publishers support the Forest Stewardship Council™ [FSC™],
the leading international forest certification organisation.
All our titles that are printed on FSC certified paper carry the FSC logo.

Typeset by Palimpsest Book Production Ltd.,
Falkirk, Stirlingshire, Scotland.
Printed and bound in Great Britain by
TJ International, Padstow, Cornwall.

DEDICATION

This book is dedicated to the memory of my beloved office staff, all of whom were buried in the back garden since I wrote my previous mystery. They were as follows:

The first one to pass was Pagan, my basenji dog. She was my office manager, and official greeter. Her 'cubicle' was an armchair placed by a sunny window. Basenji dogs originated in the Democratic Republic of the Congo area of western Africa. They cannot bark because they are a 'natural' breed. Wolves cannot bark, either. The ability to bark was a trait that was selected for ancient man. However, like wolves, basenjis can howl. Basenjis can run as fast as whippets, they move like thoroughbred horses, and they are fearless. In Africa they are even used for hunting leopards. One day at a Florida dog park, our little basenji female, all of twenty-seven pounds, stood her ground and stared down two massive wolf-hybrids that came charging at her from across the park. One snarl from Pagan, and a display of her canines, sent the wolf-hybrids racing back to their owner, who should not have had them in the park to begin with.

Next to leave a hole in my heart was my beloved Kasha, my Bengal cat. He was my typist and random editor. He enjoyed wandering back and forth across the keyboard, making interesting additions to my document, especially when it was time for him to be fed. Kasha loved to wrestle with his big sister, Pagan, and would initiate the play. To watch a cat and a dog play like that, time after time, and clearly enjoy it, was truly a privilege.

Our final loss was Dumpster Boy, whose office role was to help my printer do a quicker job. He would grab emerging pages with both front paws and pull for all he was worth. Dumpster Boy was born in a McDonald's dumpster in mid-December and spent his first year living at the veterinarian's office. The 'Boy' in his name derives from the TV show The Waltons. I believe that our pets generally behave the way in which they have been treated. I treat mine with kindness, and they have always been gentle to me and everyone else. That said, animals do have a pecking order, and poor Dumpster Boy arrived in our home as a one-year-old rescue, whereas the other two had been with us since they were babies. That put poor Dumpster Boy on the bottom. Nevertheless, this gorgeous twenty-one-pound marmalade tabby never hissed or raised a paw to his detractors. He remained sweet and loving to the end. His only fault, if it could be said to be one, was that he purred so loudly that at times it made it hard for me to concentrate. Although on the plus side, upon occasion it did drown out my husband's snoring.

ACKNOWLEDGMENTS

I would like to thank my publisher, Kate Lyall Grant, at Severn House for the opportunity to write this book. I would also like to thank my editor, Sara Porter, for her wisdom and skilful guidance. I also wish to acknowledge my copyeditor, Anna Harrison, for a bang-up job, and of course, the art department for a scrummy cover.

In addition, I am very grateful to my literary agent of twenty-seven years, Nancy Yost, of Nancy Yost Literary Agency. I want to give a shout-out to the entire team there, most especially Sarah, Natanya and Cheryl.

ONE

I don't look good in orange. I don't even look good when I'm holding the fruit. If you ask me, it's not even a colour that a God-fearing woman should be caught dead in, lest she be barred from the Pearly Gates. Trust me, you won't even find the word 'orange' in the Bible. Even harlots don't wear orange; they wear scarlet. Besides, there is not another word in the English language that rhymes with it. That should tell you something right there.

'No thank you, dear,' I said to the policewoman. 'I much prefer the colour blue – a bright, royal blue, to be specific. On second thought, the Bible does exhort us to dress modestly, so perhaps I should choose navy. What do you think?'

The officer snorted. 'I think that a self-righteous woman like yourself shouldn't commit murder in the first place. If ya didn't want to dress like a perp, then ya shouldn't have gone and killed someone.'

'Oh, *please*,' I said, 'I didn't kill anyone. Surely you can tell by the way that I'm dressed that I'm a mild-mannered, Conservative Mennonite woman. Just look at my skirt; it extends well past my knees. My blouse has elbow-length sleeves, and it is buttoned primly up to my neck. My sturdy Christian underwear alone covers more of my body than your guard outfit does. You know, if I removed the pleated white organza cap from atop my pile of braids, and was able to force my thin, withered lips into a proper smile, I might possibly be able to sneak into a Mormon community undetected.'

Officer Twaddlebottom's response was to snatch the hideous jailhouse garments from my hands and throw them violently down on a metal cot so narrow that a strand of spaghetti would have had trouble getting comfortable on it. Then she whipped a pistol out of a gleaming black holster and gave its barrel a good whack against the door of the cell.

'Get undressed,' she snapped.

'Hold your horses, dear,' I said. 'Do you realize how stupid that was? Your gun might have accidentally discharged, sending a bullet ricocheting off these bars until it eventually struck and killed me. Then *you* would be the one true murderess standing here today. No offense, dear, whereas I am unnaturally tall, and perhaps a wee bit on the gaunt side, you, on the other hand – I say this with utmost Christian charity – are more than a mite broad in the beam. Although, to be fair, you do have remarkably trim ankles, unlike mine, which would make a mother elephant proud to see them on her newborn calf. I trust that you give the Good Lord thanks on a daily basis for those mere twigs on which you manage to balance so precariously.'

Apparently Officer Twaddlebottom did not take kindly to being chided for having ignored basic gun safety etiquette. 'Strip!'

'Excuse me, dear?' I said.

'You heard me, *dear*. Take off all your clothes. Down to your bare skin. Leave nothing on.'

'Now?' I asked incredulously.

'No, silly,' Officer Twaddlebottom said. 'I was only teasing. At any minute the maid will bring us some refreshments. After that, if you've been a good girl, we can hop on the bus and take a trip to the famous Pittsburgh Zoo.'

I may not be the brightest bulb in the chandelier, but then again, neither has my pilot light gone out – if one will allow me to mix metaphors. I'm not a betting gal, but if I were, I'd almost be willing to bet dollars to donuts that there was no maid waiting in the wings with refreshments, and no trip to the zoo planned either. Given that I've so often been accused of being a pessimist, I decided to shake things up this time and trust in the Good Lord that everything would work out for the good.

'You are one fabulous lady, Miss Twaddlebottom,' I cooed. 'Snacks and a field trip into Pittsburgh sound awesome.'

Unfortunately, the policewoman was not moved by flattery. 'Strip,' she barked.

'No, ma'am,' I said resolutely.

'*What* did ya say?'

'I said, dear, that I will *not* strip. Not in front of you – certainly not in front of that camera over there. No one except my dearly beloved husband and the Lord Almighty have ever seen me naked. The Lord, by the way, has X-ray vision and can see through clothes. Even yours.'

'Amen to the Lord's X-ray vision,' said Officer Twaddlebottom. 'But that handsome hunk of flesh that you're married to now, him ain't the only man who seen you naked, is he, Mrs Yoder?'

'Really, dear,' I said, trying to stall for time, 'your grammar is atrocious. I'm sure that you must find it demoralizing, getting passed over for promotions on that account, but never fear, today is your lucky day. As a very wealthy woman, I would be happy to pay for a private English tutor.'

'Mrs Yoder, are you trying to bribe me?'

I clutched my meagre bosom in mock dismay. 'Why I never! If I was trying to bribe you, then I would dangle a ten-day Hawaiian cruise in front of—'

'Shut up!'

'Yes, ma'am,' I said. 'See? My lips are closed. Sealed with glue. I've shut my yap. I've sprung my trap. I've—'

'Not one more word,' the officer growled through clenched teeth. 'Do you understand?'

'Certainly.'

Officer Twaddlebottom closed her eyes and began breathing quite rapidly. Frankly, her behaviour was vaguely reminiscent of that exhibited by my hunky husband, whom I call the Babester, at those moments when he achieves . . . uh, marital bliss. I'm fairly certain that Officer Twaddlebottom was not on the same page. At last, my tormentor opened her eyes.

'Ya mean to say that your hunky husband is the only man to ever see ya naked?' she asked incredulously.

I recoiled like a stepped-on snake. 'Frankly, dear, that's none of your ding-dong business – oops, sorry, I didn't mean to swear.'

Officer Twaddlebottom smirked. 'Such a potty-mouth on ya, Mrs Yoder. But really, a sexy woman like ya must have had oodles of boyfriends. Surely one of them guys got lucky enough to make it past your sturdy Christian underwear.'

'Really?' I said, as I patted my mound of coiled braids. 'You think I'm sexy?'

'Like a *Playboy* centrefold – excepting one wearing granny clothes. Speaking of them clothes, Mrs Yoder, ya gotta ditch them things for the inspection.'

'What inspection?' I said. Then I remembered observing Amish horse auctions, so I pulled my withered lips away from my gums using four fingers. 'See! I still have all of my teeth, except for my wisdom teeth.' I shuffled my feet and whinnied. 'And my hoofs are in good shape as well – uh, except for a bunion on my right big toe.'

Officer Twaddlebottom didn't even chuckle. 'You're an idiot, ya know that? I gotta inspect ya where the sun don't shine.'

'No way!'

'Way. Gotta check and see that you ain't trying to smuggle in any contraband.'

Now it was my heart that was racing, but I kept my eyes wide open because I sensed that I was fighting a losing battle, one that was going to end very badly for me. Even before routine visits to my gynaecologist I require a long, relaxing bath, followed by downing a tranquilizer with a glass of warm milk. For those who wish to judge me on my pharmacological habits, try walking in my size forty-four moccasins first – or just size eleven, if you're an American.

'Look here, Officer Twaddlebottom,' I said, 'what you're suggesting is absolutely disgusting. You ought to be ashamed for even thinking such a filthy thing, much less uttering that remark. Just be glad that I'm not your mama. If I was, I'd wash your mouth out with soap, and then hang your tongue out to dry in the chicken yard.'

'*What* did you say?'

'Oops. Never mind me, Officer Twaddlebottom. I'm an idiot. Remember?'

'*Why* in the chicken yard, Miss Yoder?'

'Never mind. It's just a silly little saying that I heard somewhere.'

'Bet me. It's because chickens will eat *anything*, including chicken. Am I right? They would somehow manage to tear my tongue to shreds in a heartbeat, even if it was hanging from a clothesline.'

'Uh-oh.'

Officer Twaddlebottom took a couple of steps closer, which put her far too much inside my comfort zone. As she proceeded to scrutinize me with sudden, intense interest, I struggled futilely to ignore the plethora of scents to which I was being subjected:

cigarette smoke, beer, last night's liver and onions, scrambled eggs with green peppers and anchovies, and liquorice candy. I could scrub the woman's tongue with a strong lye soap for an hour or more, but I doubt if I could get even a single one of my chickens to peck at that thing.

'You have very nice eyes, dear,' I said, desperately hoping that flattery would work as well on her as it does on me. 'We both have mousy brown hair, but your beady dark eyes set it off nicely, whereas my faded blue eyes just make me look blah.'

Much to my relief, Officer Twaddlebottom took a giant step back. 'It *is* ya, Auntie Mags, ain't it? At first, when I read your name, I weren't sure that it was ya, because back when I knew ya, ya was skinny like a beanpole. But now ya is all filled out and has them sexy curves goin' on. Ya know, them feminine thrills. Of course now I am right positive that it is you, on account of ya made up that little saying about ya washing my mouth out with soap, and then hanging my tongue up to dry in the chicken yard. Ya did it because I was always swearing at ya and calling you a big poop-head.'

I cocked my poop-free head. I squinted. I pushed my eyelids apart, and then pulled them into slits, in vain attempts to enhance my vision. Then as I tried staring through eyeglasses formed by thumbs and rounded index fingers, an ancient memory bobbed to the surface of the soup that filled my cranium.

'Little Bindi, is that *you*?'

My jailer's response was to throw herself into my long, spindly arms and begin to pat my back. The second her wide, meaty hands began hammering away at my ribcage, I began to slap her vigorously in return. A clueless observer might be forgiven for assuming that we were both choking on inedible prison food, and gallantly trying to save the other person's life. However, someone who was born and raised either Mennonite or Amish would instantly recognize our strange behaviour as nothing more than hugging. How this custom started is anyone's guess. One theory is that folks who share my DNA are genetically unable to maintain physical contact with another human being for more than a nanosecond without having wicked thoughts enter their heads.

Officer Twaddlebottom stopped her senseless patting first. 'Ya

can give up on the back-slapping, Auntie Mags. I ain't gonna
burp like no baby. I ain't eaten cabbage nor drunked me a cola
all day.'

'Good one,' I said, as I tried to reconcile two images in my
mind. The last time that I'd seen gun-toting Officer Twaddlebottom,
she'd been a skinny nine-year-old Mennonite girl named Belinda
Rickenbacker for whom I'd been babysitting since she was six.
As far as I could remember, she'd always had dark beady eyes
and skinny ankles. The girth around her middle was new but
eating Mennonite cooking for an additional thirty-nine years
could easily explain that.

'Auntie Mags,' said Bindi Twaddlebottom, 'you and me
has ourselves a whole lot of catching up to do, but first I gotta
process ya just like everyone else.'

'Fine,' I said pleasantly. 'Pat me up, pat me down, pat me to
the right, then pat me to left, and then put your left foot in, and
shake it all around. But just so we're clear, I will not submit to
being strip-searched quietly. I will resist with every fibre of my
old, practically emaciated body. Any bruises on my thin and
easily damaged skin that may result from the drubbing that
ensues will, of course, be attributed to you. I am quite sure
that our left-leaning liberal media will be happy to take advantage of this savage and senseless attack on a pillar of the
Mennonite community, and said media will label it as prisoner
abuse. *Elder* prisoner abuse.'

Bindi laughed. '*Drubbing!* Ha! Ya ain't changed at all, Auntie
Mags. How old was ya when ya was babysitting me back then?
Like thirty, or something? Ya was using them big old-fashioned
words back then, and ya still are.'

I snorted and shook my horsey head. 'The last time that I sat
for you, I was twelve. You, on the other hand, have always had
atrocious grammar. In fact, the worst grammar I've ever heard a
Mennonite use. Possibly even anyone at all.'

'Yeah?' she said. 'Well, here's a newsflash: I ain't no Mennonite
no more. I'm C of E.'

'*Excuse* me? You're a couple of vitamins?'

'There's no excuse for ya,' Bindi said, then grinned. 'Them
initials stand for Church of England. Ya see, I married me an
Englishman, a bona fide Englishman. Me and Oliver ran into each

other by accident – a car accident. It was, like, kinda my fault, but he was real gentleman about it on account of he was an English. Back then Oliver was a student at Penn State University.

'Anyway, it turns out he ain't no ordinary Englishman neither, but one of them upper-class Englishman, the kind that don't open their mouths when they talk – just like Prince Charles. Anyway, we was married a year later in England. After he graduated, I took me some lessons on how to be a proper Anglican and all. Now I get to drink me some real wine at Holy Communion – like every week, if I wanna, and not just some stupid old grape juice twice a year. Well, except that to be a proper English lady ya ain't supposed to go to church, because almost nobody there does, on account of they prefer to stay home, drink their tea, and eat their strumpets.'

'I've heard that their strumpets are very tasty,' I said, giving her the benefit of the doubt. She was, after all, the international traveller.

'Yeah, but not as tasty as their tarts,' she said.

'And to think that you've eaten both,' I said. 'Bindi, what an exotic life you've lived compared to mine. I thought your surname Twaddlebottom sounded foreign.'

'Oh, Auntie Mags, the English are *never* foreigners, no matter where they live. Even here, Oliver refers to my family as foreigners, and we been here for over 280 years, same as you.'

'I know, dear. All of our ancestors came over on one of two ships, the *Charming Polly* in 1737, or the *Charming Nancy* in 1738.'

'Yeah. Anyway, our name ain't pronounced like ya read it; ya supposed to pronounce it "*Twddlbttm*." I don't know about them Welshes, or them Scotches, but if ya is upper-class English, ya ain't supposed to pronounce no vowels. Oliver said that's because they ain't supposed to move their lips when they talk. Anyhow, a lot of them upper-class English – them that lose their fortunes – come to America and become highly successful ventriloquists. So that's what my Oliver is: a ventriloquist. Ya ever hear of the famous Randy Upwood? That's his stage name.'

'No.'

'Oh,' she said, sounding quite devastated.

'I'm sure he's very talented,' I said kindly, 'what with all that

practice mumbling. I read once in a gossip magazine that some
aristocrats are actually quite frightened of accidentally stepping
on rusty nails in their horse paddocks. If they were to contract
lockjaw, their condition might never be diagnosed until it was
too late to do anything to treat it.'

Belinda nodded vigorously. 'That's why I insist that my Ollie
– that's what I call him – wears thick-soled cowboy boots at all
times, and denim jeans.' She paused. 'Ollie's performing right
here in Bedford, at the Black Margarine, if you wanna see him
perform when ya make bail.'

'Is the Black Margarine a – uh – bar?'

Belinda sighed. 'Jeezers wheezers. And here we was having
a normal conversation like, so I almost forgot you was still a
Mennonite. Yeah, it's a bar. But ya don't hafta drink, ya know?'

'I know. But still, no can do.'

'Hey, here's something I bet ya don't know: even lower-class
ventriloquists, *and* American ventriloquists – who are all lower
class, on account of them just being American – ain't none them
able to throw their voices.'

'Is that right,' I said, just to be agreeable, even though I did
know it.

'Yeah. That's what we in the industry *want* you to believe.
But it's all just a delusion.'

'That is absolutely fascinating, dear. But back to the business
at hand, now that we have reconnected after thirty-seven years,
and submitted to the back-whacking ritual that our people refer
to as hugs, I trust that you can see your way to relaxing the rules
a wee bit for your dear old Auntie Mags.'

Officer Twaddlebottom bit her lip as she considered my
request. 'OK,' she whispered at last, 'but you can't never tell
nobody, and ya still gotta put on these prison duds, or else it's
my job.'

I took the hideous outfit from her. 'But the bottom half of
this outfit is pants,' I *hiss*pered, which is to say that I hissed
softly. 'You know that Conservative Mennonite women don't
wear trousers.'

Bindi rolled her beady brown eyes; it was a skill that she'd
honed as a sassy urchin. 'I know, and that's crazy, if you ask
me. My mother's ancient – she's like, seventy, and she ain't never

worn no pants. But look, here's the thing: they don't make no skirt with stripes. And your prayer cap has gotta go too. Them's the regulations.'

'But that's religious discrimination!'

'No, it ain't. Last year I booked me a whole busload of nuns – some of them was even holding babies – and every one of them had to put on these here prison scrubs and lose them whippets they wear on their heads.'

'That's *wimples*, not whippets.'

'Yeah, whatever. My point is that I can't make no exceptions. *Zilch. Nada.*'

'Waah!'

'Shh. Auntie Mags, ya don't want Sheriff Stodgewiggle to hear ya hollering, do ya?'

You can bet your bippy that I didn't want to see neither hide nor hair of that corrupt sheriff ever again. To that end I closed my mouth tighter than a clam at low tide, took a deep breath and disobeyed Deuteronomy 22:5. By the time I had finished exchanging my sensible Christian garments for the sinful jail duds, I felt more degraded than a cat must feel when dressed up in doll clothes. At least a cat doesn't feel shame.

'Bindi,' I said, feeling my eyes puddle up, 'when you bring the library cart around, please make sure that it's stocked with a variety of reads. Maybe a good book will help take my mind off my dire situation.'

Bindi was gracious enough to merely snicker. 'Auntie Mags, this ain't no state prison; you're in the county jail, in a holding cell, just 'till your arraignment which some high muckety-muck has seen fit to arrange for tomorrow. You don't get no library cart, see? But there's this book somebody left out front that I've been passing around back here. It's pretty beat up by now – if ya want it, ya can have it, but just for tonight. It's a mystery novel called *Death of a Real Estate Magnet.*'

'Did you mean to say "*Magnate*"?' I asked.

'Ain't that what I said?'

'I'm sure you did,' I said quickly. 'I love reading mysteries, and this one already sounds puzzling to me.'

'Yeah, but ya see, I didn't actually read it, Auntie Mags. I did hear a review of it on one of them liberal radio stations one day on my drive into work. The reviewer said that despite the fact that some readers might complain about there being too much character development in the front half of the book, that part is actually packed with clues. And it's their loss if they miss them.

'Also, the reviewer said that some folks might say that the author used too much humour. Ya know, like she wrote a stand-up comedy routine with a dead body thrown in. Again, the reviewer lady said that if the reader didn't appreciate the humour, that was their loss.'

'Hmm. I don't like that at all,' I said. 'Never blame the reader! I'm a mild-mannered woman with a heart full of love, but I hate how some writers get us to spend our hard-earned money on worthless pieces of paper. Why, I'd throw that book across the room, and if I was outside, I'd throw that waste of time all the way to Disneyworld in Florida. That reviewer really hikes my hackles.'

'Yeah? Well, ain't ya something, Auntie Mags! But throwing that book is exactly how it got so beat up.'

Bindi's description of the *Death of a Real Estate Magnate* was, if anything, understated. The book was missing its front cover and first thirty pages. On just about every page at least one word or phrase had been underlined or highlighted, and on many there were doodles and even obscene drawings! But the worst offense, in my humble opinion, is that the last fifteen or so pages had also been ripped out. And this from a mystery! Yes, there were clever clues, despite too much character development in the first half, and far too many silly puns and alliterations, but reading it was all for naught because I never found out who the killer was. I felt like banging my head on the bars of my cell, but the only thing less attractive than a horsey head is a horsey head with long, narrow indentations.

Instead I did what every other reader of that ding-dong-dang (that's as bad as I can swear) book before me had done. I threw that book across my cell. And then I stomped on it – again and again and again.

TWO

I suppose that I should start at the beginning. You already know that I am a mild-mannered, Conservative Mennonite woman. My grandparents were Amish, and because the Amish marry strictly within their own sect, I am related by blood to almost eighty percent of them. The end result is that I am, in fact, my own cousin. Whenever I eat a sandwich outdoors, even by myself, it can be said that I am on a family picnic.

My hunky husband, on the other hand, is of the Jewish persuasion. He's a retired heart surgeon from New York City who chose our beautiful corner of Southwestern Pennsylvania to call his forever home. Gabe and I have two children: a fourteen-year-old daughter, Alison, and a two-year-old son, Jacob, whom I gave birth to when I was forty-nine.

We live in the idyllic Pennsylvania Dutch village of Hernia, population 2,169 ½ (Greta Lehman is pregnant again), where everyone knows everyone else's business before they even know their own. Case in point, twelve people knew that Greta Lehman was expecting a baby before her husband did, thanks to my blabbermouth cousin, Sam, who sold her the pregnancy testing kit at our village grocery store. The villagers live in single-family homes, many of which are two-story, Victorian-style wooden houses that sit on large lots. The streets are lined with large, mature trees and most of them lead back to Main Street. We have no stoplights, only stop signs, and many, or most, of our vehicles are horse-drawn buggies. There are hitching posts in front of the grocery store, the police station, and the feed store.

I live with my family four miles outside this throbbing hive of activity. Our home is situated on the remnants of a dairy farm, in the shadow of Buffalo Mountain. When I was in college, and my sister Susannah just ten years of age, our parents were squished to death between a truck carrying expensive athletic shoes and another one carrying unpasteurized milk. The farm had been in our family for well over a hundred years and had been paid for, and our parents' life insurance policy provided us money to live on for a while, but when it finally ran out, I had to take a long hard look at my options.

I had already sold off most of the dairy herd after our parents were killed. Now I could also sell off the land, and move into town, but then what would I do? *Or*, I could marry some farmer whom I didn't love, and immediately begin breeding little farm hands. *Or* – and this idea I lifted from a magazine at my doctor's office – I could turn our nineteenth-century farmhouse into a quaint bed- and full-board inn, in order to capitalize on the tourist trade. After all, it is a little-known fact that Lancaster, Pennsylvania does not have a monopoly on the Amish.

Our farmhouse had five upstairs bedrooms that were available for guest use, but only two baths, neither of which were en suite. But that last fact was of no consequence. I'd read about or heard enough travel stories to know that even in many old European hotels, one had to toddle down the hall in robe and slippers at night to get to the loo. What's more, in some of those places the rooms were scarcely larger than the beds, and the rooms lacked climate control, and what passed for reading lights were so dim that even a cat couldn't see to lick its tail.

Whereas my rooms were so spacious that one could dance in them (although that would surely be a sin), they were each equipped with their own thermostat, and one could actually see to read even the smallest print (in a proper King James Bible, to be sure). As for my lack of loos – well, whoopy-doo, as we say on this side of the Pond. You see, I'd concluded from those European reports that tourists will put up with just about any amount of discomfort as long as they can view it as a cultural experience. And when they travel to Asia, they lower the comfort bar even further. Why else might one stay in a dive in Delhi, a hovel in Hanoi, or a shed in Sri Lanka and still rave about one's 'awesome' experience? In some Far Eastern places, a hole in the cement floor is your toilet, thank you very much.

If folks wanted a cultural experience, I reasoned, I could give them that. I named my establishment The PennDutch Inn. Pennsylvania Dutch, incidentally, is the term that refers to the descendants of the Germans and German-speaking Swiss settlers, and their dialect, which is still spoken today by the Amish.

If folks wanted to pay outrageous European prices while they enjoyed their cultural experience, I would give them that opportunity as well. Yes, ma'am, and Bob's your uncle, my guests were going to be treated to the ultimate hotel experience. By paying mere hundreds of dollars more, these fortunate few would be able to make their own beds, clean their own rooms, clean the lavatory on a rotational basis, set the dining room table, wash up after meals, muck out the cow barn, milk my dairy cows, gather eggs, feed the chickens, sweep out the chicken coop, and replace the straw on the floor. That was just for starters, mind you – there were other chores that were more seasonal.

Take my exorbitant room prices, add my scheme for selling chores, throw in a pinch of Continental attitude (French works the best), and voila, one has the perfect recipe to appeal to the tastes of America's much-talked about one percent. Few people would be willing to shovel cow dung for two dollars an hour, but slap a fake Amish bonnet on a rich woman's head, and charge her two hundred dollars to haul manure out of the barn in a little wheelbarrow, and she'll be in 'hog heaven' – so to speak.

My business was almost an instant success. Then the murder of a United States Congressman occurred at The PennDutch Inn, and the story made national news. I held my breath for five minutes, thinking that surely no one would want to stay where there had been a violent death. But *au contraire*. God bless America, and Americans' obsession with violence – oops, perhaps a good Christian woman such as myself ought not to say that. What I meant was that virtually everyone and their pedigreed poodle was scratching at my front door begging to get on my waiting list. That meant that I could pick and choose my guests.

Just a word of advice to any would-be hoteliers, be their businesses large or small: very famous people travel with large retinues – as well as quite obnoxious people whom they call 'groupies'. Also, one might consider carefully the wisdom contained in this original saying that is sometimes attributed to Auntie Mags: 'Even the Prince of Wales puts on his knickers one leg at a time.' In case this message is still obscure, I shall be blunt. People are people, and bad behaviour is no respecter of either class or money.

Unfortunately, I am often the first person to ignore my own

words of wisdom. Also, as a simple woman, I am highly suscep-
tible to flattery, which scripture warns us to guard against in
Romans 16:18.

Approximately three months before I was thrown into the
slammer, the daughter of my erstwhile nemesis called on me. I
would have been better off pretending not to be home, but my
hunky husband deprived me of that chance by bounding to the
door. A moment later he called out, 'Hon, you have a visitor.'

'Is it a fat elf with white chin whiskers?' I asked playfully.

'No, Mags,' he said, a mite crossly, 'it's *not* my mother.'

That's when the chirpy voice of Hortense Hemphopple lilted
through the front entrance like that of a giant sparrow. Indeed,
were the common house sparrow able to mate with a human
(a sin for which they would *both* have to die according to Leviticus
20:16), their progeny would surely resemble, in all respects, our
own dear Hortense. I am not suggesting that the woman sports
a great deal of feathers. The overall avian vibe that she gives off
might have something to do with her short, spikey hairstyle,
which never fails to remind me of a badly plucked chicken, with
half its quills remaining. And I suppose that if she ditched the
yellow lipstick, her protruding upper lip might look less like a
beak – if only when viewed from the front. But then who am I
to judge?

Bless her heart, Hortense Gelato Hemphopple is the daughter
of Wanda Sissleswitzer Hemphopple, the woman who tried to
kill me and my beloved daughter Alison two years ago. Wanda
and I had been feuding since the third grade when she dipped
my braids in her inkpot. So as not to paint an unfair picture of
little Wanda, I must divulge here that the poor child was an
orphan, who was being raised by a bachelor uncle who couldn't
be bothered to wash a little girl's hair, much less braid it. My
mother, on the other hand, was a neurotic, obsessive-compulsive
neat freak who braided my hair so tightly every morning before
school that my eyes were in veritable danger of popping out and
rolling under the bus.

All through elementary school I hated Wanda, but I lacked
both the nerve and the creativity to strike back in kind. Finally,
I got my revenge in high school when, unbeknownst to Wanda, I
tucked a frankfurter down inside her beehive hairdo while she

dozed off during maths. Wanda shampooed her hair only twice a year, so she discovered the meaty addition to the matted mop atop her noggin only when the odour brought her some unwanted attention, a lot of it from flies.

After Wanda graduated from high school, her uncle moved to another state, and I am told that he eventually married a much younger woman, or a series of much younger women. It didn't matter to me. What mattered was that Wanda stayed behind in Hernia, where she married Geezer Hemphopple, who stacked lumber at Weirton Woods over in Bedford. Three months after they were married another car struck Geezer's car broadside, and he conveniently passed away at once, leaving Wanda a widow with a sizable insurance settlement. Overnight Wanda went from being nearly penniless to having enough money to open The Sausage Barn. In a very short time, the restaurant was a tremendous success. If living well is truly the best revenge, then Wanda certainly got revenge on everyone who snubbed her in high school, whether on account of her poor hygiene, or her rude behaviour.

As long as I'm being honest, then I have to admit that it wasn't just timing or insurance money that got Wanda her measure of success. That gal really knew how to cater to changing American appetites: make it greasy, or make it sweet, just make individual servings large enough to feed a family of four. Wanda's restaurant, The Sausage Barn, had a reputation for dishing up the best breakfasts in a fifty-mile radius. But then, after Wanda tried to kill us, right there in her restaurant, the place was closed down until further notice. With Wanda safely locked up in the state penitentiary for a minimum of ten years without parole, the fate of the empty building was a mocking reminder of how good we all had it.

At any rate, it came as quite a shock to find my would-be killer's progeny perched on my doorstep. As for Hortense's state of mind, I can only guess that the poor dear appeared to be shaking from nerves. Judging by her demeanour, I thought that she might turn and fly away at any second.

'Don't just stand there, Hortense,' I said kindly, 'unless you plan to chip in on our heating bill. It's been so cold lately we've been getting sympathy cards from penguins.'

'Really?' she said.

I nodded vigorously, which isn't the same as lying. 'Although frankly their writing is so illegible, they may be writing anything. I do wish they'd learn to text.'

Hortense smiled wanly. 'Miss Yoder, might I please have a few private minutes of your time?'

'Certainly. Just remember to give them all back when you're through.'

'What?'

'Never mind, dear. Step right into the parlour and I'll close the door. My family knows not to disturb me in there – well, all except for Granny Yoder, and she's dead. Granny almost never bothers anyone but me, and Police Chief Toy.'

'Boogers,' Granny said from within the parlour.

I waited long enough to see if Hortense would react to Granny's less than melodious voice. She didn't, so I ushered her into my cosy, warm parlour and directed her to sit on a hard, wooden chair with a seat that sloped forward. I intentionally designed this piece of furniture to be uncomfortable; guests should be doing chores, not lounging about on their backsides.

'I'm sitting here,' Granny said.

'Then move,' I said.

'OK,' Hortense said meekly. She headed to another chair, one which I'm proud to say was equally as uncomfortable.

'I'm sitting here now,' Granny chortled. Indeed, she was, for ghosts are capable of what I can only describe as time travel.

'Make yourself like a statue and freeze,' I said crossly.

Hortense did just that. More accurately, the young woman's limbs were locked in mid-step, her elbows akimbo, reminding me of the Pompeii victims I'd seen pictured in *National Geographic*.

'No, not you, dear,' I said to my caller. 'Please just sit anywhere.'

'You better not pass gas,' Granny growled when Hortense eventually did sit squarely on the old woman's lap – well, in a manner of speaking, since ghosts don't possess solid laps. It might be said that the two women occupied the same space at the same time. I fully realize that talk like this sounds far-fetched to some, but unless one has ever personally encountered an Apparition-American, one would be wise not to pass judgment.

'Now dear,' I said pleasantly, 'normally I might offer my guests tea and biscuits, but given that your mother tried to murder me and my sweet young daughter, and that you are an uninvited visitor, all that I am prepared to serve are fried ice and doughnut holes.'

Hortense nodded nervously. 'Fried ice and doughnut holes sound lovely.'

'Boogers,' Granny said. 'This girl has the brains of a lamppost.'

Although I hate feeling guilty, it is one thing that I am rather good at. 'I'm sorry,' I said. 'I thought that you knew: fried ice and doughnut holes are nothing more than water and air.'

Hortense frowned. 'Uh – I don't get it.'

'Never mind, dear,' I said. 'Please just tell me the nature of your visit.'

THREE

'It's about the restaurant, The Sausage Barn.'

'Ah, the site of my near demise. I made it quite clear to your mother that giving me half ownership of the restaurant was not going to make me drop the charges of attempted murder against me and my daughter Alison. Besides, it is not in my purview to dismiss homicide charges. It's not like she tried to snatch my purse, for goodness' sake. Not that it would have made any difference, because she did manage to kill that best-selling author, Ramat Sreym. And then after I refused her bribe, your mother wrote me an excoriating letter from prison because I testified against her. Talk about *chutzpah*!' Being married to a Jewish man, I pronounced it correctly, as if clearing my throat.

'You pronounced it wrong,' Granny said. 'Pronounce the first two letters like in "church".'

'How would *you* know?' I said.

'Calm down, Magdalena,' Granny said. 'You're making a scene.'

'I will most certainly *not* calm down,' I said.

Poor Hortense started to wilt before she'd even had a chance to state her business. Clearly, an audience with Magdalena Yoder and her unseen granny was no place for the faint-hearted. She fumbled inside her purse and eventually fished out a wrinkled piece of paper.

'This is a notarized copy of a new deed which makes us co-owners of The Sausage Barn. And' – she paused to suck air through her bottom teeth – 'Mama gave you sixty percent ownership and me just forty percent.'

I studied the paper. 'That's quite true, dear, but what has that to do with the price of steel in China?'

'What?' Hortense said.

'Boogers,' Granny said.

'It's *not* boogers,' I snapped in a most unchristian manner. 'The saying used to be "tea",' I said in a gentler tone. 'What I really meant to say is that I really don't understand why we are having this conversation. That restaurant is history. It's done. The Sausage Barn is kaput. Your mother – and I'll give her that much credit – was a genius at selling sugar and grease to a willing public from a most unsanitary kitchen. Even the cockroaches died in her kitchen, and she never had to worry about rats in her storeroom – they texted each other to stay away.'

Hortense smiled wanly. 'Yeah, Mama told the dishwasher to just rinse the dishes in hot water, and then wipe them down with a rag. No need to waste soap or electricity on running the machine or taking the time to actually handwash them. Do you want to know why all the plates were yellow?'

'No,' I said. 'I don't. But why is it that the Board of Health never shut her down? Never mind. Ask a silly question, you get a silly answer. Money talks, and that's the way it's always been.'

Hortense squirmed, causing Granny to make a face. 'Miss Yoder, I came here today to ask for your help.'

At last, we were getting somewhere. 'You mean like a handout?'

'No, ma'am. I don't want your charity.'

'Good for you, girlie,' Granny said.

'Then a loan?' I said. 'That's what banks are for.'

'Miss Yoder, I want – I need to get the restaurant back up and running again, because I need any income generated from it to help pay for my school expenses.'

'School expenses?' I said. 'Are you taking college courses at night? It's never too late to get an education, I always say.'

'No, ma'am,' Hortense said. 'I'll be a full-time freshman at Penn State. I start in just a week. I paid my tuition with the last of Mama's savings. Everything that was left after her trial.'

I tried not to stare too hard. 'No offense, dear, but aren't you a little long in the tooth to be a regular college student? Say twenty-five, pushing thirty?'

For the first time her yellow lips spread into a cartoon smile. 'That's the same expression that Mama says about you: "long in the tooth".'

I gasped. 'Why I never! Your mama and I are the exact same age. Come to think of it, she's six days older than I am.'

The yellow crescent morphed into a small 'o'. 'I didn't mean to offend you, Miss Yoder. Anyway, I'm nineteen.'

'Hmm,' I said. 'It's probably just because you have such

a sincere-looking face. Sincerity can often be confused with maturity.'

'What do you mean?'

I gave her my slowest and wisest smile, hoping against hope that she didn't read it as me being constipated. 'At one time or another we are all fortune cookies without messages,' I said.

Hortense tugged on her lower lip, getting its bright yellow colour on her fingers. 'And what is *that* supposed to mean?'

'It means that at other times, we are all wonton in search of soup,' I said.

Hortense nodded, perhaps acknowledging my wisdom. Or perhaps she was dozing off. I clapped my hands loudly.

'OK, dear,' I said, 'let's get on with the show. That is to say, you may continue.'

'Thank you, Miss Yoder. At Mama's trial you said that you'd forgiven her, because Jesus told us to forgive each other like a bazillion times, and somewhere I heard that you and Mama even used to be childhood friends.'

Granny giggled as I jiggled pinkies in both ears, just to make sure that they were in working order. If not properly addressed, a stopped-up ear, like a blocked toilet, can lead to avoidable regret.

'Did you read that on Facebook, dear?' I said.

'No, ma'am. Maybe I just got that impression from the fact that Mama used to talk about you all the time.'

'I'm sure she did,' I said. 'But the truth is that even when we were little girls, your mother and I were enemies. Sadly, we stayed that way. I know that sounds wrong for a church deacon to speak of herself as having an enemy, but there it is.'

'Oh, get over yourself,' Granny said. 'In my day there weren't any women deacons.'

'You know something, Miss Yoder,' Hortense said, 'when I came here, I was afraid of you because of all the things that Mama used to say – because she really did talk about you all the time – but you're much nicer than I expected.'

I leaned in her direction. 'What exactly did she say about me? Tell me the worst thing she ever said.'

Hortense scratched her receding chin. 'Hmm. That you're the Whore of Babylon?'

'Why the rising inflection, dear? Are you unsure that she said that, or are you a secret Canadian?'

'Huh?'

'Never mind.'

'Miss Yoder, *please* help me get the restaurant back up and running. I'm begging you to. You're like the world's smartest businesswoman. If you don't want it to be a breakfast place anymore, you can turn it into an Amish style restaurant. They're very trendy along the interstate highways now. Or maybe an organic vegetarian restaurant. Or even Chinese. Anything. But I have every confidence that if you set your brilliant mind to it, whatever it is will be a huge success.'

'Get behind me, Satan!' I cried.

Hortense unknowingly shrank into Granny's open arms. 'Huh?'

'Never mind, dear,' I said. 'Perhaps I got a mite carried away. It's just that flattery can lead to pride, which is a major sin.'

'And she has a big enough head as it is,' Granny said.

'On the other hand,' I said through gritted teeth, 'I do enjoy a challenge. What would you say to a hybrid restaurant, the likes of which have never been seen in these parts before? In fact, I doubt that there has ever been a restaurant like one that I am about to propose in the history of the world.'

'Hubris,' Granny said. 'I told your mother to name you that. I said it had a nice feminine sound.'

'I think that a hybrid restaurant sounds exciting,' Hortense said, sounding a tad unenthusiastic. 'But like what?'

'Well,' I said, with slow, dramatic emphasis, 'a fusion of Chinese and Amish cooking.'

Granny snorted. 'Sounds disgusting. I'm about to lose my lunch just thinking about it.'

'Hmm,' Hortense said. 'Hmm, well.' Leave it to the young to be more diplomatic.

'It's all in the marketing,' I said. 'The same folks who bought pet rocks a generation ago, and then food for their pet rocks, will buy Amish-Chinese fusion.'

'Wait a minute,' Hortense said. 'People actually bought pet rocks? Where did the rocks come from? Were they from mass breeders, you know, like pebble mills? Or from licensed Rock Hound shops?'

'Ding-a-ling,' Granny said.

'You *are* joking,' I said to Hortense. 'Aren't you?'

'Miss Yoder, because I was an only child, and because Daddy was always drunk and lying in some gutter, Mama bought me lots of stuff that she didn't need to. I not only had a pet rock, but a pet rock house that came with a pet rock *rock*ing chair.

'But about the restaurant, I really meant it when I said that I know that whatever you do with it will be a huge success. So Miss Yoder, again I'm begging you to help me. Will you?'

'*Oy vey*,' I said, having picked up that much Yiddish from my Jewish husband.

'*Pleeease*.' With that, tears the size of lollipops began rolling down her pallid cheeks.

'Don't you dare get me wet,' Granny managed to hiss without a single ess. (Ghosts can do that, but human characters in literary fiction should not.)

'But dear,' I said, 'I have a teenage daughter who can be a handful, a retired husband who's finally so into being a father that he practically ignores me – OK, let it be said that Magdalena Yoder loves a good challenge.'

'Sucker,' Granny hissed. That time she was so sibilant that she sounded like a bag full of snakes.

'Hallelujah!' Hortense shouted, betraying her affiliation with a church less sedate than we Conservative Mennonites.

'Now hold your horses, dear,' I said. 'There are going to be some ground rules. For starters, I am *not* a team player. I am good at delegating, for instance—'

'She means bossy,' Granny said.

'Miss Yoder,' Hortense said, sounding worried, 'I'm sorry about my outburst a minute ago.'

'Outburst, cloudburst, what does it matter? We're on the same team now, dear.' Ideas for implementing this innovative projective were firing off in my brain like a bag of perfectly heated popcorn.

'I can't tell you how relieved and happy that makes me, Miss Yoder.' She paused to lick her yellow lips, and perhaps fluff her hypothetical feathers – or were they petals? 'I'm just curious about one thing, and that is where are we going to find a qualified cook to add the Chinese element that we need?'

'Problem solved, dear,' I said.

'*You?*'

'Heavens no! I can't even fry ice without burning it.' I paused, giving her ample time to let her laugh at my little joke, but when she didn't even crack a smile, I ploughed on.

'However, I know a superb cook, who is an extremely hard worker. She isn't Chinese, but she *can* read. That's really all one needs to be able to do – read a recipe and then tweak it here and there as needed. You see, the recipes will need some fine-tuning to adjust for local taste and which ingredients we can – or can't – procure, but that is where the talent part of being a good cook comes in, and my gal has it in spades.'

Hortense frowned. 'But where are we going to get the recipes? I don't mind travelling around Pennsylvania, Miss Yoder, during my term breaks, but I don't see myself going to China. Besides, I don't have a passport.'

'No need to go anywhere – other than cyberspace.'

'I should go to Outer Space?'

'Ding-a-ling,' Granny said as she twirled a finger bone in tight circles next to the right side of her skull.

'Maybe *you* should go to Outer Space,' I snapped at Granny. 'After all, you're halfway there already.'

'Miss Yoder,' poor Hortense said, her face clouding over, 'did I do something to offend you?'

'Oh no, dear, not at all. Just wait until you get to be my age, then you'll sound every bit as confused. What I meant to say is that one can download tons of recipes for Chinese food from the internet. When do you want me to get started?'

Hortense hopped spritely to her feet. 'Immediately! Oh Miss Yoder, I can't tell you how excited this makes me. Now I can show Mama that I'm not the birdbrain that she always said that I was. With your help I'm going to make Asian Sensations ten times more successful than The Sausage Barn ever was. Just you wait and see.'

'*Asian Sensations?*'

'Like I said, just you wait and see.' With that the girl practically flew out of my parlour and the front door and beyond.

'*Whew,*' Granny said. 'Now that she's off my lap I can breathe again.'

'Boogers,' I said.

FOUR

News of an exotic restaurant coming to Hernia spread like influenza through a crowded church. Overall, our citizenry was happy to learn that the shuttered Sausage Barn was going to reincarnate as Asian Sensations. There were folks like my dear husband, a New Yorker, who rejoiced at the prospect of eating exotic fare, although he immediately expressed his doubts that the food would resemble anything like the 'real' Asian food he'd had the privilege of eating in the cosmopolitan city of his birth.

Now it is true that some in our community disapproved of a so-called 'foreign element' intruding into our culture through our stomachs. Others were merely afraid of going into total withdrawal, having already suffered through months of deprivation from starch, sugar and grease. Nonetheless, those folks who, on principle, were against an Asian restaurant coming to our town, were still quite happy that it was going to happen regardless, because it gave them a legitimate excuse to complain. In a community as small and inbred as ours, whinging has been elevated to an art form, and it brings meaning to many a lonely person's life.

The one complaint that I did not expect came from my Jewish mother-in-law, Ida Rosen, a.k.a. Mother Malaise, the self-styled nun who'd invented a religion based on the Theology of Disengagement. The sisters' beliefs are simple: all is lost, so nothing matters, and therefore it behoves one to simply stop caring about *anything*. Irony, however, is not Mother Malaise's forte. A year ago, she hired a bus to take her and the other forty-four nuns (two of whom are men!) on an evangelizing tour, spreading the gospel of apathy across Pennsylvania, Ohio, and Michigan. The turnout was pathetic, and no converts were made.

I think that one *should* wonder just how this recently invented religion came about, because its premise is absolutely ridiculous. And how could something that was concocted so recently be taken seriously? If I had half an imagination, I could think up my own crazy cult, declare myself its prophetess, and then go in search of a bunch of idiots who would swallow my codswallop, hook, line and sinker.

In this case, one should especially wonder why the founding of Mother Malaise's new religion coincided with my wedding to the Babester. When I made it quite clear that the woman who sneaked into our bedroom every evening to sniff her son's pillow would not be living with us at The PennDutch Inn, Ida flew into a rage.

'You vill pay for dis,' she railed repeatedly, at a volume I've heard topped only by a bull in heat.

'Ma,' Gabe said repeatedly and plaintively. I would never divulge my *most* private thoughts to a living soul. That said, although Gabe can function like a bull in some respects, when it comes to his mother, he acts more like a lamb led to the slaughter.

'Mrs Rosen,' I said, 'your son has graciously consented to give you his house, which is directly across the road from The PennDutch Inn. It's a historic house too. The Miller family built that the same year that my ancestor, Jacob the Strong, built the original part of my farmhouse that is now my inn.'

'Yah?' Ida scoffed. 'Vell, eet eez a dump.'

'Ma,' Gabe said.

'Mrs Rosen,' I said, with all the sweetness of a rhubarb stalk, 'then perhaps you should return to New York.'

'New York? Vhy?'

'Magdalena!' Gabe said.

'Because you have often spoken of how much you miss your friends there and' – I bit my tongue for a millisecond – 'how much better your life there was than it is here.'

'Den mebbe I vill!'

'Magdalena!' Gabe said.

'Yes, dear?' I said sweetly.

'This is my mother whom you're trying to banish. She's the woman who gave birth to me.'

'Yah! Tirty-six hours of de most terrible pain to birz dis man.'

'Nonsense. I know for a fact, unless your son's a liar, that he weighed a mere six pounds and that he slid out like a sardine packed in oil. From start to finish, your labour lasted less than an hour. *His* son, however, weighed—'

'Magdalena, I order you to stop haranguing my mother! Can't you see that she's crying?'

I stopped, all right. Given that I ran out of what I still considered to be Gabe's house and didn't stop until I arrived breathless back at The PennDutch Inn. At that point I was so exhausted both physically and emotionally that I couldn't have harangued an orangutan, even if I had had a banana on a pole and he'd been locked in a cage. In a word, I was a wreck.

Things have a way of sorting themselves out, and *eventually* the Babester and I got back on track. However, I stood my ground, and refused to let that four-foot-nine, not-so-divine mother of his move in with us. Likewise, she kept her word and set about making me pay for attempting to sever the apron strings of steel that connected her to her 'baby boy'.

I will give Ida credit for one thing: she can, if properly motivated, think fast on her cloven hooves. The day following our altercation, she drove into Hernia and posted a notice on the cork board just inside Sam Yoder's Corner Market. Incidentally, Sam is a double second cousin of mine, so the fact that he allowed her to do this is nothing short of betrayal. At any rate, the notice read as follows:

DO YOU JUST NOT CARE ANYMORE?
If your life seems hopeless, and you no longer care about anything, or anyone, then why bother trying to fit in with the rest of the world? If you're tired of the rat race, of trying to keep up with your neighbours, of politics – then get away from it all!
Come join the Sisters of Perpetual Apathy. We are a cloistered group of nuns who will be occupying a new Sister House opposite The PennDutch Inn. We welcome everyone over age eighteen to join, regardless of previous religious affiliation. Although our regular habits will be hooded brown robes, within the confines of the convent nudity is encouraged. Postulants are given names that connote a defeatist attitude.
Our only doctrine is: 'We don't care!'

The note also included Ida's contact information. It's been said that misery loves company. That explains why, before all was said and done, the world's shortest Jewish mother morphed into a mother superior, one Mother Malaise, with a devoted flock of forty-four nuns. Sadly, her followers weren't sincerely apathetic; they were Hernia's broken-hearted (who even knew that we had so many?). The majority of them were lonely widows, one as young as twenty-nine. Seven of them were divorcees (which is a status quite rare in these parts), and three others were women who had recently come out as lesbians (a phenomenon totally unheard of hereabouts), and of course the two men. The latter were Agnes Miller's elderly uncles, who were habitual nudists and had the bad habit of shucking their habits. Finally, Mother Malaise gave up and allowed all of her followers to prance around in their birthday suits within the confines of the convent. Mercifully, they had to wear her hideous costumes when they ventured into the outside world.

Take it from me, our conservative community was scandalized by this home-grown cult of women in coarse monks' robes and cheap plastic sandals, or less, who had so easily broken their baptismal vows to follow after the *genuine* Whore of Babylon (in other words, a New Yorker). You can bet your bippy that everyone, including my new groom, blamed me for this state of affairs.

All things must come to an end, I guess, including ill will. After a while the citizens of Hernia realized that they needed my largess, or else their property taxes would have to be increased. Likewise, the Babester concluded that he needed to come around in his thinking, if he were ever to have another opportunity to bellow like a bull again within the confines of our boudoir. Of course, Mother Malaise and her minions were quite another story.

It wasn't until after I gave birth to her grandson, Little Jacob, and had him circumcised according to the ancient Covenant, and by a proper rabbi, that she ceased to torment me. From that day forward, she merely badmouthed, pestered, and purposely annoyed me. But hey, I'm not one for complaining.

At any rate, Mother Malaise, a.k.a. Ida, showed up uninvited for breakfast just two days after Hortense came calling. On such occasions I am inclined not to answer the doorbell, but Alison dotes on her adopted grandmother, plus Gabe is tied to his mother's apron with strings of steel. Only Little Jacob, bless his toddler heart, pays as little attention to the woman as he does to developing table manners. Fortunately, on this particular day I had already managed to eat most of my meal before she appeared at the kitchen door, like a giant grey moth, shrouded as she was in her homemade habit and ridiculous wimple that extended in back as far down as the top of her buttocks. I scanned down to her extra wide men's sandals for signs of smashed dahlias. The woman is no respecter of boundaries, physical or emotional, and she often takes a shortcut to the door through my heirloom flower bed.

'*Nu*,' she said, 'vhat eez dis I hear about you, Magdalena, and a massage parlour?'

'*What?*' three of us exclaimed in unison. Little Jacob, however, was too busy rubbing soggy cereal into his hair to be startled by his grandmother's question.

'Zees Asian Zinsations. Eez a house of zin, yah?'

'What is *zin*?' Alison asked.

'Finish drinking your milk, hon,' Gabe said. 'Then go wait out front for the school bus; it will be here any minute.'

'Ah, do I hafta?' Alison moaned.

'Yes, you have to, dear,' I said.

'I ain't no baby,' Alison said. She gulped most of what was left in her glass, belched loudly, and stomped the long way out of the house, which took her through the dining room and guest reception area. Much to my surprise, Ida refrained from commenting on Alison's rude behaviour.

'Explain – *dear*,' I said to Ida, and not quite endearingly either.

First Ida shuffled around to Little Jacob's highchair and pinched both his cheeks. This supposed act of affection set the wee one bawling in pain, which in turn caused his papa to howl in sympathy, and finally, Yours Truly succumbed to temptation and scowled in indignation.

'Mother Malaise,' I said, pointedly using her religious name, 'how many times have we told you that it hurts him when you do that?'

True to character, my mother-in-law ignored my question.

'*Nu*, Magdalena, so vhy is you bringing zees streep club to our Hernia and not telling me?'

'*Strip* club?' Gabe said.

'Yah, das is vhat I said. Asian Zinsations – first dey strip, and den dey massage. I see a club wiz dis wary same name on dee U-boob.'

'You mean YouTube?' Gabe said.

His mother shrugged, an action which brought her shoulders up to her ears and which nearly forced off her wimple. Ida has no discernible neck, and her cleavage extends upwards almost to her chin. Nonetheless, the habit that she wears, which is of her own design, features a disturbingly deep neckline.

'Vhatever,' she said. 'My point eez dat zee Sisters of Perpetual Apathy und I are in need of foonds und vould like to verk der?'

'Ma,' Gabe said calmly, 'what are *foonds*? Is that a Yiddish word?'

Ida glared at her son. 'Money! Vee need money because my son, zee rich heart surgeon, don't give us enough to live on.'

'*What?*' I cried. 'Gabe, are you giving my money to that – that – cult? The Apostles of Doom?'

'Eez Sisters of Perpetual Apathy,' Ida said. 'Und vhat my son does vees *heez* money, eez *heez* business.'

'Ma,' Gabe said plaintively, 'please don't antagonize my wife.'

Ida's dark eyes flashed. 'Yah? Und who came first? Dee chicken, or dee egg?'

I raised my arm. 'I know, I know. I learned the answer to this in Sunday school when I was a little girl: the chicken came first. It says in Genesis 1:20-21 that God created birds, but it doesn't even mention eggs in the creation account, so it's safe to assume that eggs came later.'

'*Oy*,' Ida said. 'Vhat a genius dat one,' she said to Gabe, but clearly referring to me. Then, in what can only be described as a miracle, she swivelled her head completely around in my direction, and in the process lost her accent. 'So, Magdalena, I was thinking. You're going to be needing women – and a few men – to work in your strip joint and, of course, to give the massages. Well, as you know, my ladies and I, and my two men, dispense with wearing our habits every Tuesday, which is our Sabbath. This means that we are very comfortable with our bodies—'

'It's a restaurant!' I bellowed. 'Asian Sensations is a restaurant.'

Ida blinked. 'Yah? Are you *sure*?'

'I'm positive. I'm a million percent sure.'

'Vhat a pity!' Ida caught a corner of her wimple in a pudgy fist and tossed it over her shoulder in what I assumed was supposed to be a suggestive manner. Then she tugged her deep scoop neckline even lower and came dangerously close to unleashing her behemoth of a bosom.

'Ma!' Gabe said.

'Ma!' Little Jacob said from his highchair as he pounded his plastic spoon on its tray. 'Ma, Ma, Ma!'

At least Ida had the decency to pull up her neckline before blowing her grandson a kiss. 'Vell den,' she said to me, 'I vill be your cook, yah?'

'You vill be my cook, *no*,' I said.

'No, no, no,' Little Jacob sang happily as he resumed pounding his spoon, for 'no' was his new favourite word. 'No, no, no, no, no, no.'

'You tell her,' I said, in a moment of unchristian behaviour. 'And look here, since you managed to convince a group of retirees to join your cult, all of them on Social Security, and some with supplementary pensions, as well, plus you're living in a house which your son gave you, free and clear, then you should be living pretty high on the hog.'

Ida gasped with horror, feigned I have no doubt. 'Did dis vomen yoost call me a pig?'

Gabe held his handsome head in his well-groomed surgeon's hands. 'No, Ma. It's an expression that means that you should have plenty of foonds – *funds* – to live on.'

'Yah? Eez dat so?' Ida closed her eyes tightly. I could see her straining to squeeze out tears, but her ducts apparently were as dry as the Sahara desert.

'I guess that settles it,' I said with forced nonchalance. It took almost as much straining on my part not to sound exasperated.

Ida opened her eyes and wiped imaginary tears away with the burlap sleeve of her food-stained habit. 'Mebbe vee have political expirations, und vee need extra money for dee campaigns.'

'Come again?' I said.

'She means *aspirations*,' Gabe said.

'Or maybe you're just bored,' I offered.

'Yah,' my nemesis said. 'Dis could be. So, now I have another idea.'

FIVE

'You vill be needing vaitresses, yah?' Ida said to me in a much nicer tone. Fortunately I knew what she was up to. I am dense, after all, but I'm no Christmas pudding.

'Yes,' I said, 'but I need classy waitresses, not ones who dress like thirteenth-century monks.'

'Vas dat an insult?'

'No. It was only an objective description of the *shmatta* that you're wearing.'

Ida threw up her hands, precipitating an avalanche of baggy burlap sleeves that almost muffled her outcry. 'Oy! So now she speaks Yiddish already. I thought she was a *shikse*, Gabeleh.'

'She is, Ma. But maybe not for long.'

'Don't count on it, dear,' I said. I turned back to Ida. 'Who knows, maybe your son will see the light and become a Christian.'

Ida felt around through the thick fabric of her robe until she located the approximate location of her heart. 'Over my dead body.'

Before I had the chance to tell Ida just how happy I would be to gaze upon her corpse, my husband had to open his big mouth with a plan to appease his mother. At this point I feel that I should make it quite clear that not all Christians are as mean-spirited as I can be. Certainly, very few Mennonites exhibit my failings. More to the point, I doubt if any other Jewish mothers are as possessive of their sons as was Ida Rosen, and if they are, I don't see how any of their sons could be as compliant as was the Babester.

Therefore, I should be eternally grateful that before I could open my trap, Gabe clapped his hands to get his two feuding women's full attention. He clapped them hard, which got both his mother's and my attention. The gesture also inspired Little Jacob to clap his hands, which by then had been reloaded with wet oatmeal. The cereal splattered in all directions, delighting my son to no end. Frankly, I saw this as nothing short of God's grace.

'I think I have a solution,' Gabe said.

'To what?' I said. 'I'm not looking for an answer to a cross-word puzzle clue. Please allow me to reiterate my position: Asian Sensations is going to be a classy place with a dress code. Enough said. There, was that kinder this time?'

Gabe grinned. 'Yeah, maybe a bit. Mags, have you ever heard the song "Puttin' on the Ritz"?'

'Hey, I know that one,' Ida said, losing her accent again. 'It made its debut in a film back in 1930. Fred Astaire did some of his best dance moves in it. The lyrics go like this.'

Then to my utter amazement, the Babester grabbed his mother and the two of them began to dance around the kitchen, just as nimble and light-footed as fawns, and surely just as sinful as fauns, the mythical lustful hybrid which is an abomination just by itself. As for the dancing, everyone knows that we Mennonites are forbidden to have sex while in a standing position, lest that lead to dancing, so it is clearly forbidden.

But let us return to the rollicking Rosens; not only were they dancing, but they were singing. Gabe has a beautiful baritone voice. Shockingly, Ida's baritone voice is almost as pleasant. Little Jacob, a soprano, was still in the monotone stage, but he joined in nonetheless. Even I couldn't resist. You can bet your bippy that I didn't dance, although I might have tapped my right foot. Meanwhile, just to make sure that the Devil didn't get the wrong idea, I brayed some stanzas from one or two of my favourite hymns.

When the singing ended, Gabe led his precious Ma back to a chair where she made a great show of catching her breath. Because he didn't seem at all worried about the state of her health then, I concluded that the two of them had 'tripped the light fantastic' together before. I had heard that curious phrase used by my worldly sister Susannah, and subsequently looked it up in the library in Bedford. It refers to dancing, and its origin is to be found in a poem by John Milton titled 'L'Allegro'.

While Ida panted, and Little Jacob splashed merrily in the remnants of his breakfast, Gabriel and I had a breakthrough conversation. I take that back. If I had been a castle door, and

my husband a battering ram, then yes, one could rightly say that
a breakthrough occurred. As it was, I capitulated. I did so because
it was the course of least resistance, and I thought that it might
offer me at least a temporary reprieve from my mother-in-law's
incessant hectoring.

'You see,' Gabe explained, 'for the umpteenth time, the lyrics
to "Puddin' on the Ritz" are all about how what you wear can
change how you feel. Trust me, I've travelled extensively and
seen some grinding poverty. I've seen people living in shanties
that are constructed from corrugated iron and even cardboard
boxes, but to the best of their abilities, they keep their personal
space – their bodies and their clothes – clean and neat.'

'Yes,' I said, 'the Sisters of Perpetual Apathy might live in
crowded conditions, but that's by their own doing. And they have
money. They don't need "foonds".'

'I'm not finished making my case,' Gabe said.

'By all means, proceed,' I said. I know, sarcasm does not
become me. Perhaps if I had my tongue pierced like so many of
the young people that I see today, I would be reminded not to
let it wag unless it had good things to say.

To his credit, the Babester dove straight back into his spiel.
'I believe that the common denominator among these women is
depression. Not just sadness, or a case of "the blues", but real
clinical depression. Ma just happened to tap into their vulnera-
bility on that score.'

'What you're saying is that she's using them.'

Gabe flushed. 'Uh – that's a little harsh, isn't it? Never mind,
let's concentrate on something positive. We can take a lesson
from those song lyrics, and the slum-dwellers and dress up the
Sisters of Perpetual Apathy. Have them "put on the Ritz", so to
speak. I bet that they'd have a whole new lease on life, and you
might find yourself three presentable waitresses.'

Ida ceased to pant. 'Vhat? No vay! Vee vill not change habits.'

'Good habits, Ma, not bad habits.'

'Nu, you vant dat I should look frumpy like dis one?' Ida
pointed at me.

'Ma, *this one* is my wife!'

'Yah? Mebbe.'

'Gabe,' I said, 'I really don't have time for this.'

To everyone's astonishment, including his own, Gabe threw himself down on one knee and grabbed both of my hands in his. If it hadn't been for his strong grip, I would have toppled over backward in my chair.

For her part, Ida squawked in indignation.

'Da-dee down,' Little Jacob chortled. 'Da-dee down.'

'Hon,' the Babester said, 'I'm picturing smartly tailored tuxedos – styled for women, of course, so that they don't break any laws in Leviticus. Yeah, I know, a lot of people would interpret that verse as meaning that women should only wear dresses, and men should only wear pants. But the truth is, back in those days everyone wore robes and tunics, which are nothing more than dresses. Besides, pants are a heck of a lot more modest than skirts, because a man can't pretend to drop change on the floor, and then sneak a peek on the pretext of picking it up.'

'Harrumph,' I said. 'Jonathan Beiler tried that stunt in front of my locker in high school, but since I was wearing sturdy Christian underwear, he may as well have been looking up at a concrete wall.'

Gabe grinned. 'Same impression I had on our wedding night. Anyway, these tuxedos will be trimmed in satin, with pearl buttons, and the ladies will be wearing black patent leather pumps.'

'What about their hair?' I said. 'They're not going to wear their brown burlap hoods, will they? You know, to cover up what's left of their locks after being shorn with a big old hedge trimmer.'

Just when I'd almost been persuaded, Ida piped up. 'Eet vasn't a big old hedge treemers. Eet vas a leetle garden shears.'

Gabe squeezed my hands tighter. 'Focus, Mags. Please. I promise. No hoods, just normal, easy to maintain hairstyles. Pick any three of Ma's disciples whom you please. I'll drive them into Pittsburgh, to a first-class beauty salon, and see that they get a total makeover. Hair, nails, the works. I'll take them to a tailor and get them measured for their uniforms.

'What I don't know is if any of these ladies have ever worked in a restaurant or have ever had a job that involved serving the public. That might be something you might want to look for when you select your three – or however many that you want – trainees.'

'I'll think about it,' I said.

The Babester lowered his voice to a whisper. 'Sweetheart, by hiring your waitresses from among Ma's followers, you will be achieving three things: you will be getting Ma off your back, you will be calling off the pit bull named Ida Rosen, and you will be giving her one last reason to give you a pain in your *tuchas*.'

'OK,' I whispered. 'But I'm doing it for *shalom bah-yeet*.'

'Way to go,' Gabe said proudly. 'You remembered the Hebrew expression for "peace in the house". I'll tell Ma.'

He stood. 'Ma, my wife will employ three of your women in Asian Sensations. But Magdalena will do the interviewing and the hiring, and have final say on their uniforms. Is that understood?'

'Vhat is she,' Ida mumbled, 'a dictator?'

'I heard that,' I said.

'You didn't hear nothing,' Ida said.

'Ma,' Gabe said sternly, 'may I remind you that my wife can hear a rose petal land on a pool of water. So, I suggest that if you really want your ladies to work as waitresses, you start playing nice.'

'Nice, nice,' Little Jacob chanted. 'Pway nice.'

Despite the extraordinarily keen hearing attributed to me by my Dearly Beloved, I could only imagine that I heard Ida's dentures grinding in agitation. At the moment the ball was in my court; I could either swallow my pride, thereby pleasing my family, or else demand that the domineering, accent-switching mother-in-law from the Lake of Eternal Fire apologize and promise to toe the line – perhaps even to curtsy to me.

I forced my lips into what I hoped resembled a somewhat gracious smile. But without showing any teeth, I reminded myself. I'd recently read an article stating that the English are critical of the way we Americans insist on baring our fangs when we greet them. (Truly, the majority of us do not mean to eat them when we smile.) Since the English are the undisputed arbiters of good manners, I henceforth intended to mend my toothy ways, even if it did make me look constipated.

Having smiled correctly, I had to manually return my lips to speaking mode. 'Ida, dear, I am delighted to welcome three of your most *vivacious* ladies to the wait staff of Asian Sensations. I am quite sure that they will be a wonderful, *enthusiastic*, and, of course, *energetic*, addition to our well-oiled team.'

'Vhat?' Ida turned back to her son. 'You see? Dat vife of yours is crazy, I tell you. Zee Seesters vill not like zee oil, Gabeleh. Dey are not wrestlers; dey are noons.'

I try to be a good Christian, but that woman is like a burr under my saddle. '*Me* crazy? Gabe, your mother's wheel is spinning, but her hamster is dead!'

'Ladies, please,' my husband begged, 'leave me out of this. I love you both. Don't force me to mediate your little squabbles.'

'Und for zees I gave you life,' Ida said.

'And for this I gave you a healthy, happy, bouncing baby boy,' I said, 'one who will give you many grandchildren, both boys and girls.'

'*Oy gevalt*,' Ida said, throwing up her hands in submission. At least she set aside her accent for the third time. 'OK, you have a deal. But that's only because we Sisters of Perpetual Apathy really could use some outside income.'

'I don't understand,' Gabe said. 'I thought all your postulants had to sign over all their assets to the convent before they could officially be inducted into the – uh—'

'Cult,' I said.

'I vas hoodvinked,' Ida said. 'Some of zee vomen still sink dat zee Sisters is yoost for having a good time.'

'How many is some?' I asked hopefully.

'Mebbe most.'

My heart soared with gratitude (metaphorically, of course). That lasted just for a second, before my heart plummeted, weighed down by guilt and shame. Jews, and even Catholics, do not have the market cornered on guilt. Look the word 'guilt' up in any dictionary, and if 'Mennonite' is not listed as its first definition, I will eat a pair of my sturdy Christian underwear.

'Well, if it's any consolation,' I said, 'since this will be an upscale restaurant, unlike the former Sausage Barn, your ladies will be paid a fair hourly wage, plus they could receive some handsome tips. In fact, some celebrities have been known to go overboard and leave really extravagant tips.'

That's when the Babester actually stepped up to the plate. 'But

that will only happen, Ma, if your ladies act like they're "Puttin'
on the Ritz". No more of those blank stares that you had them
learn. Those expressions freak people out.'

'Fweek, fweek,' said little Jacob.

For the first time ever, Ida glared at her grandson. 'Shtop dat!'

'Ma,' Gabe said plaintively, 'he's just having a good time.'

'Yah? Is dat so?' I have absolutely no imagination, but even
then, I thought I observed wisps of steam emanating from Ida's
ears.

'You know that you're his favourite grandparent,' I said. I
grabbed her voluminous sleeve and tried to steer her from the
room, before she could recall that both my parents were dead.

'Yah?'

'You bet your bippy, dear,' I said. 'Now let's focus on the
money that your ladies will soon be bringing in. Nice, green
dollar bills.'

Ida smiled slowly. 'So now mebbe I'm not sorry dat I tell
zee man I vill not sell him zee convent.'

'What man?' Gabe said.

'Frum big religious real estate company,' Ida said. 'Dey vant
to make big tourist teem park, like zee Noah's Ark in Kentucky,
but much bigger. Dis von they call Armageddon. Vhat is
Armageddon, son?'

'Ma, it's nothing you want to get involved with. Trust me.'

Ida's head bobbled. 'No matter, because vhen he asks if
convent is inside Hernia, or outside, and I say "inside", den he
doesn't vant. Gabeleh, mebbe if not for your Magdalene, den I
make a lot of money.'

I released my mother-in-law's *shmatta*. 'Hold your horses,
You Homespun Holiness! I wasn't the only one who voted to
incorporate the former Miller farm into Hernia proper. By the
way, that could only have been done with the consent of the
present owner, who did so when he realized that his precious
Ma was going to turn a once productive Mennonite farm into a
rest home for a tribe of dropout geriatric whackadoodles.'

'Doo-dee, doo-dee, doo-dee, doo-dee.'

I'm sure that the majority of mental health professionals would
have been appalled at the grownups' behaviour that morning.
I'm also positive that they would have been quite certain that

Little Jacob had been profoundly affected by our bad behaviour, even though it was obvious that he was not in the least bit traumatized. Or was he? Perhaps only time would tell.

In the meantime, my revelation appeared to have stunned my querulous nemesis into silence. When she'd regained a modicum of composure, she shot daggers at her son, but not me, and then made a beeline for the back door. As for the Babester, he seemed strangely at peace. If pressed to hazard a guess, I would opine that my husband was relieved that his mother had finally been told of his betrayal. Of course, only a fool, or a psychiatrist, would dare wager that Gabe and his mother would let such a trifling thing as this come between them.

As for Little Jacob, almost immediately he started singing a new tune, and quite merrily as well. 'Daddy doo-dee, Daddy doo-dee, Daddy-doo-dah!' It had several more verses, all punctuated by giggles, but they all involved 'doo-dee', and were therefore not entirely spiritually uplifting.

Although Gabe has the patience of Job when it comes to his offspring, nevertheless, I didn't want to push my luck that morning. To that end I scooped up my sweet son and strode from the room. My exit could not have been better timed, because as I left through the door that opens into our master bedroom suite, a storm blew into the kitchen from the outside.

SIX

There is just so long that one can ignore the sound of slamming cupboard doors and the crash of pots and pans upon our cast-iron stove and polished concrete floors. Finally, I had to return to the kitchen and face the discordant music, if only to halt the wear and tear on my implements and furnishings.

The 'musician', as I knew it would be, was my kinswoman Freni Hostetler. The dear woman is Amish, which means that she is considerably more conservative than I am. Freni wears a longish black skirt, navy blouses, black bibbed aprons, and white pleated bonnets with the strings hanging untied over her collarbones. Outdoors she dons a black bonnet. Freni and her husband, Mose, travel only by horse and buggy.

Both Freni and Mose Hostetler are more closely related by blood to me than I am to Bindi Stodgewiggle. Freni and I could share the same shadow, were I not tall and spindly and Freni short and squat – bear in mind I say that with a good deal of Christian love. But even if I was cut off at the knees (as some have threatened to do to me), or Freni was stretched on a rack, we still wouldn't look alike, because Freni was my mother's contemporary. However, despite the fact that Freni is twenty-six years my senior, I am her boss.

The reason that Freni is usually found in my kitchen is because she works as my cook. Although she is many years past the age when many women would retire, Freni and her husband live with their only son and his wife, because the Amish don't believe in collecting Social Security. This poses a problem, because Freni can't stand her daughter-in-law Barbara. All that aside, there was absolutely no reason for a seventy-six-year-old woman to be bashing pots and pans about as if she were trying to exterminate an invasion of rats.

'What in tarnation is going on?' I shouted above the din. For the record, by then the Babester must have fled from the premises entirely, for he was nowhere in sight.

Using both hands Freni raised a cast-iron skillet to shoulder level and slammed it down on our six-burner stove. The exertion required to do this left her momentarily breathless. It also set into motion her not insignificant, and quite unfettered breasts (her sect does not believe in wearing brassieres). Freni is constructed rather similarly to Mother Malaise, but unlike the latter, Freni does have a hint of a neck. Also, Freni's mother was a Yoder, which means that she was cursed with the infamous Yoder ankles. That is to say, their circumference exceeded that of the aforementioned cast-iron skillet.

Having at last succeeded in getting my attention, Freni turned her fury on me. 'You, Magdalena! You are the problem.'

'*Moi?*' I asked sweetly. Quite frankly, I was astonished at the level at which she was expressing her anger. Amish and Mennonites have the reputation as a gentle and peaceful people, who seldom raise their voices. We are human, of course, and we do reach our limits when our buttons are pushed just like people everywhere. However, by and large, we strive mightily to live by the wisdom found in that Beatles' song 'Let It Be'. Yes, I know, I am a country bumpkin, and a Conservative Mennonite woman who ought to have never heard of this song, but bear in mind, that I am married to a liberal Jewish man from New York. So, let it be.

'What is this *moi* mean, Magdalena?' Freni said. 'You know that I do not speak this foreign language.' Already I could feel her wrath turning – away from me and to the contents of the white enamel pot at the back of the stove. In order to reach it, Freni had to drag over a low wooden stool and mash her bodacious bosom into the cold burners of the stove. Of course, she could have asked for my help, but she would sooner have died, and had I offered assistance, she most probably would have stomped out of the kitchen and returned home. She might even have threatened to quit working for me. No, she *would* have quit.

'Freni, dear, I say "*moi*" all the time. You know what it means.'

'So?'

'Hmm. Since you're already mad at me, I think I'll press my luck. Have you suddenly decided to go "fancy"?' Heaven forfend that any Amish person should dress in clothing other than that proscribed by the bishop or drive a buggy that didn't conform to the community standard. To do so, was to become 'fancy', and could eventually lead to shunning for unrepentant church members.

Poor Freni recoiled, snapping her head back as far as her hint of a neck permitted. 'Ach! What do you mean?'

'Well, as soon as you took off your black travelling bonnet, I noticed that you have a ring of rose petals tucked inside each of the pleats of your white bonnet. What's up with that?'

Freni whipped off her white bonnet and squawked with dismay. Then she muttered up a storm in Pennsylvania Dutch as she shook the white bonnet in all directions, but with the vigour one might shake a can of spray paint that needed a good mixing. Rose petals flew everywhere, drifting to my kitchen floor like giant pink snowflakes. By then my kinswoman was quite out of breath, so I pushed a sturdy chair under her enviably ample behind and bade her catch her breath. I also brought her a glass of cool, but not cold, water. I'd seen enough of Gabe's movies to know that water was de rigueur in traumatic situations, but Freni waved away my proffering.

'It must have been my granddaughter,' she said at last. 'The one I named after you. This is your fault, Magdalena.'

I was dumbstruck, but of course not for long. 'And just how old is Little Magdalena?'

'You know.'

'How old?'

'Six.'

'Aha. Were you dozing off on the front porch after breakfast again this morning, Freni?'

'So?'

'So? Your six-year-old granddaughter lovingly decorated your plain white bonnet with rose petals this morning. You blew the incident all out of proportion and blamed it on me. Clearly something is bugging you.'

'Bugging?'

'Yes. The way you were slamming pots and pans around when you came in – why, you were so worked up about something that I thought you were going to have kittens.'

Freni managed to drag a gargantuan enamelled pot off the stove and hoisted it onto our wide granite island. I suppose that she gave me the evil eye, although given the fact that she wears bottle-thick glasses, it is hard to be sure.

'Always with the riddles, Magdalena,' she said. 'Bugs and kittens. Who has time for such nonsense?'

'They're metaphors for asking what has gotten you so riled up.'

'Ach, again with the riddles.' Freni grabbed two handfuls of flour from a canister and expertly spread a thin layer across the long granite island. Next, she uncovered the white enamel pot and hauled out an enormous blob of semi-sticky dough. Although I am an essentially humourless woman, I couldn't help but snort with mirth.

'What is so funny now?' she demanded.

'The dough,' I said quickly. 'Last summer Gabe took us up to Lake Erie for a couple of days, and this big glistening lump of dough resembles the bellies of most of the men on the beach. Lots of the women too.'

Freni's head turned on her sliver of neck. 'They were naked?'

'No, dear. The men were wearing short pants, and the women were wearing – well, it is hard to describe if you've never seen a bikini. But trust me, three men's handkerchiefs and a few bits of string are the only things needed to make one. You wouldn't believe how much it all jiggles when the women walk.'

Freni clapped her hand over her ears. 'Stop! If your dear mother, my best friend, could hear such sinful talk, she would wash your mouth out with soap and hang it out to dry in the chicken yard.'

'OK, OK, don't get your knickers in a knot.'

'*Ach du leiber!* Will these riddles *never* stop?'

'Certainly, dear,' I said, 'and I'm sorry.' I meant it too, because I knew full well why Freni was upset. I'd hired her much disliked – in a Christian way, of course – daughter-in-law Barbara to be the chef for Asian Sensations. I concede that the word 'chef' might be too grandiose a term for an imitation Asian establishment, but overstatement is the American way of life, and I am, without a doubt, a patriotic citizen.

Freni didn't acknowledge my apology. Instead she expertly cleaved the massive lump of dough in two equal halves with the side of a small, calloused hand. One half she pushed toward me with a grunt.

'That woman, Magdalena. Why *that* woman?'

I sighed. 'Freni, you know as well as I do that, with the exception of you, *that* woman – whose name is *Barbara* – is the best cook in the county. She can make anything taste Chinese. Even Amish food.' All right then, perhaps that was what our daughter Alison calls a 'fib', but nowhere in the Bible does it say, 'Thou shall not fib.'

'Yah?' Freni said. 'You have eaten Amish food made to taste Chinese?'

'Let's not split hairs, dear – oops, look at me, riddling away again like nobody's business. Sorry about that.'

'Hmph.' Freni didn't possess a drop of English blood, upper class or lower; she was merely quite vexed. She began to vigorously knead her massive lump of dough with her strong little hands in controlled, rhythmic motions. Because I'd forced myself to watch a minute or two of the video that Gabe rented in the hotel on our wedding night, I hastily concluded that what Freni was doing to her dough ball was vaguely pornographic.

I felt rather awkward just standing there, and since idle hands are the Devil's playground, I decided that I should also assault the glistening glob of gluten in front of me. However, perhaps I did so with a bit less fervour than Freni.

'May we at least talk about it?' I said.

'Talk is cheap,' Freni said. 'Is that enough riddle for you?'

'Not really dear; everyone knows that saying.'

'Yah?' Freni stopped massaging the dough and began punching the dough with her tiny fists. Under normal circumstances, this was actually the method by which she broke up the air bubbles trapped in the dough that had accumulated during the overnight leavening process. However, on those other occasions she neither grunted, nor threatened to send the dough back to the State of Iowa for misbehaving.

I tried my hardest not to even smile. 'Freni, dear, just because Barbara is from Iowa, that doesn't make her a bad person.'

She gave an extra hard punch with her left fist. 'You have been to this Iowa?'

'No, but—'

'That woman is too tall.'

'How can anyone that the Good Lord made be *too* tall? Barbara's six foot two, has eyes of blue, chickens cluck and cows go moo. Skippity-dippitiy-do-da-doo.'

Freni pummelled the dough with both fists. 'Forgive me,

Magdalena, but you talk crazy, yah? For another thing, who will take care of my grandchildren when this woman is working in your Asian Sinsation?'

Having been somewhat coerced into bread-making without having time to put on an apron, I wiped my hands on my skirt before spinning Freni around to face me. Given that she's stout, with elephantine ankles, it was no easy task, so perhaps 'spinning' is not the best word, but at least that was my intention. Freni squawked in protest and took a large amount of our future bread supply for the next three days with her. Had she not been born Amish, I'm quite sure that Freni could have had a bright future as a professional discus thrower. I base that observation on the incredible strength which she exhibited, and the height that she achieved, when she managed to sling, quite accidentally, approximately five pounds of wet dough squarely into my face. The impact knocked me to the floor where, thank heavens, I landed on my bony behind. Remarkably, but not surprisingly, the airborne slab did not break my prominent Yoder proboscis. (By the next morning, however, a large portion of my heinie had turned as black as bituminous coal.)

Freni has been like a mother figure to me ever since my parents were squished to death between two trucks in the infamously long Allegheny tunnel when I was just twenty years old. Thus, I was surprised, saddened, and a bit miffed that she appeared unfazed by what had just happened. Instead of offering to help me to my feet, or simply inquiring after my well-being, she merely retrieved the erstwhile missile of wheat and flour and returned it to her work surface. There she folded it into the main body of dough and resumed her abuse of our future comestibles.

'Freni, don't you have anything you need to say to me?'

'Yah. Do not grab me like that. I get the jumps, yah?'

'You could say that you're sorry. The English are always saying sorry. We could learn from them.'

'Yah? Maybe Barbara is English. Are there many English in Iowa, Magdalena?'

'I think that Barbara is terrified of you, Freni. Maybe that's why she's always apologizing.'

Freni was able to achieve a textbook quarter turn on her thick

Yoder ankles. Frankly, I was gobsmacked. For the most part I consider television to be the Devil's toolbox, but the Babester once coaxed me to watch ice skating in the Winter Olympics along with his old movies. Given her physical and cultural handicap, Freni's maneuver was every bit as impressive as any of those skaters.

'That woman, she is twice as tall as a real person. How can she be afraid?'

'The Bible says that Goliath was also a giant,' I reminded her, 'and yet a little shepherd boy named David managed to kill him with a single stone from a slingshot.'

Freni is a faithful Bible reader, although she reads it in the German tongue of her forbears, not the King James English that Jesus spoke. Nonetheless, she understood my reference and burst out laughing. The rarity of such an event can only be likened to the Republicans and Democrats holding a slumber party in pink pyjamas, or the British people overwhelmingly proclaiming their love for Americanisms. I came so close to fainting in astonishment that I was barely able to enjoy the moment. Truthfully, all that I can report is that a laughing Freni sounds a bit like a cross between a drunken bullfrog and a strangled magpie. Not that I've ever encountered either creature in that condition before.

'So,' she finally said, 'you think I am like King David?'

Not wanting her head to swell too large to fit inside her bonnet, I had no choice but to answer appropriately. 'Not when he was King David, but when he was the shepherd boy, David, yes.'

Surprisingly, that satisfied her. 'Yah. Still, about my grandchildren, who will watch them when the giant is away at Sinsations?'

'It is *Sen*sations, dear,' I said, tiring of her game, for I knew her well enough to know it was just that. '*You* will take care of your grandchildren. Isn't that what you've been whinging about – I mean something you've been wanting to do ever since they were born? Don't you think that you can do a better job of turning them into good Amish than that giant from Iowa, who might really be a secret Englishwoman?'

I waited expectantly for another glorious belly laugh from the taciturn woman, but none was forthcoming. She merely nodded and continued working.

SEVEN

Later that morning I rang my best friend Agnes, but when I couldn't get her on the phone, I hopped into my rather ancient, but quite reliable, Ford and motored over to her farm on the opposite side of Hernia. Incidentally, my second-hand car was originally painted a proper Christian black, but over the years the sun has faded it to fifty shades of grey. Sadly, my mode of transportation hasn't always been so modest. I once drove a sinfully red BMW that, you can be sure, was the talk of the town. The Presbyterians and Episcopalians expressed a mixture of admiration and envy. Most of the Baptists and liberal Mennonites kept mum, but as for the conservative wing in our community – well, I did hear the phrase 'harlot with the scarlet car' bandied about. Anyway, the phrase was a misnomer given that my then much-cherished 'chariot' was more of a red-orange than scarlet.

Agnes Miller Shafer and I have known each other since we were infants. We were bathed together as babies. We were class-mates together through high school. Just like Freni, Agnes is a cousin of mine in some degree – related to me through both my parents. We both like to read, to meet interesting people, and discuss the events of the day. However, the similarities stop there.

While I resemble a beanpole with perhaps a few sticks tied across it to represent human limbs, dear sweet Agnes is shaped more like a bowling ball that rests atop a pair of shoes. This is mere observation; there is not an inkling of judgment intended. Of course, Agnes possesses a head, albeit a very small one, and deep green eyes, rather like the colour of magnolia leaves. What Agnes doesn't have are wrinkles. She claims that's because 'fat don't crack'. In short, Agnes is prettier than I am.

At any rate, she only recently became the owner of this farm when her husband Doc Shafer died. Doc, by the way, was another of my dear friends, and quite frankly, he was a would-be para-mour of *mine*. In fact, I am quite certain that he fancied me much more than he ever did Agnes.

Every time that we were alone, the wily octogenarian attempted to talk his way past my sturdy Christian underwear and thick woollen stockings, in order to gain access to my treasure chest of purity – if you get my drift. Because Doc was merely persistent, and I knew that he would never force himself on me, we had had some wonderful deep discussions. Frankly, and I will admit this to no one, when eighty-seven-year-old Doc Shafer married Agnes Miller after dating her for just a fortnight, I might have felt a wee bit of jealousy. I mean, let's face it, Agnes may be a liberal Mennonite with a four-year college degree under her belt, but at the risk of tooting my own horn, I'm a mite scrappier, and the old coot always liked to take as good as he gave.

Never mind all that, Doc was dead now, and the woman who was arguably my best friend was now a freshly minted widow, and I was in need of comfort. Still, as I drove up the long dirt lane to the traditional Pennsylvania farmhouse, I couldn't help fantasizing what life would be like if I'd married Doc instead of Gabe. Doc had been the community's veterinarian for sixty-plus years, and had birthed a goodly number of human babies, as well as assisted in difficult animal deliveries. Our police chief estimated that well over a thousand people attended Doc Shafer's funeral up on Stucky Ridge, making it the largest send-off of its kind in the county. Even the governor made a brief appearance.

Please don't get me wrong – I'm not saying that Agnes doesn't deserve to be old Doc's widow – but truthfully, how well did she know him? Did she know him well enough to get the female lead in the biggest public drama ever to play itself out in Hernia, Pennsylvania? More to the point, it was Magdalena who had held Doc's hand – literally – after his first wife died twenty-five years ago and put him back together – metaphorically – after their only child, an alcoholic son, committed suicide in New York City.

After a quarter century of enduring friendship, and fending off his advances, was it unreasonable for Magdalena to expect that Doc might bequeath her a few pennies in his will? Not that I needed it; in fact, I would have given away everything that Doc left me. The only thing that Agnes ever did for my beloved old friend was to succumb to his advances within two weeks of their first date. If you must know, fifty-year-old Agnes was a virgin when they started dating, which leads me to conclude that she was either an incredibly fast learner of the 'mattress mambo,' or else Doc felt guilty for having robbed my friend of her maidenhood.

At any rate, it used to be that one couldn't drive up the lane to Doc's farmhouse without having one's heart skip with joy at the sight of all the animals frolicking about in his rich green pastures. Also, despite the fact that he really was of pure Swiss stock, as were the rest of us Amish descendants, old Doc claimed to be one eighth English. This, he claimed, was the reason he was not embarrassed to enjoy growing flowers, as are many other so-called 'red-blooded' American men. And what a garden Doc had! Every summer he exhibited specimens in the Pennsylvania State Fair and collected blue ribbons. Why, one year he perfected his own variety of black dahlia that he named 'Satan's Bride', which caused an enormous sensation in gardening circles every-where, even across the Pond. But apparently the Good Lord was not pleased with the flower's name. Before Doc could propagate enough specimens to ensure its survival in the trade, his billy goat, Gruff, crawled under a fence on his knees, his massive horns notwithstanding. Free to wreak havoc on Doc's garden, Gruff devoured Satan's Bride while Doc was away delivering a calf that had presented itself in a breech position.

On the day I drove out to see Agnes there was no sign of Doc's garden, nor did I spot any frolicking animals. Not anymore. Finally, at his age, old doc had been forced to choose between performing his husbandly duties and caring for his livestock. To everyone's surprise, Doc's resident four-legged critters, barnyard fowl, and prize-winning flowers, all lost out to his rotund bride. Oh, what a horrible word for me to use when describing the very best friend a gal could ever have. Thank the Good Lord that He made it impossible for anyone to read our private thoughts. I, for one, couldn't stand to know what others thought of me. I take that back; I would like to know, but only if the thoughts were truly lovely.

That said, upon arriving at the house I was a trifle concerned to find Agnes's solid wooden door standing wide open, and the screen on the outer door torn almost completely out of its frame. The correct response should have been for me to call the police on my cell phone. On the other hand, as mayor, and as unofficial lady detective for the freakishly high rate of murder in our otherwise happy hamlet, I am essentially an extension of our little police department. Besides, I would have bet dollars to doughnuts (*if* I were the betting sort), that the torn screen on the door was Agnes's doing.

The truth of the matter is my dear, spherical friend is about as accident prone as a rogue elephant in a Limoges factory. She also is slow to tidy up after herself, which meant that the rip in the door could have happened weeks ago. She once dropped a jar of beef gravy on the floor the evening before leaving on a two-week holiday and left the mess laying there until she returned. Tell me, who on earth does such an appalling thing? (I mean, who *buys* beef gravy in a jar?) No good Mennonite of Amish descent, that's who!

Anyway, after I called Agnes by name a few times, and then called her a few names a couple of times, I ventured in for a semi-official investigation. I am not licensed to carry a gun, nor would I use one if I had one. That said, I do wield a mean broom if need be when it comes to fending off vicious field mice who have invaded my kitchen – well, that's not quite true either. I can, however, use the bristle end of the broom to guide the little darlings as I sweep them gently out the door and into the field from whence they came.

As it happened, I spotted what looked like a brand-new broom just inside the kitchen doors, so I armed myself with that, gripping it in my right fist. Next to the broom was a metal, colour-coordinated dust bin, which I scooped up with my left hand to use as a shield. As long as Agnes's perpetrator was firing nothing more lethal than paper clips, and aimed for the centre of my shield, I might come out of the skirmish just fine.

Oh, silly me. There wasn't just a new broom in Agnes's kitchen, there was a new stove, a new refrigerator, a new dishwasher, new granite countertops – why even the Doc's disgusting, cracked and curled, fifty-year-old linoleum flooring had been replaced with ceramic tiles. In the middle of the kitchen, where Doc used to serve me lunch (with a side dish of wisdom) on his Formica table, was now the *de rigueur* island, without which no modern house is complete. I glanced up to see that no longer was there a bare lightbulb dangling from the stained ceiling. The water stains were gone, and in their place was a rectangular silver bar from which hung brightly coloured glass light fixtures, each one no larger than a jam jar. No doubt the light that they managed to cast would turn the task of chopping vegetables into a game of Russian roulette.

'Well, well,' I mumbled, 'you have certainly abandoned your penny-pinching ways. What's more, except for those jam jars that some big city designer talked you into buying, instead of installing decent lighting, you have actually exhibited fairly good taste.'

Thank heavens the dear gal wasn't around to hear my critique. I walked into the dining room and was shocked again. Doc's painted grey dining room table, which he'd made himself from salvaged lumber, was gone, along with the motley assortment of wobbly chairs that usually surrounded it. In their place was a stunning mahogany showstopper that could seat twelve, and around it, arranged with the precision that one would expect from a footman employed at Buckingham Palace, were Queen Anne-style mahogany chairs. The table surface was as smooth and glossy as a peeled hard-boiled egg – that is, except for a single dust mote. Aha! Dear, sweet Agnes had gone totally bonkers: she'd gone and hired a housekeeper!

But wait, there was more – so much more! The large dining room was literally lined with credenzas and breakfronts and china cabinets. Wherever space permitted the walls were chock-a-block with paintings, two of which were massive. Being the simple-minded country bumpkin that I am, I have no appreciation for anything but representational art. They say that art is in the eye of the beholder, but when this beholder beholds a picture of someone with three eyes, then I say that there is no art to behold. Just my opinion, and I am welcome to it.

But moving right along. I shan't even begin to describe the treasures contained in the sitting room, except to say that even King Tut would have tutted at the sight of such over-the-top luxuries. Interspersed twixt gasps of admiration and clenched-teeth tuts, I continued to call Agnes's name, as next I headed for the master bedroom which is still on the ground floor.

When I reached the open door to her bedroom I nearly fainted, for there was Agnes in her king-size, four-poster bed, with the bedclothes pulled up to her chin, and snuggled next to her, also under the covers, was a billy goat. Gruff is not just any billy goat; he is an old goat with a long white beard, long curved horns, and light brown eyes that manage to seem both disconcertingly human and diabolical. It wouldn't take much to convince me that he was the Devil incarnate.

'Ach,' I gasped.

'Magdalena,' my best friend cried, as she struggled to clear herself of the weight of the cumbersome bedclothes and get to her tiny feet.

Once upon a time, long, long ago, we primitive colonists made do with items that we called sheets and blankets. The blankets were relatively lightweight, and since we had central heating, one was able to add or subtract a blanket as needed throughout the night. This practice was especially convenient for menopausal women who suffered from hot flashes. Then someone – perhaps a Francophile – decided that blankets were only for horses and that we ignorant yokels must now learn the joys of the 'duvet'. Now when one travels Stateside and sleeps in a hotel or a motor lodge, one is forced to either sleep under a mattress stuffed between an envelope of sheets, called a duvet (with the thermostat turned down to Arctic temperatures), or sleep without a cover. But I digress.

'Agnes,' I hollered happily, exceedingly pleased at her reaction to seeing me. After all, I'd worn a very dark shade of grey to her wedding. That's what the colour code said on the label, but I preferred to call it 'light black' which, in my opinion, is the correct colour to wear when one is in semi-mourning.

Because we are both of Amish-Mennonite stock – although she is of a more liberal branch – we shared as many ancestors as a pond full of koi. The goat, however, was not closely related to either of us. What I'm getting at, is that when we hugged, we commenced to patting each other's backs half a dozen times as if we were babies who needed burping – that is, until inspiration struck. I actually did burp. On *purpose*. It was a wee burp, a mini-belch, one might say. However, I most certainly did not intend for the goat to burp in return.

'Did you hear that?' Agnes said, clearly delighted. 'Billy is talking to you!'

'Billy is disgusting,' I said. 'Why on earth do you have a barnyard animal in bed with you?'

'Oh, Mags, don't be so judgmental. If other people can have cats and dogs on their beds, why can't I have a goat? Think of Billy as my comfort animal. Besides, I gave him a bath with puppy shampoo, and I even polished his hooves and his horns with moustache wax.'

Incidentally, Agnes is one of only three people whom I tolerate calling me 'Mags'. The other two who have permission to truncate my given name are Gabe and my sister Susannah. By the way, the latter is serving a lengthy prison sentence for being an accessory to attempted murder. The victim of this foiled murder plot is none other than me.

I took both of Agnes's hands in mine and led her all of three feet back to the bed and had us sit. I was about to point out that cats and dogs normally sleep *atop* their owners' bedding, when the beast suddenly bleated just as loudly as my smoke alarm.

'Oh, shut up!' I said crossly. My comment was directed at the goat, not at Agnes. I had not intended for old Billy to bolt from the bed, leaving his diaper behind, weighed down as it were, beneath the meter-thick duvet.

'Am I really that whacky, Mags?' she sobbed, as she attempted to bury her head into my bony shoulder.

'Absolutely not,' I said. 'But we've always been a tidy people, and letting farm animals share our beds goes against four hundred years of our inbred family history, probably beginning with Menno Simons and his followers. Then again, I could be wrong; I was wrong in 1965, 1987, and then also in 2003.'

'What about that time in 1998?'

'Oh yeah. I'd just as soon forget about that. Anyway, did you ever see your parents display any signs of physical affection?'

She nodded as she smeared the tears across her round cheeks with her arm. 'Once. Papa tripped on an electrical cord, and when he fell, his lips touched Mama's.'

It had been a shocking revelation, one that practically made my heart race, but there was no time to revel in sins of the flesh. 'Agnes, I need your help.'

EIGHT

'You *do?*' Agnes was instantly transformed. She clapped her small but plump hands and bounced up and down on the bed just like Little Jacob does sometimes. 'Who's been murdered? Do you have any good clues?'

In all fairness, Agnes *has* helped me do a little sleuthing in the past; she has been the Dr Watson to my Sherlock Holmes, if you will. Not that I've been a drug addict, mind you. She has a good head on her round shoulders. She's brave, she's far more techno-savvy than I am, and above all, she's loyal to a fault.

'Agnes,' I said, 'I'm not here about a murder, or any sort of crime. I'm here to offer you a job.'

I could feel the excitement drain from her like water from a cheap plastic bottle. 'Mags, as much as I love your kids, I really don't see myself being their nanny.'

'That's good, because watching after them is what their father loves doing most in life.'

'Oh? What is it then?' Burble, burble, my bestie was getting excited again.

'Hold on to your hat, dear – well, at least hold on to this stupid duvet, because you're not going to believe this. This has to do with the really wacky woman, Wanda Hemphopple—'

'And you say that with no judgment?'

'Are you judging *me?*'

'Sorry, go on.'

Sometimes it takes a minute or two to stop feeling aggravated when one has just been criticized. Other times it takes longer than that. On this occasion it was expedient to swallow my irritation and move on. Besides, I've been told that irritation contains very few calories.

'Anyway, I am going to reopen her Sausage Barn,' I said pleasantly.

'*What?*' Agnes said.

'Hortense came to see me. She brought with her a notarized

deed. Wanda has given me sixty percent ownership of the place, and Hortense the other forty percent.'

'Why, Mags? You know that Wanda is crazy. Stark raving mad. You're not really considering accepting ownership of The Sausage Barn, are you?'

'I already have. It's not for me; it's for Hortense.'

'But Mags, that evil Wanda tried to kill both you, and your precious Alison, in that very place.'

'You think that I've forgotten? I still have nightmares about it. But Hortense needs this. She's working hard to put her life back together after everything that happened, and all the subsequent media attention she's received. She's even gotten death threats.'

'Shut the front door!' Agnes said.

'I did,' I said quite crossly. 'And for your information, missy, I found it wide open when I arrived.'

Agnes had the temerity to laugh. 'Calm yourself, Mags. That's just an expression of astonishment. Death threats, huh? From whom?'

'We didn't talk about that, and this is just between you and me, and your sinfully expensive French silk drapes, but I heard about the threats from Police Chief Toy Graham a while back.'

Agnes smirked. 'Figures. The two of you are as tight as two ticks on a Mexican hairless dog. Now let's pivot back to The Sausage Barn. Are you and Hortense going to be running the restaurant together?'

'Absolutely not. Did you realize that Hortense is only nineteen, and will be a college freshman?'

'Goodness me, I thought for sure she was closer to thirty.'

'Bingo! I did too. Anyway, the poor girl ran through all her mother's savings after the murder trial, but she is determined not to let her dream of a college education be ripped from her grasp by a mother who is behind bars for a murder, and two more attempted murder convictions. In order to follow through on her goal, Hortense has asked me to run the restaurant for her while she finishes college. Anyway, I agreed. She said that I could do anything that I want with the place, and I decided that it is going to be an Asian restaurant.'

Agnes clapped her petite, but nonetheless pudgy, hands. 'Oh goody! I love Asian food. *Ramen* noodles are my favourite.'

'*Ramen* noodles aren't quite what I had in mind. Listen, the reason that I'm here – besides the fact that I haven't seen you in a month of Sundays – is that I want you to be the manager.'

'Get out of town and back! Did you say that you want *me* to manage it?'

'Yesiree, and Bob's your uncle.' For the record, Agnes really does have an Uncle Bob. Or Robert, at any rate.

'But why me?'

I did something which would have been unthinkable before I married a touchy-feely New York Jew. I slung a bony arm (one of mine, of course) around Agnes's shoulders. Given her body shape, and the slippery texture of her nightgown, said arm slid off, and I had to launch it around her shoulder again. This time I stuck a landing, and thus was able to draw her to me in a semi-embrace.

'I'm choosing you because – with the possible exception of Gabe – you are the brightest person I know.'

She turned to me with enthusiasm, causing my lanky limb to slip yet again. '*Really?*'

'You bet your bippy. And also, because you have great people skills. Look how you've handled those two doddering nude uncles that lived with you until Mother Malaise enticed them into her cult.'

'Yeah, I guess. But Magdalena, you know that I don't care much for Hortense after her mother tried to kill you and Alison. I know it's not her fault, but don't you think that Hortense and Wanda kind of look alike?'

'Kind of? Why if Hortense was thirty years older, gained twenty pounds, broke her nose in two places, but didn't bother to reset it, lost a few teeth, put her hair up in a French twist and forgot to wash it for three decades, she'd be the spitting image of her mother.'

Agnes stared at me opened-mouthed. 'I can't tell if you're being kind, or if you're being judgmental.'

'Both. For penance, I'll work on the latter later, on a lopsided ladder lapping a latte. Now, dear, you needn't worry about running into Hortense too much. She wants to be a partner in name only. Another thing, when I said it was going to be an Asian restaurant, what I really meant is it's going to be a *pan*-Asian restaurant.' I giggled. 'Oh, I just made a delightful little pun – pan-Asian. Get it?'

Agnes rolled her very round eyes and groaned, as seemingly everyone does when a good pun is delivered. 'So,' she said, 'have you managed to *stir* up any good Asian cooks yet?'

I groaned in retaliation, which is what I am wont to do, given that I am six weeks younger than her, and ergo not quite as mature. 'We're not going to have an Asian cook. Traditional Chinese, Thai, Indian, what-have-you restaurants are so yesterday's news. No, this is an original Magdalena Yoder-Rosen concept: Amish-Asian Fusion, only we don't advertise that part until our guests get in the door. Our sign will simply say Asian Sensations.'

The expression on Agnes's face reminded me of how Gabe looked when I told him I was pregnant at age forty-nine. 'Mags, either you've finally lost your last marble, gone bonkers, nuts, Loony Tunes, aren't playing a full deck, etc., etc., or else you might have accidentally hit on another potential winner. It's definitely unique. As are you.'

'Thank you,' I said to Agnes somewhat warily. 'Anyway, I've lined up Freni's much maligned daughter-in-law, Barbara Hostetler as our chef, but I need to come up with at least three others to work under her in the kitchen. I was thinking of Marigold Flanagan – you know, the woman who pretended to be Hindu for a year because she had a distinctive age spot developing between her eyes, and she wears wreathes of marigolds displayed prominently like in an Indian documentary. She's not Amish, of course, but her grandmother was. Marigold was raised on traditional Amish cooking.'

I'm quite certain that the sound of Agnes sucking in air between her teeth could be heard all the way down in the State of Maryland, possibly even over in Kerala, India. I braced for her comment. No doubt I had done it again: being politically incorrect with my Hindu comment. But it wasn't *me* who had pretended to be someone of another faith. It was Marigold Flanagan.

'Mags, didn't I tell you the terrible thing that Barbara Hostetler did to me?'

'*What?* Barbara's a good Christian woman. She's Amish for heaven's sake. She doesn't have a mean bone in her vertically-enhanced body.'

'Ha!' Agnes snorted. And here I thought that only horses could snort. 'Barbara fat-shamed me.'

'She fat-shamed you? That's a thing?'

'Sheesh, sometimes I forget just how out of touch you Conservative Mennonites are. Anyway, you know that Barbara's an excellent seamstress, as well as a fair-to-middling cook—'

'She's an *excellent* cook!'

'Don't interrupt me, Mags. I hate it when you do that.'

'Touché, toots. See? I'm not so out of touch with your modern type's lingo, am I?'

Agnes inexplicably rolled her eyes, then jumped right back into her story. 'I needed a new dress for a wedding at a Mennonite church in Berne, Indiana. It's hard to find something stylish for girls my size.' My friend paused for me to nod in agreement, but the truth is Agnes hasn't been a *girl* for the better part of half a century. 'Anyway, their organist, Grace Wulliman, is playing a recital the afternoon prior to that. That church has a massive organ and she is supposed to be a top-notch organist. It's a shame you Conservative Mennonites don't allow instrumental music in your churches.'

'When we get to heaven, I'll let you plunk my harp for all eternity if you move your tale of woe along,' I said wearily.

'Why I never!' Then she grinned. 'Really?'

'Absolutely. I'll even let you beat my drums and fiddle with my fiddle.'

'In that case, it went down like this. During the fitting, that woman had the nerve to complain about my figure. Do you want to hear what she said?'

I had no choice *but* to hear. Even if a flock of angels tried to pull me away, a herd of demons would have tugged me right back to listen to what promised to be a juicy, albeit sad, account of the dress-fitting session. Barbara was raised to tell the truth at all times. It was a trait that I found endearing, but it didn't always go over well with her clients.

'At first Barbara told me that I was shaped like a glob, and that the dress I envisioned wouldn't work,' Agnes said.

'What is a glob shaped like?' I said.

'That's what I asked. So, then she said it was shaped like the earth, but in a ball form, similar to the one that she saw in her one-room schoolhouse back in Iowa. What she really meant was a *globe*.'

'I don't get it,' I said. 'I know that Barbara can be straight-forward, but I've never known her to be rude. Why would she volunteer such a thing?'

Agnes sighed. 'Maybe because I wanted a sheath dress made from silk.'

'Oh.'

'That's *it*? Just "oh?"'

'Oh – that was indeed untoward of her. So, then what happened?'

'I called her a giraffe who was so freakishly tall that her head was in the clouds.'

'You didn't!'

'I certainly did. I hate that woman.'

'You do not,' I said. 'You're just miffed. And F.Y.I., she's not *that* tall. Did you know that Princess Diana was five feet ten? Barbara is only four inches taller than that.'

'First of all,' Agnes said, still quite steamed, '*I* would never have divorced a studmuffin like Prince Charles. And secondly, does this mean that you're taking Barbara's side against me?'

'Of course not,' I said, although of course I was. 'How could you say such a thing? Do you mind telling me now who's making this lovely frock for you?'

OK, so I fibbed when I said I hadn't sided with Barbara, but I needed Agnes to manage Asian Sensations, and clearly, she needed a job. From the standpoint of hygiene alone, sharing one's bed with a quadruped is not a good idea. But cuddling with the beast that snacked on the Bride of Satan, was flirting with demonic possession if you ask me.

'Mags, you're such a hoot,' Agnes said. 'You and your archaic use of English. "Frock" indeed. It almost sounds like a swear word. No, I don't mind telling you. Lydia Burkholder, that's who.'

'Oh, my word!'

'What is that supposed to mean?'

'Nothing. Nothing at all, dear.'

'Out with it, Mags. You know that you can't keep secrets.'

'All right, I capitulate,' I said, if only because I had important

information to share, and not because I am a gossip – which I
most certainly am not. 'Well, Lydia and Ezekiel Burkholder have
fifteen children in all, thanks to the Amish need for farm hands.
Freni told me – and you can't tell anyone – that poor Lydia is
on the verge of a nervous breakdown and is desperate to get
out of the house. Their oldest child is eighteen and is still unmar-
ried, and quite capable of taking care of the little ones, even
though she has a nervous tick. Matilda has the tick, not Lydia.'

'*So?*' Agnes demanded.

'So, I offered Lydia a job as assistant chef at Asian Sensations,'
I said. 'This will give her a chance to get out of the house, and
out from under Ezekiel – so to speak.'

'No, you didn't just hire her to work under Barbara!'

'I just said that I did.'

'It's a way of speaking. Never mind. While she was taking
my measurements, Lydia and I got to talking about Barbara and
why she didn't fit in here in Hernia, and Lydia told me that all
the other Amish women say that Barbara's too outspoken, sometimes to the point of rudeness. Kind of like you, Mags.'

I hopped off that goat-scented bed and sputtered like a flooded
car engine. 'S-s-so that's what you think of me?' I hollered. 'You
think I'm rude?'

Instead of a snappy rejoinder, Agnes began to sob. As Agnes
is my very best friend, I shall never, ever, even on pain of death,
reveal what an ugly crier she is. There is possibly only one person
in the entire world who presents a more disagreeable visage when
shedding tears, and that is Yours Truly. The one thing that I know
having grown up with Agnes is that we both hate it when anyone
tries to hug us and offer such meaningless platitudes as 'There,
there.' 'Where, where?' we are wont to respond.

There was really nothing that I could do but sit back down on
the odoriferous duvet and wait until the monsoon had passed. I
briefly entertained the idea of going all 'English' on her and
fixing a 'cuppa', given that Agnes is such an Anglophile that she
could rule the waves with one hand tied behind her back, but
then I decided that she might feel abandoned if I left the room.
Besides, there was simply no telling if the horny beast with the
horns would try to sneak his way back into Agnes's bed during
my absence.

At long last the sobs were replaced by a fair bit of sniffling, followed by a good deal of throat clearing. Eventually my childhood friend smiled gratefully. 'I'm sorry that I called you rude,' she said. 'I shouldn't have said it, even though sometimes it's true. Thank you for letting me have a good cry. There's nothing like letting it all out, is there? I've been so incredibly lonely. Mags, that's why I bought all the stuff you saw on your way coming in. I was trying to fill up the hole in my heart.'

'Because you loved Doc so much?' I asked incredulously.

'Mags, you sound jealous, but don't be. I never really loved Doc all that much, and I know that he didn't love me. It was you, and only you whom he loved.'

I said nothing. What could I say? I had indeed been jealous of my best friend's marriage to Doc, but I had never lusted after the grizzled old man. Having lost my own father early in life, Doc had always been more of a wise father figure to me, albeit one with boundary issues.

It's a fact that we voluble Americans cannot abide silence. 'And I want you to know,' Agnes said, 'that I paid for all those items with my own savings. I'm actually penniless on account of that. By the way, Doc was broke as well when I married him. He didn't have one thin dime to his name.'

I gasped, which was a huge mistake, as it caused me to inhale several goat hairs. 'I don't believe it!'

'You better believe it. I have all his banking and investment records to prove it.'

I slumped, but immediately straightened, thanks to 'bouquet d'barnyard'. 'Everyone in Hernia believes he was a millionaire.'

'Why?' Agnes asked fiercely. 'Doc was only a country veterinarian. He had a kind and generous heart. Too many people took advantage of that.'

'But most of us are good Christians. We don't steal. Not paying our bills would be stealing.'

Agnes sighed, sending a flurry of goat hair and dust particles into the air. Who knew that goats had such lightweight hair? Perhaps it belonged to some other hideous mammal, and I shuddered to think of the possibilities.

'Look at it this way, Mags: a farmer gets a poor return on his corn crop, so he's strapped for cash. In the meantime, one of his cows gets sick. Doc treats the cow and tells the farmer to pay him back when he can. In the meantime, there are three more bad crops, and two more sick cows, and well – at least one of those treatments gets lost in the shuffle because of Doc's kind heart.

'Mags, if I work for you as manager at Asian Sensations, aren't folks going to think it odd? I mean, aren't they going to wonder why a millionaire's wife is managing a restaurant?'

I blew at the air, which only made matters worse. 'The way I see it, you have two options. The first one is that you start telling people the truth – beginning with Marigold Flanagan, surely our biggest gossip here in Hernia – and then you hold your head high. Your second option, should anyone question your need for employment, is to simply tell them that you enjoy managing people. That will set them in their place.'

Agnes giggled, something she is surprisingly good at for a woman of a certain age. 'You see what I mean about you being rude?'

NINE

We Mennonites are a humble people. Quite a few of us, myself included, have always been proud of our humility. Yes, I am perhaps more outspoken than most Mennonite women, and it has been said of me that I have a tongue that could slice Swiss cheese, but that is a slight exaggeration. A mild cheddar is more like it.

With my equine face, mousy brown hair, and prominent teeth, I look like the reflection of an anaemic horse in a silt-laden pond. Even though my doctor husband claims that this is not the case, and that I can't see myself for who I am, thanks to a hypercritical mother and a sexually-repressed culture, I didn't believe it was worth taking any chances. To that end, I hired the most unattractive woman I could find to replace my beloved kinswoman, Freni.

Thelma Bontrager has a lopsided face that only a mother could love – that was Thelma's own description, not mine. The Babester, with a wink, told her that 'no', Picasso would also have loved her face, which caused the woman to blush the colour of a ripe pomegranate. From that moment on she became his adoring puppy dog until I put a stop to it with my rude, cheese-slicing tongue. What I said was: 'Less looking, and more cooking.' How is *that* rude?

Anyway, I wasn't all that worried that my Honey Buns would do anything untoward with our new cook, because Thelma was sixty-two years old, and as for her figure, try to imagine a Bactrian camel crossed with a gunny sack filled with large Idaho potatoes. Which are the camel humps, and which parts are the potato lumps? I'll leave that up to the imagination.

The important thing is that Thelma's less than stellar looks enabled me to leave the inn and concentrate on the restaurant without having to worry that my handsome groom of just three years might yield to temptation and do the mattress mambo while I was gone. Speaking frankly, every working wife with a stay-at-home husband should have a 'Thelma'. Due to Thelma's presence, my inimitable mother-in-law, Ida, a.k.a. Mother Malaise, stayed away. Completely. Whatever Ida's problem was with Thelma, I dared not ask. I was just happy to have the time to spend getting the restaurant up and running.

My, what fun it was! With the possible exception of my honeymoon, I've never enjoyed something quite so much. Sure, there were no moments when I gouged the headboard with my fingernails, or when fireworks went off in my head and I actually burst into a rousing rendition of: 'Oh sweet mystery of life at last I found you!'. Nonetheless, my soul soared.

Of course, no woman who is more than half a century old, and long in the tooth (quite literally), should be surprised to discover a fly in her happiness ointment. Yet by the time Asian Sensations had its grand opening on the first day of summer, it was impossible to keep all the flies out.

TEN

Perhaps I really was responsible for the murder that landed me in the Bedford County Jail – which I most certainly did not commit, by the way. What I mean to say is that it was my cockeyed approach to finding a culinary niche that set everything in motion. Plus, if it hadn't been for my God-given ability to spin straw into gold, none of what follows would have happened.

After careful consideration, I came to the conclusion that an advertising campaign that described Asian Sensation's unique contribution to the culinary scene was the smartest approach. I studied press releases and then wrote my own with input from my imaginative, fourteen-year-old daughter Alison, who wants to be a novelist, movie star, astronaut, U.S. president, royal duchess, and a race car driver. Meanwhile my sophisticated New York hunk of a husband practically wrung his surgeon hands in horror when he read our finished product. He claimed that no legitimate newspapers would print, for free, what were so clearly advertisements.

The Babester was wrong. Even *before* Asian Sensations opened, we became the darling of media. The 'weekend' sections of the largest newspapers in Pittsburgh, Harrisburg, Washington, D.C., and New York City were all keenly interested in exploring the 'next new phenomena' and sent feature editors to The PennDutch Inn to interview me. The amount of free advertising that we received was priceless.

Alison is a chip off the old block. My darling daughter had taken a page from my success with The PennDutch Inn, wherein bored, rich, city folk will drive ridiculously long distances, and pay through the nose, to be the first in their social set to have some exotic new experience. I don't mean to disparage the weaker sex, but yes, it *is* usually the men who fall for this trap, or should I say 'claptrap'. At any rate, I insisted that she sit in on all the interviews, and it was really Alison who got the feature editors' juices flowing, and eventually led to a feeding frenzy of media attention.

'AMISH MEETS SECHUAN' screamed the headlines in the food section of the nation's largest paper. 'TIKKA MASALA MENNONITE STYLE' read its competitor. Foodies from as far away as Chicago flocked to my (OK, *our*) restaurant. Eventually, after the first rave review, it was reservations only, a fact which frustrated motorists passing nearby on the Pennsylvania Turnpike, not to mention the citizens of Hernia. On the plus side, with all the people vying for a seat at the trough, we could afford to jack up the prices, which I did.

My best friend has always had a wee bit of a bossy nature. This is not a judgment, merely a statement of fact. Agnes soon discovered that she actually enjoyed turning folks away from Asian Sensations in a fake English accent. American Anglophiles derive enormous pleasure from copying the accents that they hear on such popular programs as *Downton Abbey*, and from what I've been told, they mangle those accents terribly. On the other hand, it is a pity that the British, with the exception of actors, almost never attempt to mimic our more mellifluous way of speaking.

But back to Agnes. That woman blossomed like a patch of fertilized dandelions on a warm spring day. Although I had envisioned her manning the cash register, she had a vision of her own. In fact, in her vision she rose above her assigned station in the restaurant, even *before* Asian Sensations opened. Hers involved getting a new hairstyle, going on a crash diet, buying a number of fancy-schmancy outfits in Pittsburgh with my money, and playing the part of hostess with the mostest to the hilt.

The clothes she bought looked to me like red silk pyjamas with gold dragons embroidered on them. However, Agnes insisted that she bought them at the Asian market, and that red symbolizes happiness and good luck in China.

'They are *not* pyjamas,' she insisted. 'You're just jealous because your strict religious hang-ups preclude any kind of comfort.'

I gasped with righteous indignation. 'Why, I never!'

'Exactly. If you tried to wear an outfit like this, all the thick straps and buckles on your so-called "sturdy Christian underwear" would stand out like walnuts on a slice of buttered bread – if they didn't snag this fine silk to smithereens first.'

'Harrumph!' I said. 'You too could wear sturdy Christian underwear. Verily, I say unto thee, Agnes, forsake your modern Mennonite ways and embrace my Conservative Mennonite customs. I daresay that sturdy foundation undergarments, ones which provide ample coverage, are the foundation of a strong moral character.'

I should have known better than to give my best buddy moral and spiritual advice together in the same sentence. She commenced huffing, and puffing, and nearly blew my house down. Thank heavens we were in my bedroom at The PennDutch Inn, and not somewhere more public, like the dining room at the restaurant.

'Are you saying that *I* lack strong moral values?' she said. 'And don't you dare bring up the goat in my bed thing again, or I'll pull one of the chopsticks out of my bun and jab you in the right eye.'

I nodded warily, as Agnes is a woman of her word. 'Okey dokey, Annie Oakley. But speaking of your chopsticks, what are they doing in your hair? Isn't that a trifle unsanitary?'

'Mags, haven't you ever seen pictures of geishas?'

'Agnes. I'm not a country bumpkin; I only come across that way. For your information, geishas use hair sticks in their hair, not chopsticks. There is a difference.'

If we hadn't been sitting on my bed, Agnes's bottom jaw would have hit the floor. 'How do *you* know that?'

'Because I read. By the way, wearing hair sticks will be seen as cultural appropriation, so I can't allow it.'

'You're kidding!'

'Kidding is when goats deliver their young, and I won't allow that in the restaurant either.'

'Mags, stop it! Are you joking, or not?'

'Yes and no. Here's the bottom line: no cultural appropriation in Asian Sensations other than from our own culture, except for inspiration for the menu. You can keep the silk pyjamas for your own use at home, and I'll give you double that budget to return to Pittsburgh and find yourself a suitable hostess ensemble. And remember, you're going to be on your feet for eight or more hours, so buy sensible shoes.' I fished one of my boat-size black brogans off the floor and waved it aloft. 'I can recommend—'

'No, thank you!' Agnes ripped the chopsticks out of her bun, and threw them to the floor, where they landed with a clatter. Unfortunately for Agnes, her body shape, coupled with her short arms, made it impossible for her to slam the door behind her without it bouncing off her bum.

In deference to our friendship, I pretended not to see her clumsy exit from my boudoir. But there was something else that I couldn't see either, and that was the fracture that had been developing in our relationship ever since I married the Babester three years ago. Perhaps I hadn't recognized it at first, because the growing rift started as a thin line, like a hairline fracture, but unless we both put the brakes on our emotions it could escalate until it was as big and dangerous as the San Andreas Fault.

No pun intended, but who was at fault for starting this rift? Why is it that some people like you only when you are down? Why do some folks collect as friends only those people who have less material wealth, or whose relationships can't hold a candle to yours? Yes, Agnes and I had started out together in adjacent prams, but when in middle life, a rich handsome man came along for me – a knight in shining armour (although chained to his mama) – she started putting distance between us.

That afternoon, with the chopsticks still lying on the floor, I slipped to my bony knees. I should have prayed, but instead I sobbed. Trust me, for what was about to happen at Asian Sensations, crying was a waste of time.

ELEVEN

I must confess that on opening day Agnes looked like a million bucks. When she saw me, she flashed me a smile so bright I had to blink three times in order to regain my indoor vision. Before I could say anything, she pulled me aside.

'Are these women with you my waitresses?'

'Technically they're mine and Hortense's waitresses. But practically speaking, yes, they're yours.'

'Wow. They really look fancy. Are those tuxedos that they're wearing?'

'Those are women's tuxedos. If I dressed them in men's clothes, then that would be a sin, wouldn't it?'

'Mags, do you always have to quote scripture? I'm trying to give you a compliment, by telling you that these women really look sharp.'

'Thanks. So do you.'

'Really? You're not just saying that?'

'No, the words "a million bucks" is what popped into my mind the second I saw you.'

Agnes beamed. 'I could kiss you right now, but you'd probably run away screaming. Or at the very least, throw some Bible verse at me.'

'Probably. By the way, these sharp-looking waitresses, who are standing there idly, waiting for their instructions, are none other than Sisters of Perpetual Apathy.'

'No way!'

'Way.'

'But how?'

'Why, it was no trouble at all. I simply caved in to my mother-in-law's cajoling, but instead of hiring her – which would have been a terrible mistake – I got these three ladies for a pittance. Besides, since they get to take their earnings back to the convent, including tips, it's a win-win situation for everyone. Also, I checked to see that they all have their own teeth, so you won't have to worry about any dentures falling onto a customer's plate.'

'B-b-but,' she stammered, 'how did you get the so-called Sisters to shed their burlap monks' robes and don tuxedos? They're also wearing black patent leather pumps and earrings!'

'I guess I should give credit where credit is due,' I said somewhat reluctantly. 'Have you ever heard of a song called "Puttin' on the Ritz"?'

'Everybody has! It was written by Irving Berlin and a musical based on it was made into a film in 1930. Oh, that's right, you don't watch movies, especially if they involve dancing.' She winked.

'Show off, you fount of knowledge. At any rate, first Ida wanted to work here as a cook, but I refused. Then she tried badgering me to hire her followers as waitresses. Again, I refused. I told her that my concept was a high-end mash-up of Amish and Asian cuisine, not something Dr Frankenstein dreamed up.'

'Very good, Mags. Most people think that Frankenstein was the monster's name.'

'That depends on your point of view,' I said. 'And by the way, I read the book – I didn't see the film. Back to my relentless mother-in-law. When Gabe mentioned the song, "Puttin' on the Ritz", he grabbed Ida, and the two of them danced around my kitchen as if they were a pair still in their twenties. As sinful a sight as it was, I found myself tapping my feet.'

'Oh boy, you've just boarded the fast train to Hell,' Agnes said. As a General Conference Mennonite, she could afford her more liberal views as regards dancing, but if you ask me, sarcasm never becomes anyone.

'I plan to hop off that train at the next stop,' I said. 'The point is, who knew that an old – uh – woman, had so much energy. Anyway, Gabe explained that the lyrics of the song were about making people feel good on the inside by what they wore. Long story, short, I agreed to take three depressed old women and turn them into the stunners standing over there awaiting your orders. Also, remember the Earl and Countess who were guests at my inn last year?'

'Yes,' Agnes said warily, for that particular English couple had proved to be rather a handful.

'If you'll recall, she explained that what we call dessert here in America is called pudding in Great Britain. After some consideration, I've decided that the best of the cooks whom I hired should be the one to concentrate on the so-called puddings. In this case, our to-die-for American fruit pies and rich, mouthwatering cakes. Think of it as *"Puddin' on the Ritz".*' I didn't mean to neigh like a horse, but given my unfortunate features, that's the sound that came out when I laughed.

My dear friend wordlessly wiped the spittle from her face. 'Just tell me that you didn't capitulate so far that you hired Mother Holy Terror for the job.'

'Heaven forfend,' I said. 'I'd sooner take on the post myself, despite the fact that you once accused me of being unable to boil water, even if I had detailed instructions typed in large print. No, our mistress of desserts is Barbara Hostetler.'

'Whatever,' Agnes said, in the same passive-aggressive tone that teenage Alison uses when she wants to shut down a conversation.

'Hmm,' I said. 'I thought you'd have more of a reaction, one way or another, given how much you hate Barbara, and were upset that I'd made her chef.'

'Yeah, well, maybe "hate" was too strong a word to use. I'm in a better place now, Mags. But does this mean that now Lydia Burkholder will be chef?'

'Confidentially,' I said, 'Lydia seems a little too high-strung and fragile right now to handle that much stress, and so she's still an assistant chef. It's Marigold Flanagan, Hernia's ex-faux Hindu, who gets top billing in the kitchen, and who will be in charge of creating our so-called mash-up sensations. Do you have any questions, dear?' I gave her one of my barn-pleasing, bucktooth grins, although I'm quite sure that most Brits would have winced at the sight of my incisors.

Agnes rewarded me by smiling as well. 'I could be mean, and ask where your whip is, but instead, I'm curious to know if the Grand Poohbah of this operation is finally wearing a touch of lipstick.'

I felt my cheeks redden, whereas the lip balm that I was wearing was called 'Barely Pink'. 'Yes,' I said, feeling a bit like a tart. 'But it was Alison's idea. It's not too much, is it?'

'Are you kidding? I think it's a riot.'

So it was that on opening day, Agnes and I were feeling good about each other. Also, Asian Sensations was a smashing success. As it was the following day. And the next. I'm speaking from a purely business point of view, of course. Putting Barbara in charge of making all the desserts was an absolutely brilliant move on my part, if I do say so myself.

Prior to this job she had already established a reputation in the Amish community for making the best pies and cakes in a three-county radius, which she brought to barn-raisings and church dinners. Although the Amish, who eschew praise, were not wont to heap it on Barbara, especially given her outsider status, they sure let her know by voting with their stomachs. At every communal meal, the second that the 'amen' had been uttered, there was a mad dash straight to whichever dessert Barbara Hostetler had brought. Freni said that she used to stare at this scramble of grown men, children, and even a few women, and wonder what magic ingredient it was that her daughter-in-law had put into her baking. She'd even considered the possibility that her daughter-in-law was in league with the Devil.

I hate to admit it, but I was wrong yet again. The naysayer who'd predicted that the Amish-Asian craze would be a flash in the pan was right. It was like those Cro-Magnon doughnuts, or whatever those hybrid doughnuts were that had folks lining up around the block in New York some years ago. People might still be eating them, but you don't hear about them in the news anymore. Well, the same thing would have happened to Asian Sensations, because frankly, the flavour combinations were truly terrible. In the words of one down-to-earth reporter, 'the desserts are sublime, but even the most palatable entrée is not something that you would wish to see fed to your worst wartime enemy. Perhaps you would feed these disgusting concoctions to the members of your rival political party, but even that might be going too far.'

Little by little, my well-heeled society folks drifted away. After all, novelty has a short shelf-life. However, things that taste delicious are always in style. We Americans are unjustly criticized because our desserts are too sweet, or too buttery, but that's like saying Mount Everest is too tall, or the Pacific Ocean is too deep. Those things simply do not compute. A proper pudding (to use the 'posh' English term), should pack the pounds on one's posterior while one is still seated at the dinner table. End of discussion.

TWELVE

Fortunately for me, and more so for young Hortense, some customers discovered the joys of Barbara's rich, calorie-laden desserts before the restaurant had to be closed. Then word spread online, and in other media outlets. As new customers found us, I phased out the Asian influence, and soon all the entrées were hearty Amish dishes. I can't describe how thrilled I was when another review was published extolling the desserts, this time by our nation's premier rag. The reviewer was a young man in his twenties who wrote that he actually liked our entrées. He also said that if he had to choose between eating one of Barbara's desserts every day for the rest of his life, in prison, or being a free man and eating his fiancée's cooking, he would pick the first option. 'Then lock me up and let me eat cake!' That is a direct quote. A few days later I read an article in the same newspaper that his fiancée had dumped him.

However, this young man's excessive enthusiasm for Barbara's baking did result in a promotional idea. Given that edible treats are sometimes described as 'sinfully good', I promptly changed the name of the restaurant that Hortense and I jointly owned from Asian Sensations to Amish Sinsations. Anyway, the fact that it had been Barbara who'd been singled out for praise by this reviewer rankled the other two cooks. They threw her dirty looks, jostled her when she was measuring ingredients, slammed cupboard doors when she was baking, and muttered constantly under their breath. Marigold was a Presbyterian, but Lydia, an Amish woman, was supposed to be a good Christian! How could either of them be envious of an interloper from faraway Iowa? And a giantess at that!

On one hand, Christians should obey the Ten Commandments. The tenth commandment states that one should not 'covet their neighbour's ass, nor anything else that is your neighbour's', which would presumably include the praise that they get for their work. On the other hand, Marigold and Lydia were only human.

Nonetheless, it deeply saddened me that nobody warmed to Barbara. But for the life of me, I couldn't think of any reason why the Sisters of Perpetual Apathy should have a grievance with her. Sister Disenchanted was particularly rude, despite her snazzy outfit. One day, whenever the so-called nun came to the serving window to pick up one of Barbara's mouth-watering desserts, she flicked her tongue at my chef, like the monitor lizard I'd seen once on my husband's gargantuan TV. This bizarre behaviour prompted Barbara, a faithful Christian woman, to wonder aloud if the not-so-good sister might be possessed by the Devil. Compounding this problem was the fact that Lydia thought that Barbara was overreacting to a simple practical joke, and soon the story of Barbara and the serpent's tongue – for that's how Barbara viewed it – spread like head lice at a little girls' sleepover.

You can bet your bippy that the stout mini-Madre of the Sisters of Malicious Machinations jumped into the fray with both of her cloven hooves. Once, in a rare moment of generosity, I gave her a key to the back door, which opens directly into the kitchen. This is a privilege which she frequently abuses. She walks in uninvited at mealtimes and cuts my husband's meat for him, even if it is only a ground beef patty. She's been known to barge into our bedroom on a Saturday morning, and squirm her way between us before we're awake, so that she might be the one to stir her beloved son with a kiss.

The morning after the tongue-flicking incident, I was having breakfast with my family in the kitchen, when the back door flew open, and in burst a short, squat pseudo-nun.

'Gamma,' cried our two-year-old son, as he joyfully clapped his chubby, jam-smeared hands. Christianity teaches that we are born into sin because of Adam and Eve's fall, but Gabe's Judaism teaches that we are born with pure, unblemished souls. I hate to admit it, but so far, Little Jacob must be taking after his father's faith.

'Hey,' grunted Alison, who has a good heart, but who at four-teen has had the veil of innocence stripped from her eyes. I know she loves her adopted dad's mother, but she is also quite aware that whenever Grandmother Ida a.k.a. Mother Malaise drops in unannounced, chaos is sure to follow. This time, it was Sister Disenchanted who followed, and she was back to wearing her dismal habit. As the two self-proclaimed sisters remained standing between the table and the open door, it was obvious to me that they were up to no good.

'Welcome, dear,' I said, looking solely at Sister Disenchanted. 'As our second uninvited guest of the morning, you may help yourself to whatever is left on the table, or cook your own breakfast.'

'Mags!' Gabe said. 'Is that any way to speak to our guest?'

'Outta here,' Alison said, and scooted from the room.

'Und you see how dis one ignored me?' Ida said.

'Ma!' Gabe said. 'Don't start. Please? You're my two favourite women, and all you ever do is go for each other's throats.'

At that, the door from the dining room slammed open. 'What am I?' shrieked Alison. 'Chopped liver? Huh, Dad? Huh, Dad. Huh?'

'No, honey,' he said, 'of course not. I *had* to say that because one of them is my mother, and the other one is the mother of my son.'

'Oh, yeah? So where do I fit in?' Alison pointed at me. 'How come ya didn't say that she's the mother of your daughter? It's because I'm adopted, ain't it?'

'Of course not!'

'Then tell me something.' Alison's voice quavered like a violin bow drawn across the smooth edge of a saw blade. 'If it was me, Little Jacob, Mom, and that old woman who is supposed to be my grandma, and we was all drowning in, like, the Atlantic Ocean, or somewhere, and ya could save everybody, *except* for one, which one of us would ya let be dinner for the fishes?'

'Ya, vich von?' said Mother Malaise, her eyes gleaming expectantly. I have no doubt that she was quite sure that she would be the first one to be plucked out of the drink by her devoted progeny.

'Bon, bon,' said Little Jacob, beating his Sippy cup against the tray of his highchair.

Gabe, heretofore unequivocally known as the Babester, cleared his throat. 'Well, uh, you see, Ma raised my sister and me all by herself while holding down two jobs. And I met and fell in love with your mother before I met you. As for your brother, he's just a baby who can't swim, but you can.'

'I knew it,' Alison screeched. 'I don't belong in this family! I never did. You're all a bunch of fakes, liars, and hypocrites.'

'But I don't even work for the government,' I said.

'Eeeeeeeg,' Alison screeched again. 'Mom, all ya ever do is try ta change the subject with your stupid jokes. Well, I got news for ya: they ain't even funny. Not ever, ever, ever!'

'Ebah, ebah, ebah,' said Little Jacob, still pounding away merrily with his Sippy cup.

Alison pointed at her baby brother. 'Ooh, I hate ya so much, ya spoiled little brat! I wish that ya had never been born. In fact, I wish ya'd fall out of your highchair and break your head open like Humpty Dumpty, that's what I wish.'

'Alison,' Gabe said sharply. 'Go to your room! If anyone's acting like a brat now, it's you.'

Our fourteen-year-old daughter's eyes blazed at her father. 'I hate you more,' she rasped.

'Right now, I don't like you very much either,' he said. He turned to me. 'Now look what you made me say?'

'*Me?*' I said. 'I didn't make you say anything.'

At this point Alison was fit to be tied. 'Mom, why does everything hafta be about you? Dad and me was having a fight and now ya has to jump in. It ain't fair! I betcha don't love me neither. No way, no how, ain't nobody ever gonna love me, or take my side.'

She stomped away with such force that the hanging pots acted as chimes, the water glasses tinkled, and the china in the cabinets rattled. Throw in Little Jacob's Sippy cup performance, and we had ourselves a proper mini-symphony.

Gabe shot to his feet, knocking over his chair. Seconds later I could hear him chasing Alison up the stairs and down the hall to her room. Then there came the sound of more slamming.

That's when my mother-in-law turned to me. '*Nu?* How could you do a ting like dis?'

I prayed for patience before answering. It is my least answered prayer.

'The show is over, dear,' I said. 'Now the audience must go home.'

Ida refused to budge. Too bad I hadn't prayed that a very strong angel would whisk her and her dour companion back across Hertzler Road to the Convent of Perpetual Apathy. Only the Good Lord knew the purpose of their most unfortunate visit that morning. However, one thing was clear: if Sister Disenchanted showed up at the newly renamed Amish Sinsations the next day looking like that, she was out of a job. For another thing, while my mother-in-law's supposed purpose in starting this cult was to provide a place for folks who had given up on life, almost from the very beginning it seemed that she used her power as Mother Malaise to drive a wedge between the Babester and me.

'It vill never voik,' Ida said. 'Dis ting dat you did.'

'*Excuse* me?' I said. So help me, I was on the verge of pushing her out myself.

I lunged past the despondent duo and grabbed a large broom that I keep by the back door. 'You have thirty seconds to explain yourselves. If you can't, I can sweep you out, or you can hop on this, and take a ride back to your convent.'

THIRTEEN

'Your shmeer campaign against Sister Disenchanted,' Ida
said. 'Das vhy I'm here.'

I was taken off-guard, and so was my mouth. 'Isn't a
shmeer like a portion of cream cheese spread across a bagel?'

'Oy, must you always mock an old woman?' Ida said.

'Believe me, I try very hard not to. But there isn't a smear
campaign being conducted against Sister Disenchanted. Whatever
makes you think so?'

Ida came all the way into the kitchen and hauled her ample
patooty up onto the nearest chair. Now it was going to take *two*
strong angels to cart her off, and unless they showed up before
Gabe got back downstairs, I was going to have to forfeit my
planned morning at home. Thank heavens Little Jacob was
gleefully occupied with giving himself an oatmeal facial.

Mother Malaise wagged a gnarled finger at me. 'Den, vhy vas
it, last night, at da convent, my nuns dat used to be Aye-mish,
dey get phone calls from der friends on de outside dat say all
everybody talks about is da vaitress vid da snake tongue?'

'Give me a break,' I said. 'For starters, you've lived here too
long – I mean, long enough to know that the word is pronounced
AH-mish, with a short "a", like in the word "American". And
secondly, I don't like conspiracy theories, so just back off on
that score. *Capiche?*'

'Vhat is dis void, capiche?' Ida said fiercely. 'Some Mennonite
food dat you make for my boys now?'

'Ay-yi-yi,' I said, tugging at my neatly braided hair.

'Yi-yi-yi,' Little Jacob mimicked proudly, as he gave himself
an oatmeal shampoo.

I stamped my oversize feet and waved the broom. 'Ida, your
son is a heart surgeon; he is not a boy. Now go!'

She stood with exaggerated slowness, a smile on her lipless
face. 'Yah, I vill go now. But just so you know, Magdalena, your

fancy-schmancy restaurant vill fail. Dis I can promise.' She smiled
again. Broadly. 'You vant to ask me vhy?'

'No.'

'Den goot, I vill tell you anyvay. Eet is a crazy idea, and you
are *meshuggah* to vaste my son's goot money on eet, dat's vhy.
Eet is a fad, und fads dunt last, dat I can tell you.'

'And you know this how?' I said.

'People are saying,' she said.

Left without options to preserve my sanity I took my baby
son, who really *was* a boy, and whisked him off to my bedroom.
After locking the door, I jammed a chair under the doorknob just
to make sure that my nightmare didn't follow me in. Then I
called the Hernia Police Department and reported that two
intruders had broken into The PennDutch Inn.

'Hey Madam Mayor,' a jovial male voice said.

'Toy,' I said to the Chief of Police, 'I'd like to report a break-
in.' As a matter of interest, other than our disproportionally high
rate of murder, we good citizens are quite law-abiding, and thus
Chief Toy Graham is our only police officer. Also, Toy originally
hails from the South where men named Toy are not unheard of.
Toy has the most delightful Carolina accent, which brings to
mind languorous summer days filled with the scent of magnolia
blossoms, and the taste of sweet tea and fried green tomatoes.
Don't get me wrong when I say that this man, who is half my
age, is as cute as an eight-week-old puppy, and if he were my
puppy, I'd put him on a leash and take him for a lot of long,
slow walks. Maybe even a few cuddles.

On the other end of the line, Toy chuckled. 'Magdalena, does
one of your intruders stand four-feet-nine inches tall in her support
stockings and wear a habit? Also, might she be the same woman
that I've heard you refer to as Mother Despicable?'

'You've read my little mind,' I said. 'Isn't there anything that
I can do?'

'We've been over this a million times, boss. You can't get a
restraining order unless your better-half signs off on one. Maybe
you can get your mother-in-law mad enough to hit you. Then I
can haul her in on assault charges.'

'*Really?*'

'Magdalena! Frankly, I'm—'

'No, I didn't mean it. Well, I did, but I shouldn't have, and I take back my evil thoughts. It's just that she makes me so miserable.'

Toy chuckled. 'I was about to say that, frankly, I'm proud of you.'

'You are?' My shrivelled old heart began beating sinfully fast.

'From what I've learned about you Mennonites and Amish in the year I've lived in Hernia, you really are the pacifists whom you claim to be. If a Methodist man hits an Amish man, the Amish man will just turn and walk away. It's the same with you Mennonites too, right? You'll also just walk away.'

'Jesus told us to turn the other cheek,' I said. 'It's in the Bible.'

'Yeah, well, maybe that's how it's supposed to be, and it is – most of the time. But we both know that Obadiah Rupp pummelled his pregnant wife in the abdomen so many times that she miscarried in the fourth month and lost the baby. And we know that Dorcas Gundy poisoned her husband and three of her eleven children, by putting eye drops in their food every day for a week.'

One can get irritated at even puppy-dog cute men in uniforms. 'So, what's your point?' I said.

'No, what's your mother-in-law's point? By now I'm beginning to suspect that woman is up to something more than just sabotaging your marriage. Her insistence on having Sister Disgusting working in your restaurant has the workings of a sinister plot, if you ask me, and I'm not one to buy into conspiracy theories. I fielded calls all evening from women claiming to have witnessed a brouhaha at Amish Sinsations that apparently didn't happen. Am I right?'

'Wow! Actually, her name is Sister Disenchantment, although I like your moniker better. But you're right as rain. I'm sure it was disgusting, and terribly unsettling, from poor Barbara Hostetler's point of view, but my elite customers were never aware of the pseudo-nun's snake imitation. There wasn't any sort of disturbance, I assure you.'

'Well then, get this: most of the calls I got were from supposed customers of yours. But here's the thing, they were from this area code, and they spoke with Hernia accents.'

If devilishly attractive Toy and I had been having this

conversation in person, I would have cocked a sparse, mousey-brown eyebrow. I might even have giggled coquettishly before framing a careful reply. Instead, I merely made a point of clearing my throat. 'They were definitely *not* New Yorkers or Bostonians. Or from Chicago for that matter.'

'Toy, you are from the South and have that charming Southern accent. You only just moved up here, above the Mason-Dixon Line, a little more than a year ago. Is it possible that all Yankees sound the same to you?'

'Ouch! Allow me to fine tune my answer a bit, and I know this will come across as snobby. Some of the callers who claimed to be well-heeled, high society people from the East Coast, sounded like they'd never graduated from high school. Plus, even a Charlottean like me can recognize a New Yorker, or a Bostonian, unless they've gone into broadcasting, or acting.'

'Message received. I'm sorry for offending you.'

He laughed. 'That's OK. Some Southerners take a dim view on immigrants from the North who want to fit into our culture. "Just because a cat has kittens in the oven," they say, "that don't make them biscuits."'

I tried to laugh. 'Somehow I don't think that you're trying to fit into our culture. But if you are, you can always forsake your loose Episcopalian ways, and become a Mennonite. One of the liberal Mennonites like Agnes. However, you would never make it as an Amish man. No electricity, no television *ever*, and no computers.'

Precious minutes flew by while Police Chief Toy Graham enjoyed a belly laugh. By the time he finally came to his senses, I was on the verge of having a panic attack. After all, at any minute Gabe, or the nightmare who birthed him, could be at the door, demanding entrance.

'Hey, boss,' Toy finally said, 'are you still there?'

'No, this is your mother, and she wants you to brush your teeth twice a day and floss at least one. But your boss wants to know some of the specifics of those calls, because I thought Barbara handled herself very well.'

'Yeah, a couple of callers whom I questioned further reported that you remained calm as well. Look, I'm not trying to argue, Magdalena, but many of the callers were Amish women. They called from the public phone at Yoder's Corner Market, because as you know, the Amish around here are about the strictest there are, and don't allow cell phones. Two men called to offer their support for Barbara, but I recognized their voices. One was her husband Jonathan, and the other male caller was her father-in-law.'

'And my dear, dear cousin Freni? I know that she's so jealous of her daughter-in-law that she can't stand it. Did Freni call?'

Toy was silent for far too long. 'Magdalena, boss, will you at least listen to what I am going to say next, even if you don't heed my advice?'

'OK but speak fast. I hear Gabe calling me.'

Toy spoke with the speed of an auctioneer. 'Your hybrid restaurant idea was brilliant while it lasted. Emphasizing Barbara's rich, moist, mouth-watering desserts was a brilliant decision. It's obviously been a huge success, but you need to fire all your staff, except for Agnes and Barbara, and start over. Barbara is a sweetheart, but she's a pariah, because she's from someplace else. Believe me, *I* get that.

'The really bad news is that reptilian with the flicking tongue, Sister Dystopia, or whatever her name is. She's been inserted there by your mother-in-law from Hell, and I think that what happened yesterday is just the tip of the iceberg. At the very least get rid of that Sister.'

'But Gabe will be so angry—'

I had missed the doorknob turning. Perhaps this way and that, and perhaps several times.

'Magdalena, are you in there?' Gabe called softly. 'Of course you are. I can hear you talking on the phone.'

'Official business,' I said sweetly. 'I'll be right there.' I quickly ended my call with Toy.

'Why was the door locked?' Gabe said, after I let him in.

'One can't be too careful,' I said, which wasn't a lie. 'The fruit of your loins is fast asleep on our bed. Whilst your ravishingly beautiful wife was fulfilling her mayoral duties, you wouldn't want the little tyke to toddle off into harm's way now, would you?'

'Harm's way?' Gabe said. 'Mags, there's no harm out there. Just Ma looking all hurt and confused.'

'Oh, is she still here?' I would have batted my eyes, but my colourless lashes are as effective as a pair of dead fly wings.

'Yeah, she's still here. Mags, she claims that Barbara Hostetler is spreading ugly rumours about one of the disciples at Amish Sinsations. Do you know anything about this matter?'

'Unfortunately, I know more than I care to. That's what I was on the phone talking about with Toy. Your mother and her denizens of society's dropouts have launched a campaign aimed at having poor Barbara Hostetler quit her job.'

'Why the heck would Ma do that?'

'Because your mother wanted the job of chef for herself. She begged me for it – no, she demanded that I make her my chef, but I refused. Now look what's happened!'

'But that's crazy! Ma is old; she is way past retirement age. Besides, she enjoys playing the part of a Mother Superior, in what you know is in a made-up religious organization. You're always accusing her of running a scam, of conning these women. You can't deny that.'

'Gabe, don't you get it? It's not really about the cooking. Your mother doesn't *really* want to be chef; she just wants to get back at *me*. She wants to do anything that she can to mess up my life.'

Gabe stared at me with perhaps the same amount of comprehension that I once used when regarding a photo of a Jackson Pollock painting. My clueless husband jiggled his pinkies in both ears, but I think that it was to test for wax, not to see if they were still functioning. Then he groaned.

'Mags, you're being paranoid,' he said.

'I am not. Face it: your mother can't stand the fact that there is another woman in her son's life.'

'Oh, not that again.'

I wanted to grab my handsome doctor husband and shake him until at least one of his outrageously expensive caps fell off his teeth. Of course, I didn't. That sort of behaviour wouldn't have been good for our marriage, and it would have violated my pacifist beliefs. Instead I sucked it up, as they say nowadays, and changed the subject.

'How is our precious daughter doing?' I said.

'Better,' Gabe said. 'I think I got through to her that I misspoke, that I didn't express myself well. I think it's important that I start doing more things with her when it is just the two of us. You know, to make her feel special. I emphasized that she is my *only* daughter, and that I love her very much.'

I nodded. 'Good start. I'm proud of you for that. Now my turn. Back to your mother and me. The Bible says that you're supposed to leave your parents and cleave unto your wife – or husband, as the case may be. If you could save only one of us, who would it be?'

My answer was a slammed door. I waited until I heard Ida's nasal voice silenced by the kitchen door. A few minutes later I heard Gabe's car crunching out of the driveway, so I guessed he was either giving the women a lift back to the convent, or else he was running errands. Although to be perfectly honest, the Devil did make me hope that he was running her over in the driveway – but I only thought that for a second, and then I quickly repented of that evil thought. Father Joijuice, the Episcopalian minister in Bedford, said on the radio that we are not responsible for the thoughts that just flicker through our brains, but that sounds contrary to Matthew 5:28. Besides, Episcopalians are the American variety of Anglicans, and Henry VIII who started that faith did some rather unsavoury things, and well – I'm just saying.

Back to my Dearly Beloved, and why he felt the need to jump in his car and drive away. Perhaps he was just driving about aimlessly to 'let off steam', as he calls it. In my opinion, jogging would have been a better option than driving, even if there wasn't the slightest chance that he would have accidentally backed over his mother. There, you see? I'm not quite the horrible person that some people think that I am. Anyway, Gabe knows cardiology, and Magdalena knows how to milk cows, which means that we're supposed to stay in our own lanes. End of story.

When I was confident that the coast was clear, I went upstairs and knocked on Alison's door. As her mother, I pay no attention to the carefully lettered sign that she posted two years ago when she was twelve that reads:

GO AWAY!
DONT EVEN NOCK!

But I also respect her privacy to the extent that I do the forbidden action, and always knock before entering her room if she is at home. If she is not home, then her privacy is not in play, and since this is my house, and she is my daughter, I feel free to enter her room whenever I please. As a good mother, it is my responsibility to do so. Who else is going to put away her clean clothes, sweep under her bed for dust bunnies, and look under her mattress for little bags of marijuana?

That day when I knocked, I received the usual response. 'Go away!' Alison bellowed.

'I'm here to stay!' I bellowed back. 'And if we wake up your brother, you're the one who will have to change his next diaper.'

'Aw, Mom! Then come on in.'

One of my daughter's soul-crushing chores is to keep her room 'somewhat neat'. The definition of 'neat' had broadened over the last year, beginning with 'a few things left on the floor', practically to the point of 'was there ever really a floor in the first place?'. Because entering her room always causes my stomach to churn, and often leads to me grounding her, I try to limit my visits as much as possible.

That morning, with Gabe off who knows where, I tried to keep my focus strictly on Alison. All the rooms in my restored farm-house, The PennDutch Inn, are quite large. Therefore, it was a challenge negotiating my way through slippery piles of paper, plastic, and piles of dirty clothing, all the while trying hard not to really see anything out of the corner of my eyes, except for Alison.

It wasn't until I was looming over her that I noticed she was reading a Harry Potter book. I don't recall which one, but it doesn't matter. I'm not the only Christian who disapproves of their content. The Bible forbids us to practice sorcery. In fact, it states in plain English that mediums and conjurers are to be put to death.

'Alison,' I asked in horror, 'where did you get that book?'

Alison looked up slowly, defiantly. 'From the library in Bedford. Dad took me there last week. I got three Harry Potter books. I've already read two.'

I was stunned. I knew that the girl was clever, and that her terrible grammar was a combination of laziness and a gambit to get under our skin as teenagers are wont to do. However, I hadn't the foggiest notion that she had the stamina to plough her way through a book longer than a comic book, much less a tome so thick that she had to prop it up with a pillow.

'But you know that I don't approve of magic and witchcraft,' I said, as I tried to keep any hint of admiration off my face.

'Yeah, but Dad said was it all right. In fact, he checked them out on his card.'

'Is that so, huh? Well, we'll just see about that.'

Alison snickered. 'Mom, ya do know that in your half of the Bible, the one that Dad doesn't approve of, it says that the husband should be the head of the wife. And then it says something like, "wife obey your husband".'

I could feel my face redden. That has always been one of the most difficult verses in the New Testament for me to wrap my mind around. But the thing is, if you try to wrap your mind around something too far, then your brain gets twisted, and you end up becoming a Presbyterian, like my sister Susannah, who is in prison, or even worse, like Toy, the Episcopalian.

The Bible is full of *supposed* contradictions. According to one website there were 196 of these contradictions in the New Testament alone. In fact, Pastor Diffledorf calls them riddles, and said that God will supply the answers to all of them when we get to Heaven. Pastor says that Christians shouldn't waste their time trying to second guess the Lord, and this is what *faith* is all about. For the record, nearly everyone at Beechy Grove Mennonite Church has observed Daphne Diffledorf shamelessly bossing her husband around. What's more, the couple is not only childless, they seem positively allergic to teenagers.

'So, Mom,' Alison said when I was slow to respond, 'whatcha gonna do, huh? Ya gonna be the wimpy wife like your half of the Bible says ya supposed to be, or ya gonna let Dad win, and let me get away with reading this book about sorcerers and spells?'

I braved a billion cooties and plonked my bony caboose down beside her. 'Scoot over, toots. I want you to read me some of this heathen book.'

'You mean, like, *aloud*?'

'Yes, aloud, dear. You know that, like all mothers, I have eyes in the back of my head, and the hearing of an owl – which is pretty keen. But I won't be able to hear you, if you read silently, because this book was written in Great Britain. The English that they speak over there has a funny accent, and the sound waves required to turn the words into proper American English can't be transmitted through skull bones.'

'No way!'

'No way, indeed,' I said, with a wry smile, for by repeating her response I had just undone my little white lie.

'OK, here goes,' she said. Alison leaned back, and we snuggled together on her bed as she read to me for almost an hour. I didn't have her stop until I heard Little Jacob wake up, thanks to the portable baby monitor which I carry in my skirt pocket at all times when I'm home.

You can bet your bippy that I was horrified by the contents of the book – had it been a more perfect world than what we were living in, I might have wrested it from her hands and grounded her further. But what can I say? At least when she's reading, Alison's grammar remains consistent, and that's something.

Experts say that when it comes to raising children, we should choose our battles. Harry Potter and his friends were fighting evil with good magic spells; they weren't selling drugs or assaulting girls. In the interest of what Gabe calls *shalom bayit*, 'peace in the home', I decided to *try* to think kinder thoughts about his mother. And I certainly had no intention of bringing up the Harry Potter episode.

FOURTEEN

'Vanity of vanities,' says the Preacher; 'Vanity of vanities, all is vanity.' Ecclesiastes 1:2.

We Americans are a church-going people. We have one of the highest rates of church attendance in the world. Those of us who do make it a habit to show up at God's House every Sunday also own a copy of his written word, the Holy Bible – hopefully the King James Version, which I am sure is the one that Jesus himself must have read.

Although I make it part of my routine, as do many other American Christians, to work their way through the entire Bible every year, I will admit that there are parts that I tend to skim. For instance, do I really need to know how to make a portable meeting house that can be lugged around in the desert for forty years?

Or how about the parts that challenge my cherished beliefs, and which Pastor Diffledorf can't answer. For example, in the Book of Jeremiah, God curses King Jeconiah (a Davidic King) and says that none of his descendants will ever sit on the throne of David. But in the Book of Matthew, King Jeconiah is listed as one of Jesus's direct ancestors. The problem is that in order to fulfil the messianic prophecy, Jesus had to be descended from the House of David, which stopped with King Jeconiah. *Oy vey*, as my Jewish husband would say, if that were one of *his* theological puzzles – which it isn't. Pastor Diffledorf says that I'll just have to ask the Lord for the answer when I get to Heaven.

But oh, how I've digressed, just to avoid a painful subject: that of my vanity. Although I've always possessed an admirable amount of humility, the sudden success of Amish Sinsations must have gone to my head. That's the only way that I can explain the disastrous chain of events that was about to upend my life.

By then, Amish *Sin*sations was an even a bigger hit with the so-called one percent than its predecessor had been, and I had every confidence that it was what Agnes called 'a keeper'. We

Pennsylvania Dutch have traditionally subscribed to the dictum that 'fat's where it's at' when it comes to our cooking. If you ask me, that's how the Good Lord designed us, otherwise we wouldn't be drawn to a perfectly marbled steak, or bacon, or cinnamon rolls, or even just bread warm from the oven that's been slathered in real creamery butter.

Now let's talk about sugar: white granulated sugar, powdered sugar, dark brown sugar, medium brown sugar, and light brown sugar. All of these are a party for one's mouth. Honey is as well. Of course, one would be sadly remiss not to mention the Crown Jewel of North America: maple syrup. Why else did God create sugar maples, if not for us to enjoy their wonderful bounty on our pancakes, candy, and even in our coffee?

One day, when the sun was shining brightly, and birds were singing in the lilac bushes on either side of the nursery window, I received a call from Sarah Conway, the personal assistant to the editor of *A Woman's Place*. This highly esteemed homemaker's magazine combines mouth-watering recipes, housekeeping tips, gardening, and lots of scripture, within its pages. It is issued monthly, and I know many women for whom this publication constitutes their only reading material, other than their Bible and daily devotions guide.

One can only imagine then how thrilled I was to have the editor of this esteemed magazine request a stay at The PennDutch Inn. This was especially the case since Sarah, the assistant, let it be known that her boss, Gordon Gaiters, had read about my 'esteemed' establishment in *Condor's Nest Travel,* another highly esteemed publication. In addition to booking the entire inn (to ensure his privacy, Sarah said), Mr Gaiters wished to eat several of his meals at Amish Sinsations. Would I be willing to accommodate him? You bet your bippy I would. It was all so perfect!

Or not. How could I have allowed myself to be seduced by the flattering words Sarah Conway had thrown at me? Was she an evil temptress like the serpent in the perfect Garden of Eden? How stupid of me to have gotten carried away like that. I had forgotten that I was supposed to be a businesswoman of integrity. In order to accommodate Gordon Gaiters' request for use of the entire inn, I was going to have to call every guest who had confirmed reservations for the week of his stay and tell each one of them that their reservation was not going to be honoured. Some of these guests might feel less than pleased to learn that the holiday they'd been planning for a year or more had to be scratched. Some might even get it into their heads to sue.

There was another downside to Gordon Gaiters' sudden visit. This aspect was even more troubling than having to deal with an angry, hysterical public threatening to blackball my inn and the restaurant, both actions which were likely to happen when I pulled the plug on my highly prized reservations. What caused my stomach to churn, and my hand to reach for antacids, was my growing awareness that I no longer could stand shoulder to shoulder with the underlying premise in each issue of *A Woman's Place* magazine. Inside the publication, the first page following the Table of Contents is illustrated with the facsimile of an ancient scroll. Written across the scroll are words that are supposed to look like Hebrew but are actually English. The author is the Apostle Paul and the quote I refer to is Ephesians 5:22-23a in the New King James Version of the New Testament: 'Wives, submit to your own husbands, as to the Lord. For the husband is the head of the wife.'

Well, for one thing, Paul was never married, and for another, he made it pretty clear in other passages that he wasn't too fond of women. That's just my opinion, of course, and who am I to argue with a man who had a divine revelation with the risen Jesus on the road to Damascus, and thereafter claimed that he knew Jesus better than anyone who'd actually prayed, touched, sweated, walked, and tarried with the bodily Jesus for thirty-three long years? I'm just saying, I'm just a woman, I'm just Magdalena Portulacca Yoder. That's a lot of 'justs' in order to justify myself. We still have freedom of religion in this country, so I don't have to agree with those verses that say that a man is the head of the wife, and that a woman should submit to him.

I think that Paul said those things, but I don't believe that Jesus said them. So there! I certainly don't want Alison to grow up to be submissive. That would break my heart – and to think that some folks say that I don't have a heart. My heart may be tiny and shrivelled, but I know that I still have one, because my doctor heard a faint beating sound in my chest at my last physical check-up. Well, either that, or it was my acid reflux acting up, she wasn't sure.

It was around the time that I became an inadvertent adulteress that I began to have serious issues with the content of *A Woman's Place*. At first, I foolishly attempted to express my opinions by writing letters to the editor. Long, instructive letters – for I am a passionate woman, if you will. Most of my letters were published, but only after they'd been chopped to bits by the editor, thereby making me out to sound foolish, perhaps even mad. After that I simply let my subscription to *A Woman's Place* lapse. In all honesty, before Sarah Conway called to book the entire inn, I had not once, in six years, picked up an issue of her employer's magazine. Although I had spotted some well-thumbed ones lying about in various homes I'd visited during that time frame, I'd heard almost no one speak of *A Woman's Place* anymore. My friends are loyal and considerate of my feelings, unlike Gordon Gaiters, who had taken my letters and twisted them into pithy bits of mockery – aimed at *me*! And all because I disagreed with some of the content in his magazine. Talk about hubris!

Why then, one might ask, did I agree to let him have use of all my rooms for a week? Because of hubris. Like Granny said, the word did have a pleasant, feminine sound. Sort of like the female equivalent of Hubert. Although nicknames would be a bit awkward, given that 'bris' is the Hebrew word for ritual circumcision. A Jewish couple would probably wish to refrain from having to introduce their boy and girl twins as 'these are our children, Bert and Circumcision'. Back to my sin of pride: since Gordon Gaiters had shredded my self-worth six years ago, it was important to me, in a big way, to show him that not only had I survived, but that I had *thrived*.

So there you have it. And once having fully committed to Gordon Gaiters' imminent visit, I was feeling both extremely excited, and at the same time, full of dread. These two emotions, duelling for supremacy, even caused me to break out with a few pimples, as if I were a teenager again. At least Alison and I had something to bond over throughout the coming days – if only she would lift a page out of my childhood, and be one of those children who was seen, but never heard. Realistically, that was about as likely as a snowstorm in August.

Given that it was still early August, school was not yet back in session, so I encouraged – nay, practically begged – our daughter to arrange a sleepover at a friend's home. Better yet, a series of friends' homes. Despite her bad grammar, Alison is a surprisingly popular girl, not only with her peers, but with their parents. Gabe thinks that may be because she has learned to 'play the game', as he calls it. Several times when he has gone early to pick her up from an overnight stay at a friend's house, he has caught her helping the mother washing up in the kitchen and speaking to her in Standard English.

I am so ashamed to admit that I even tried bribing Alison with cash to stay away from The PennDutch Inn, but to no avail. When that didn't work, I tried luring her into the lounge area of our master bedroom where Gabe keeps his sinfully large flat-screen television, with the added bonus of unlimited snacks, both sugary and savoury, but she wouldn't bite. Finally, at my wit's end, I finished where I should have begun, which was on my knees, imploring God to keep her mouth firmly shut, just like the angel did to the mouths of the lions who would have torn the Prophet Daniel limb from limb.

Whatever game Alison was playing on the day of Gordon Gaiters' arrival, I couldn't help but admire her pluck and enthusiasm. Since she's not my biological daughter, I can't rightly say that she's a 'chip off the old block', but as we share cousinship in so many family lines, it's not totally beyond the realm of possibility that she's my very much younger identical twin sister.

That said, the afternoon when Gordon Gaiters arrived, chauffeured by Sarah Conway, my dear sweet husband and me had long since kissed and made up. The details are, of course, nobody's business. Gabe and I strive not to go to bed angry with each other, and if the circumstances are such that one of us has to retire in a foul mood, we both agree that it had better be him. Gabe awakes each morning with his mind a blank slate, whereas my mind still has scribbles etched on it from forty years ago.

When Alison espied Gordon Gaiters' sleek car from her bedroom window, she flew down from upstairs like Harry Potter himself, and out to greet him. I hadn't been sure if Alison had ever read *A Woman's Place*, and had been afraid to ask, but she acted as if he was a rock star, or a famous actor. Her motive,

I had no doubt, was to rack up 'brownie points' with me, so that I would overlook her choice of reading material.

But when Sarah Conway stepped out of the sleek new automobile with the Missouri license plates, Alison stopped dead in her tracks. Her eyes widened to the size of manhole covers, and her lower jaw swung back and forth just above her bare feet. That may have been a slight exaggeration, but I too was stunned by what I beheld.

Sarah Conway bore a striking resemblance to Hernia's very own Barbara Hostetler. She was sinfully tall (at least she would have seemed so to Freni), she had Barbara's green eyes, the same rich brown hair, bordering on auburn (although hers was lightly streaked with grey), and the same pleasant features. Where they differed the most physically was that Sarah Conway appeared to be a generation older than Barbara Hostetler, which would have put Sarah at around sixty. What was not immediately noticeable, was that she had apparently spent a good deal of time outdoors in the sun, without having first applied sunscreen. At any rate, a more imaginative woman than I am might have entertained the idea, however briefly, that Sarah Conway was Barbara Conway's mother come to pay a surprise visit.

It is no secret that I have often been accused of being one muffin shy of a gift basket. In my defence, I wish to state that although Barbara Hostetler is a legitimate Amish woman, from a well-known Amish community in Iowa, she came to Pennsylvania to marry Freni's son Jonathan. Jonathan did not go there to seek a bride. What's more, Barbara Hostetler was a so-called foundling. She had been found in a barn as a newborn, most likely abandoned by an Amish teenager who had left the community to sow her 'wild oats' during the years of teenage leniency called *rumschpringe*, and then returned home.

Besides their obvious difference in age, they were also dressed quite differently. Whereas Barbara Hostetler wears dresses sewn out of plain coloured cloth, and keeps her hair covered unless she is sleeping, Sarah Conway was dressed in the style to which some very conservative evangelical groups adhere. Sarah's light blue shirtdress with its tiny flower print was even more modest than Barbara's with its ankle length skirt, long sleeves, and stand-up collar, which she wore buttoned to her throat. Her still gorgeous hair, which the Bible states is a woman's 'crowning glory', although braided and coiled around her head in the identical manner as Barbara's, seemed strangely naked in its uncovered state.

'Wow,' Alison said, when she'd found her tongue. 'Who are you?'

'You will address me as "Miss Conway",' the new arrival said.

'Ya sure ya ain't Barbara Hostetler's mom?' Alison said.

Sarah Conway stiffened. 'Are you sure that you're not being incredibly rude?'

'Maybe I am, or maybe I ain't,' Alison said.

'So you are just being rude. And you're immodestly dressed, too, I see. And here I thought this was a Conservative Mennonite establishment. Or are you just an uncouth neighbourhood girl? I can't imagine that Miss Yoder would hire a maid the likes of you.'

A more responsible parent upon reading this verbal exchange transcribed on a page, might conclude that I should have chastised my child for having sassed Sarah Conway in the first place. That's what my mama would have done, had I dared speak to an adult the way Alison had. However, that never would have happened, because back then I didn't even have the chutzpah to speak to my dolls that way. At any rate, Sarah Conway's harsh criticism of Alison caused me to react to her in a most unchristian manner. One might say that the Devil made me do it.

'Miss Sarah Conway,' I roared. 'You are unworthy of touching the hem of this girl's garment, to borrow a phrase from the Good Lord himself. Alison may be rude, and crude, and socially unacceptable, but she has a heart of gold, and she is my beloved daughter. Nobody can point out her many and obvious faults except her father and me. Have I made myself clear?'

Much to my great surprise Sarah Conway's green eyes smiled. Not her lips, mind you, but her eyes.

'Well then,' she said, 'now that introductions have been made, I must attend to my employer.'

When the Barbara Hostetler lookalike headed around the bonnet of the sleek automobile to assist Gordon Gaiters, my dear, sweet Alison flew into action. Perhaps she wished to prove herself hospitable after all, although the result was that she and Sarah

Conway practically came to blows to see who would be the one
to open the car door for the elderly gent. It was a foregone
conclusion, however, as few living people possess elbows
sharper than Alison's.

'Mr Gaiters,' she shouted into the man's ear. 'How ya doing?'

'He's just fine,' I heard Sarah Conway say a bit crossly.

OK, I might have lagged some five yards or so behind my
daughter, but my hearing is still so sharp that I can hear the
Babester clip his toenails when I'm in our barn, and he's back
in our master bathroom. To be fair, Sarah Conway was only
trying to do her job when my rude, but altogether endearing,
daughter butted in.

'Good,' Alison said, 'then I can walk the old man up to the
house.'

'I beg your pardon!' Sarah Conway said.

'Nah,' Alison said, 'ya ain't gotta beg for nothing, lady. Not
with this fancy-schmancy car ya been driving.' She reached for
Gordon Gaiters' arm, but he snatched it away as fast as greased
lightning. Believe you me, that old man was mighty impressive
for someone who I assumed was looking eighty in the rear-view
mirror.

'It's not her car, little girl, it's mine.'

'Is that so, huh? Then why ain't ya the one driving it? And
just so ya know, I ain't no little girl.'

Before Alison could launch another verbal assault on my
guests, Sarah Conway launched a physical assault on her. With
her gloved hands she literally gave my daughter a hard push that
sent the dear child toppling backward to the rough asphalt drive.
Alison thrust out her arm in an attempt to break her fall, but still
ended up lying on her back, her knees spread, and the skirt of
her sundress flipped back.

'Hey!' she shouted as she went down. Then she lay there
moaning, while I stood there staring, dumbstruck, for far too
long. There are times, sadly, when it is impossible to process
what one has just seen. At least that happens to me.

Sarah Conway, on the other hand, had a shorter reaction time
than I did. 'Oh, I am so sorry,' she gushed. 'Sometimes I don't
know my own strength.' She extended a hand to Alison before
I could even move. 'Here girl. Upsy-daisy.'

Alison merely glared at the woman. That's when I rushed in. 'How bad is it, dear? Do I need to call Gabe?'

Alison sat slowly and showed me a bloody right palm to which tiny bits of asphalt adhered. With her other hand she rubbed her back as she straightened it. Then she twisted her head this way and that, and I could hear her neck 'crack'. Getting her cartilage to crack is one of my young teen's favourite ways to frighten and annoy me.

'Nah, I'll live.'

'In that case,' Gordon Gaiters said, 'you might do me the great favour of putting your knees together as soon as possible. No Christian child should be seen in such a compromising position.'

'Why, I never!' I said.

Alison jumped to feet. 'That's OK, Mom.' She turned to face Gordon Gaiters. 'When I actually *was* a little girl, I was very shy. I used to think that if I couldn't see someone, then that person couldn't see me. So I used to do this.'

Alison yanked her skirt as high as it would go, which was over her head, and which subsequently exposed not only London and France, but possibly even Scotland and the New Hebrides. The naughty maneuver was over almost before it began; that's how fast her skirt came down. If the soft snicker that escaped Sarah Conway's lips was the only response to Alison's prank, then I might have thought that my eyes had literally deceived me. But there was corroborating testimony.

'Shame on you, little girl,' Gordon Gaiters said, wagging an arthritic finger inches from Alison's nose. 'That's how harlots get started.'

Alison snorted. 'By getting pushed to the ground by old ladies?'

'No,' Gordon Gaiters said. 'Harlots get started by acting like heathens. Is that what you are? A little heathen?'

I watched in escalating horror, and mounting pride, as my daughter stood up to a bully many times her age. 'Maybe I *am* a heathen,' she said, 'but I sure ain't no Mennonite, nor no Amish neither, because I don't wanna turn the other cheek, just because some man in the olden days says that I hafta. I used ta say that I was Jewish like my dad is, but now that I been reading them Harry Potter books, I've been thinking about maybe becoming a witch.'

I gasped.

'Get behind me, Satan,' my guests said in unison.

'Don't get me wrong,' Alison said calmly. 'I wouldn't be one of them bad kinda witches. I wouldn't be no black witch. And just so ya know, that ain't no racist thing. Black witches just mean they are the kind that practice black magic, you know, the kind that puts curses on people and the like. I'd be what they call a white witch; I'd do just good spells. Good luck type stuff.'

'Get behind me Satan,' *I* said to my daughter. Any kind of witch was expressly forbidden in the Bible. In fact, witches were to be stoned to death. I'm fairly certain that commandment was the origin of the infamous Salem Witch Trials.

'Hey,' Alison said brightly, 'how about I take ya guys up ta your rooms? Mom's giving ya the entire upstairs floor. She's even kicking me outta my room and putting me down in the nursery with my baby brother. I'll even carry your luggage for ya, if ya want. Course ya gotta tip, just like if I was really a bona fide porter in a swanky-dank hotel, not that this ain't. Ya get my drift?'

Perhaps somewhat misguided, but goodhearted to the core, my sweet daughter headed around to the rear of the car to fetch my guests' luggage. Just how on earth she planned to accomplish this task with a scraped and bloody palm, still with bits of asphalt embedded in it, was beyond me. The odds were that Alison hadn't given her injured hand another moment's thought, and wouldn't again, until its nerve endings were pressed against a hard surface.

'No, don't!' Sarah Conway trotted after Alison on ridiculously high heels. Who wears heels to stay on a farm, I ask?

'You heard the lady,' Gordon Gaiters said. 'We don't want you touching our suitcases.'

'Why?' I demanded. 'Is that because she's a heathen?'

'Miss Yoder, I can't believe you would ask me that.'

'Then is it because her father is Jewish? Are you anti-Semitic?'

FIFTEEN

Gordon Gaiters appeared to be genuinely taken aback. 'Miss Yoder, have you forgotten that both Mary and Joseph were Jewish?'

'Indeed, I have not. Then what is so all-fired ding-dong-dang important that my daughter not touch your ding-dong-dang luggage? And while I'm sorry for my French, I'll have you know that those swear words are as bad as any that have ever exited my potty mouth.'

Gordon Gaiters sighed heavily. 'OK, if you must know – oh heck, you're going to find out shortly anyway, so I might as well tell you now. My suitcases are albino ostrich skin, and Miss Conway's are even rarer natural pink ostrich skin. Both sets are brand new and are – uh – rather pricey. But you know what they say: you get what you pay for.'

'And I'll have *you* know that I do swear from time to time. My mama – she was a simple woman, may she rest in peace – used to say that cussing, as she called it, was God's way of letting us get the Devil out. According to her, Jesus lives in our hearts, but Satan lives in our brains, where he stockpiles wicked thoughts. A good cussing session helps clear the mind of that, just like a productive cough clears the throat of phlegm. Perhaps you should meditate on my mama's wisdom, Mrs Yoder, because frankly, your curse words aren't worth a Hoover Dam.'

'I certainly shall,' I said. 'And I appreciate your equivocation, as I am but a spiritual infant, especially when compared to such an august presence as yourself.' Clearly it was the Devil who made me say such a rude thing to a coveted guest, and who but the Devil caused me to roll my faded blue peepers, albeit with my face turned discreetly away?

If he'd caught on to my shameful performance, the elderly gent did not let on. 'By the way,' he said, 'perhaps you could clear something up for me.'

'Absolutely. Just don't ask me my shoe size.'

Gordon Gaiters had a smoker's laugh. 'Why would I ask your shoe size? Even Noah's Ark wasn't quite that large.'

'That was mean.'

'Oh, I was merely having fun. Come on, admit it: they are exceptionally big, right. Remember that nursery rhyme about the old woman who lived in a shoe, and had so many children, that she didn't know what to do? Well, she really could have lived in one of yours. Maybe even rented out the extra space for conventions.'

'Was that a kind thing to say?' I said, even as *I* was not thinking very kind thoughts. If the editor's mama was right, then before this visit was over, Gabe was going to have to teach me some New York swear words, so that I could release some of the pent-up Devil pressure I could feel building in my brain.

But before Gordon Gaiters could apologize, along came Sarah Conway, teetering on her spikey heels, and weighed down by the weight of two enormous suitcases. Within breathing distance stumbled my clumsy and vociferous daughter, running her mouth off at a mile a minute.

'Why don't them things have wheels on them? Ya never did say.'

'Because wheels would compromise their beauty,' Sarah Conway said. However, each word was delivered after a gasp for air.

'If ya want my opinion, that's just stupid,' Alison said.

'No more stupid than you people not providing a luggage trolley for your guests,' Sarah Conway snapped.

'Touchy, touchy,' Alison, although I'm sure she meant touché. It's one of those words that ignorant Americans, like myself, occasionally read, and having never heard them spoken, haven't a clue as to how they are pronounced.

'Well, dear,' I said, in an attempt to defuse the situation, 'we at The PennDutch Inn believe in offering our guests unlimited opportunities to lean into the traditional Amish lifestyle. A.L.P.O., we call it. It stands for Amish Lifestyle Plan Option.'

'It's also the name of a popular dog food,' Sarah Conway said.

'Yeah?' Alison said. 'Mom, ya hear that?'

What a loyal child. She'd actually heard that dozens of times, and always pretended that each time was the first. Since she was only acting, and her game hurt no one, then surely it was over-reaching to label that behaviour as a lie. Even a white lie.

'Anyway,' I said, getting right back to business, 'I will be charging you an extra fifty dollars for the privilege of toting in your bags. It's a bargain, really at twenty-five dollars for each bag.'

When an eighty-year-old man snickers, it is a frightening sound. When a sixty-year-old woman, who still possesses most of her teeth, gnashes them, it is equally as unnerving. Veins protruded on Sarah Conway's temples and forehead where previously only wrinkles had been present. Even more interesting was the fact that her rather small dewlap morphed into so many cords that her neck resembled the trunk of a bonsai banyan tree. I assumed that these obvious signs of stress were the result of her desire to set down the ridiculously expensive suitcases.

'This is highway robbery,' she finally managed to say as she continued to teeter up the walk to my front steps.

Her intense agitation only served to gladden the heart of my heathen daughter. 'Hey lady, I see them little holes in the leather where the ostrich feathers was. Did them ostriches scream in pain when they was yanked out? 'Cause I'm telling ya, if you was ta pull out some of my hair, I would be screaming bloody murder.'

Alison threw back her head and emitted a scream that instantly set Eldon Krebiel's bloodhound to braying. Eldon's farm backs up to mine. In addition to Maisey, his bloodhound, he owns six beagles and two plough mules, Lilibet and Guadalupe, all of which got caught up in a choir of somewhat discordant voices.

'I surrender, you little witch,' Sarah Conway shouted. She kicked off her sinfully tall, high-heeled shoes and lurched the final distance to the veranda. Upon encountering the steps, she grunted like a discus thrower, and with a mighty lunge, managed to get both suitcases to rest simultaneously up to the next level. Unfortunately, this meant that the albino and pink skin valises had to briefly rest on a wooden surface. At least it wasn't black, crumbly asphalt. At any rate, after repeating that remarkable action three times, Sarah Conway managed to reach the front door, which Alison so graciously opened for her.

'Here you go, madam,' my daughter said. 'If ya wanna, ya

can muck out the barn, for the low fare of only two hundred dollars a day. Feeding them cows is just fifty dollars a day, but if ya wanna milk them, and we only got two of them cows – Betsy and Flora Bell – ya gotta pay twenty bucks a teat. Ya guys know what a teat is?'

'Just shut up, kid,' Sarah Conway said. 'I can't stand it anymore.'

'Now was *that* kind?' I said.

Gordon Gaiters grabbed my elbow with his gnarled fingers as we ascended the stairs behind Alison and Sarah Conway. I couldn't tell if he did so because he needed to be physically supported, or because he wanted to restrain me. Perhaps he thought I might assault his assistant for an excessively strong rebuke of my child. If that was the case, then Gordon Gaiters did not understand my people. My great-grandmother, six generations back, was scalped by the Delaware Indians because her husband Jacob Hochstetler would not pick up his hunting gun and defend her.

Gordon Gaiters let go of my arm when we reached the door. 'Go ahead, madam,' he said, with mock gallantry. 'Or is it mademoiselle?'

'Excuse me?'

'That's what I was attempting to ask you when I said I wanted you to clear something up for me, but then I made that wisecrack about your foot size.'

'So ask.'

'Which moniker do you prefer? I understand that your husband is a Jew by the name of Rosen, but at your delightful restaurant today, your staff either referred to yourself as Mags, or *Miss* Yoder.'

I gasped. '*What?* I was hoping that tomorrow would be your first time. I wanted to see your reaction when you took your first bite of one of our sublime creations, made especially for you by the deft hand of our much-lauded pastry chef, Barbara Hostetler.'

'Don't worry, uh – whatever your name is. I plan to go back tomorrow.'

'Really? You liked it that much?'

'Now, did I say that?'

'Well, what did you mean then?' I was beginning to sound like a fire engine with a malfunctioning siren.

'Give him a break,' Sarah Conway snapped. 'Can't you see that he's tired?'

'Yoder was my maiden name, and I kept it when I met Dr Rosen,' I said, thinking I might never have another chance the way the conversation was going. 'Mags is only for people who know me very, *very* well. If you were to call me that, I suppose it would be akin to me calling you Gordy.'

'Understood. When is dinner?'

'Just as soon as your Sherpa totes your bags up our impossibly steep stairs to your rooms. Alison can give you the full tour. On the way up she can tell you all about how that poor Japanese girl – oh, never mind that. I had to remove the elevator in order to get the stench out, and of course that wasn't enough. One never gets the smell of a corpse out of particle board, does one?'

'I wouldn't know,' Gordon Gaiters said somewhat frostily.

'Well, let me assure that is the case. We had to rip out all the particle board. But as you can see, I had this lovely little alcove panelled with oak all the way up to the ceiling of the second floor – or, if one was British, then I guess that would make it only the "first" floor. At any rate, please note the simple wooden bench where, I suggest, a man of your advanced age might wish to regroup his strength before ascending my infamously tortuous stairs.'

He snorted. 'You're full of prunes.'

I was so taken aback that I had to make use of the simple wooden bench myself. My mother used that same expression all the time on me. Being the dimwit that I am, I never understood its meaning, until my doctor husband reminded me of the connection between a belly full of prunes, and what normally comes after.

'That was very rude of you,' I finally said.

'Not really,' Gordon Gaiters said. 'I believe that in one's eighth decade of life, one should be able to speak one's mind. That's all.'

'Perhaps. But why be unkind?'

'Miss Yoder, why should that be any concern of yours? Besides, from what I understand, you are famous for having a tongue that can slice through Swiss cheese.'

I hopped to my feet, ready to defend my honour. 'Who told you that? Was it my best friend Agnes? I'm telling you, that woman is skating on thin ice, and she has been for some time. Was it one of the kitchen staff who tattled? Or one of the waitresses? By the way, those waitresses are not who they seem; they are actually sex-starved, religious extremists who belong to a godless cult headed by my mother-in-law. Yes, I know, being a godless religious extremist is an oxymoron, but these ladies are morons at the very least, and I wouldn't put it past them to be high on the drug OxyContin.'

As I was speaking Gordon Gaiters was continually backing away, until he was pressed against the bannister of my wicked stairs. 'Whew,' he said, 'you spit when you get excited. Nonetheless, I have always enjoyed the company of a passionate woman.'

'Come again?'

'You heard me. Is your husband here?'

That's when the Devil spoke loudly into my left ear. It's always the left one. I'd already regretted inviting the man and his assistant to The PennDutch Inn, so with a little help from the man in red with the horns and pitchfork, I was going to make short shrift of this visit. Of course, I don't literally envision the Devil *quite* that way, and I wasn't eliciting his help, but I did nothing to question the source of my diabolical plan either.

'Dr Rosen is out running errands, dear. Do you have something in mind?' I attempted to waggle my sparse mousey-brown eyebrows in what I hoped was a seductive manner. When I first tried that trick on Gabe, he thought I might be experiencing a stroke.

'Well then,' Gordon Gaiters said, 'we might have enough time.'

I shamefully prayed that Gabe might dawdle at Amish Sinsations where he'd been sent to pick up tonight's dinner. And why not, I ask? Neither Thelma Bontrager, The PennDutch Inn's new cook, nor I, can whip up a meal anywhere near as good as Barbara Hostetler can. But in regard to my shameful shenanigans, rest assured that they were a trap.

'Shall we retire to the master bedroom then?' I said.

He had the temerity to stare into my faded blue eyes without blinking once. 'I don't see why we can't do it here.'

'*Here?*'

'Right next to that little bench would be perfect.'

'On the hard floor?'

'Come on, Miss Yoder, don't tell me that Mennonites are too proud to do it on the floor. I thought humility was your thing. I do it on the floor all the time with Miss Conway. In fact, give her a shout with your loud, country voice, because I know that she's been looking forward to doing it with you.'

I was so flabbergasted, so gobsmacked, so flummoxed, so – well, you name it – by his statements that I just stood there, as rigid and mute as Lot's wife, *after* God turned her into a pillar of salt.

'That's settled then,' he said. 'The three of us will do it right here. Shall we ask your daughter to join us as well? I know that Miss Conway would really like that. Your daughter can always watch, if she doesn't participate directly.'

In retrospect, I was probably not justified in slapping the editor of *A Woman's Place.* More accurately, I walloped him. In doing so, I dishonoured five hundred years of pacifist ancestors, some of whom were tortured and died for their faith. And I most certainly should not have threatened Gordon Gaiters.

'I'm going to kill you both!' I screamed. Of course, I didn't mean it. It was hyperbole. They were words from a hysterical mother who had just heard an octogenarian suggest a threesome with her fourteen-year-old daughter. Honestly, I am unwilling to let Gabe set mousetraps in the attic.

Gordon Gaiters was already leaning back against the banister post, so he couldn't very well escape altogether. However, he didn't seem as if he felt the need to escape.

'Why would you want to kill me for suggesting that your daughter pray with us?' he said calmly. 'I was quite serious about that. I'm not like that pastor in South Carolina who believed that God doesn't hear the prayers of Jewish people. If that was the case, we wouldn't have King David and his beautiful psalms, for starters.'

'Uh – I – you really were talking about prayer?'

'What else could I have been speaking about?' He removed

his wire-rimmed glasses, fogged them up with his breath, and began studiously cleaning them on a shirttail that he'd just untucked.

I was too ashamed to answer. While I cast about in my pitiful brain for an answer that would sound less spiritually incriminating than what I'd been thinking, I cast glances around the lobby of my inn. Imagine my horror when I beheld Alison and the acid-tongued Sarah Conway frozen on the stairway just steps above Gordon Gaiters' head, as well as my beloved Babester, standing in the doorway that led in from the dining room.

Had any of them witnessed me slapping Gordon Gaiters? On second thought, judging by their expressions, they all had. I'd been helping Toy with his law-enforcing duties long enough to know that Gordon Gaiters could have me arrested on assault charges if he wished. But the situation could get even uglier than that, depending on how much of our conversation the three onlookers had heard? If they'd been standing there long enough, they might be able to put it into context, and draw the same conclusion that I did. What were the chances that any of them could *really* think that I was serious when I said that I was *going* to kill the editor of *A Woman's Place* and his assistant?

Give me a break! How stupid would that have been of me? How might I have done it – yank out one of my manifold number of bobby pins and stab him in the jugular vein? Right there in the stairwell/ex-lift area of my inn, right off the lobby? If one was still in doubt, then they should ask him or herself, is she the sort of person who would ruin her oak floors with a cascade of blood?

Again, I stood there as speechless as the sheep who had been asked an algebra question. Although this time the sheep was able to answer the question correctly, before I found my tongue.

Gordon Gaiters put his hands together in a playful pose. 'Miss Yoder, I asked what you thought I might have been thinking when I declined your invitation to visit your bedroom, and instead suggested that we move next to that little bench and get down on the floor. I submit that you thought that I was making a sexual advance. Am I correct in my assumption?'

'Yes!'

'It is also my assumption that you didn't really mean it when you said that you were going to kill me. Is that right?'

'Yes, yes, yes, quadruple yes,' I said.

'In that case,' Gordon Gaiters said, tapping the tips of his folded fingers to the bottom of his chin, 'I forgive you. In fact, I forgive you for everything rude that you've said to me thus far.' He sighed deeply. 'Now, might we finally get around to eating?'

'I shall make haste!' I was so relieved to be forgiven, and so focused on staying in Gordon Gaiters' good graces, that I charged out of the lobby like a blindfolded bull. I didn't even notice that Gabe was standing in the middle of the dining room door. Fortunately, he saw me in time to step aside with all the grace of a Spanish bullfighter.

'Ah, just a minute,' Gordon Gaiters called out. 'Before dinner I am desirous of freshening up. And as I am now rather exhausted, due to my long journey, but more especially to our rather emotional exchange of words, I will be unable to haul my ancient body up your admittedly dangerous – dare I say, libellous – stairs. Therefore, please point me to the nearest downstairs bathroom.'

That request brought me to a full stop. 'Ahem. In the interest of authenticity – no, I cannot tell a lie. I remodelled the inn after the tornado that blew it off its foundation and into a distant cow pasture where I landed face down in a cow patty. By the way, do you know what a cow patty is?'

Alison giggled, breaking some of the tension in the area, at least for me.

'Miss Yoder,' Gordon Gaiters said, 'with every passing second my need grows strong. After all, I am eighty.'

'But you don't look a day over seventy-nine,' I quipped.

Alison giggled again, sweet girl that she is.

'Tell him, Miss Yoder!' Sarah Conway barked. 'Why are you stalling?'

'Because there are no public guest facilities on the ground floor. There was a roomy half-bath off the parlour, but I needed the space to add to my new master bedroom plan. My guests all come to experience a genuine old-time Pennsylvania Dutch experience, so they never – or seldom – complain about having to go upstairs to use the facilities. Even the English Lord and Lady who stayed here recently. It's all in the brochure.'

'What about your help?' Sarah Conway was still barking her demands.

'The help is you, dear, since *you* are supposed to sign up and do the cleaning. The only other help is the cook, who is Amish. For her, we maintain a very attractive outhouse on the south side of the barn. The original, built by my great-grandfather, was a six-seater. Remember the motto: "the family that prays together, stays together?" Well, great-grandfather believed that "the family that sprayed together, stayed together".'

'That's disgusting,' Sarah Conway said over Alison's giggles.

'Miss Yoder,' Gordon Gaiters said, his legs crossed, and while hopping in place, 'this is an emergency.'

'Oh, all right. You may use our bathroom in the master suite. But don't go snooping around and touching things unnecessarily.'

The master suite is located downstairs, at the back of the house. For privacy sake, it can only be entered through the kitchen, and off of a secluded rear patio. This meant that I had to lead Gordon Gaiters through the dining room and through the kitchen. The problem with this was that Gabe had not had time to hide the carryout parcels of food which he'd brought home from Amish Sinsations. It's not as if we were going to lie about the dinner's origins – not exactly – we would just fail to *disclose* certain bits of information. If our guests were to ask who cooked the meal, then I would have to answer truthfully, but if they merely complimented the meal, then I would smile and thank them.

I looked beseechingly at Gabe for advice on how to handle this dicey situation, but I needn't have worried. To my immense relief he winked and flashed me a thumbs up.

'Then don't stand here a second longer,' I chirped. 'My husband there will escort you to the little boy's room.'

SIXTEEN

As Gordon Gaiters hopped off, cross-legged, and trailed Gabe, I turned to Sarah Conway. 'In the meantime, I'd like you to come meet my granny.'

'Ooooooh,' Alison said. 'I gotta see this.'

'You're in for a treat,' I said.

Alison, who'd surprised me by becoming chummy with Sarah Conway, led her by the hand, and bade her sit in Granny's favourite rocking chair. My guest took one look at the chair's unpadded seat and clucked like an angry hen.

'What's the matter with you, girlie?' Granny said. 'You too proud to plop your sitter down where generations of hard-working Yoder women have sat?'

Sarah Conway nearly jumped out of her Manolo Blahnik heels. 'What kind of sick joke is this?' she said angrily.

'It ain't a joke,' Alison said. 'Ya is a lucky woman. I can't hear my great-granny Yoder, but Mom can. And our Chief of Police can. But most folks can't.'

'I don't believe this manure!' (She actually said a word that I can't repeat!) 'Miss Yoder, you should be ashamed of yourself. This is some of that evil sorcery that your daughter picked up from reading those Harry Potter novels. The next thing you know she'll be casting voodoo spells and dancing naked in bars that have peanut shells on the floor. Thanks to you, the Devil might have her so tightly in his clutches by now, that he's training her to be the Whore of Babylon!'

'Ah, shut yer trap,' Granny said.

Sarah Conway spun around. 'Where's the speaker? Show me the speaker!'

'T'aint no speaker,' Alison said, then giggled. 'What did Great-Granny say?'

'None of your business,' Sarah Conway snapped.

'I can see through your clothes, girlie,' Granny said.

'You cannot!' Sarah Conway said.

'Oh yes, she can do that,' I said. 'She is a ghost, after all. They have X-ray vision.'

'What can Granny do?' Alison said.

'She can see through clothes, dear. But you already knew that.'

'Yeah. Ain't that the reason you put on clean Christian underwear every day.'

I frowned at my daughter. 'That's not the only reason that I do it; I am a clean person.'

'Hey, Mom, have Granny prove to this lady that she can see through clothes.' Alison turned to Sarah Conway. 'Don't worry, lady, Great-Granny don't never leave this room.'

'I don't doubt that,' Sarah Conway said smugly. 'At least not yet, because you don't have the speakers and whatnot set up anywhere else.'

That did it. That hiked my hackles higher than the ones on our Rhode Island Red rooster.

'OK, Granny,' I directed her. 'Tell us what you see.'

Only once before has Granny Yoder's chair rocked without a corporeal being having their tuchas planted in it. This was the second time. Granted, the movement probably wasn't enough to soothe a colicky infant, but it was sufficient to elicit reactions from both first-time observers. Predictably, Sarah Conway patted the chair and turned it on its side, looking for electrical wires and/or mechanical devices.

'Cool!' Alison said. 'Great-Granny, ya da best!'

'Put me back, right-side up,' Granny snapped. 'And you're the one who should be ashamed of yourself. That thing you're wearing has less fabric than even half of a woman's hanky. Why, it doesn't even cover any of your buttocks – none of it at all. It's like someone took a strip of banana peel to use as a pattern, laid it on a piece of cloth, cut it out, and then tied bits of string to it. Speaking of the Whore of Babylon, even she wouldn't wear it. And oh, my gracious, look at that!'

'Look at what?' I implored Granny, because she paused a millisecond.

'She has a butterfly tattoo on her left cheek,' Granny said, 'and a moth tattoo on her right cheek.'

'It's not a moth!' Sarah yelled at the chair. 'It's another

butterfly. That was my first tattoo and I didn't do diligent research on the artist.'

'Magdalena,' Granny said, 'you know that I always got bogged down reading those passages in the Bible about laws, but isn't there one that forbids getting a tattoo?'

'Absolutely,' I said.

'B-but how did she see through my Ralph Lauren dress?' Sarah Conway needed a place to sit and made the mistake of plonking her ample patooty on the nearest available chair.

'Get off my lap, girlie.' Because her body is buried up in Settlers' Cemetery, Granny is literally covered in dirt, and metaphorically speaking, she is older than dirt, but she can growl like a mother grizzly when properly motivated.

'I think I need a drink – I mean some aspirin, or something,' Sarah Conway said.

'I can offer you some wine,' Gabe said from the parlour door.

'It's just because he's Jewish,' I said, always quick to exonerate myself.

'It's for Kaddish,' Alison said. 'And I'm Jewish too.'

'Kaddish is the memorial prayer for the dead, honey,' Gabe said gently. 'Kiddush is the blessing over wine.'

'Which he only does on Friday nights, and even then, sometimes he forgets,' I said. 'And I never touch the stuff,' I added quickly.

'That's true,' Gabe said. 'Although that puzzles me, given that Jesus turned water into wine at a wedding, and this was *after* they'd already run through their booze supply.'

I was mortified. 'Please, dear, some folks believe that He turned the water into grape juice.'

'Ha. Then they have no understanding of ancient near-Eastern cultures, nor any knowledge of Ancient Greek, in which that particular Gospel of John was written.'

'My dad's very smart,' Alison proudly.

'My husband's a smart-aleck,' I said.

'Now I need that drink more than ever,' Sarah Conway said.

'Well then,' Gabe said, 'let's head on into the dining room, because the food's getting cold.' He winked at me.

'Where's Gordon?' Sarah Conway said.

'He's already sitting down, waiting,' Gabe said.

We filed in and took our rightful places. A husband and wife should always sit at the ends of the table, not along on the sides like some modernists do. A family is headed by the parents, or parent, and not by its children. Alison sat on my left, facing the kitchen door, which of course placed my guests on my right. That way they were able to look past Alison, and as it was still light outside, enjoy our wonderful view. With any luck an Amish buggy or two would come clopping along during dinner. If so, I would encourage them to rush to the windows to enhance their dining experience. They might even wish to take photos of those on their phones – assuming that they'd paid the two hundred and fifty dollars surcharge for the privilege of keeping them during their authentic Amish-lifestyle stay.

I will give kudos to the Babester for having thought of every-thing. The two entrées and various side dishes that he'd brought home from Amish Sinsations were now in our tureens, bowls and platters. Thank heavens that Gordon Gaiters had taken such a long time to relieve himself in our master bath. I just hoped that he hadn't done too much snooping while my beloved was busy being sneaky about our dinner preparations. It would be bad enough if he peeked in the cabinet over the vanity, but if he rifled through my dresser drawers, I would be livid. Just the thought of it made my heart race.

As I said earlier, we weren't planning to outright lie if either of them asked who cooked the food. That would be a sin. We'd rehearsed this scenario several times, mind you, so we knew what we were doing. The only possible fly in this proverbial ointment was that Gabe had brought home a variety of desserts. How on God's green earth were our guests to believe that I baked all those sweets for them? That very day, no less? What makes the desserts at Amish Sinsations so sinfully delicious is that Barbara bakes everything fresh each morning. None of our baked goods are frozen or refrigerated for later use.

And what's more, my dear beloved husband had taken his selection of desserts and spread them across the sideboard against the kitchen wall. The sideboard was custom built by a local Amish man who goes by the nickname Eight Finger Dan, and it is ten feet long. That evening there wasn't a square inch not covered by 'potential tooth decay on a plate'. There were slices of chocolate cake, German chocolate cake, coconut cake, Devil's food cake, strawberry cake, lemon cake, angel food cake; wedges of fruit pie, cream pies; squares of brownies with nuts, brownies without nuts; butterscotch bars, toffee bars, lemon squares; peach cobblers, blueberry cobblers, cherry cobblers, and apple brown Bettys.

Last, but not least, there was a single slice of our speciality, a dessert called Blitz Torte. I will be the first to confess that I have a low threshold for irritability. I've been told that it is a character flaw that showed up shortly after I first encountered people. That said, one might understand that it annoyed me to see that two servings of Blitz Torte were already on the dining room table, placed directly in front of where our guests were to sit. That is not how things are supposed to be done. One is supposed to clean one's plate – eat every last morsel, whilst considering the starving children in India, or China if need be. Only then is one to be rewarded with dessert. Otherwise, one is excused from the table and sent to one's room. But that was in the old days. Now, if one's father is named Gabe, one can get away with just about anything.

'Hon, I know what you are thinking,' said Gabe, whispering into my ear, 'but you've got it wrong. The old geezer came wandering out of our bedroom when I was dashing about putting food into serving dishes. He immediately started poking into the pastry boxes. When he saw the Blitz Tortes, he asked that I put them by their plates. He wanted to make sure that no one else snapped them up. After all, I only brought three in that selection.'

'You should have brought more!'

'Everyone's waiting,' the Babester said gently. 'Let's get this show on the road.'

I put on my hostess face and everyone under eighty sat. Although Gabe and I worship the same God, our approach is quite different. Therefore, we don't say grace *together* before meals. Instead each of us offers up the prayer suitable to his or her own tradition. Alison does as she pleases, which is often nothing. That evening as soon as she was seated, she grabbed a fresh dinner roll and shoved it into her mouth.

'My, you *are* a little heathen, aren't you?' Gordon Gaiters said.

'Cooth meh?' Alison said. In her defence, proper diction is rather difficult with a wad of bread in the way of one's tongue.

'How absolutely revolting,' Sarah Conway said.

'Sweetie,' Gabe said, patting our dear Alison's arm. 'Chew it twenty times, and then swallow.' He then turned to Gordon Gaiters. 'Now, what's this about you calling my daughter a heathen?'

The editor of *A Woman's Place* was not easily intimidated. He looked the much younger man straight in the eye, and when he spoke, even his smoker's voice lost some of its raspy quality.

'She reads those Harry Portnoy books, doesn't she?'

'That's Harry Potter. So what?'

'No Christian should read them.'

'She's not a Christian,' Gabe said.

'Nevertheless, just now she started eating before saying grace. Only heathens do that.'

'Say grace,' Gabe said to Alison.

I shot Alison a meaningful look. 'No, dear, please don't do it,' I said.

'But it would be my pleasure,' Alison said, as she stood and waved her arms dramatically. 'Rub-a-dub-dub. Thanks for the grub. Yay God!' Then she plopped back on her chair and jammed the roll back in her mouth.

'That's sacrilegious,' Gordon Gaiters growled, his smoker's voice having returned.

'So help me,' Sarah Conway said, 'if I don't get that wine now, I think my head's going to explode.'

'Coming right up,' Gabe said cheerily. He poured red wine into three goblets and placed two of them in front of our guests, reserving one for himself. But when Sarah Conway brought hers desperately up to her lips, Gabe stopped her.

'In this house, because I'm Jewish, we pray before drinking wine. It's in Hebrew, but it thanks God, who is King of the Universe, for creating the fruit of the vine. Alison, will you join me?'

'Sure thing,' Alison said. She was beaming with pride.

'*Ba-ruch a-tah A-do-nai*,' they sang. '*El-o-hay-nu mel-ech ha-o-lahm, bo-rei p'ree ha-gah-fen.*'

'Harrumph,' Gordon Gaiters said. 'That sounded like so much

gibberish to me. How do we know it wasn't Ancient Greek? Or even Mandarin?'

'Now may I drink?' Sarah Conway said. '*Please?*'

'Yes,' I said, glaring at her boss. 'It's at times like these, that I wish that I drank as well.'

'Perhaps you should drink, Miss Yoder,' Gordon Gaiters said. 'Then you wouldn't be such a nervous flibbertigibbet. Somewhere in the Book of Psalms we are told that wine makes glad the heart.'

'It's Psalm 104, verse 15, the first line, *dear*.' I took a deep breath and exhaled my sarcasm. 'Permit me to quote the entire first verse of the Book of Proverbs, Chapter 20. "Wine is a mocker, intoxicating drink arouses brawling, and whoever is led astray by it is not wise."'

'Easy, hon,' Gabe said.

'You go, Mom!' Alison said.

'Ugh,' Sarah Conway said spitting into her now empty wine glass. 'That stuff will rot your teeth. What was it? Cough syrup?'

'It's a traditional, sweet, kosher wine that I reserve for Friday nights. It's to remind us just how sweet the Sabbath is.'

'The Sabbath is Sunday, not Saturday,' Gordon Gaiters said.

This time I looked at our guest imploringly. 'Please don't get Dr Rosen started,' I said. 'My Jewish husband knows the history of the early Christian Church better than you do. I guarantee that.'

Gordon Gaiters wagged an accusing finger at me. 'How do you know he's not lying to you? After all, you're unequally yoked.'

'I beg your pardon?'

'If you know your Bible so well, you know what I mean. Scripture warns believers not to be paired with unbelievers – "yoked" it says – or they'll be led asunder. Even in this man's Old Testament, there's a law against yoking an ox together with an ass.'

Gabe, who normally shies away from confrontation pounded the table with his fist. 'Are you calling my wife an ass?'

I don't express my emotions physically, just hysterically. 'He didn't say that *I* was the ass, did he? Maybe I'm the ox, and you're the ass!'

'Hee-haw, hee-haw,' Alison brayed. In retrospect I don't blame the kid. The tension in the room was so thick, that one could slice it with a paper knife.

'That display of incivility is disgusting,' Sarah Conway said.

'You're the pot calling the kettle black, dear. Now I, for one, wish to eat this delicious dinner which is cooling before our very eyes. Gabe, be a dear, and help yourself to some Swiss steak on yon platter, and pass it to Miss Conway, who will pass it to her right to Mr Gaiters. Mr Gaiters, will you be a dear, and help yourself to the sweet corn and cream casserole in front of you, and then please pass it to your left to Miss Conway, who will then pass it to me. And Miss Conway, will you—'

'I get the picture,' Sarah Conway said. 'I'm not some dumb, country hick. And don't even think about calling me "dear". We're nothing to each other.'

'That's not exactly true,' said Gabe. 'I read this book—'

I shot my Dearly Beloved a look that could have shrivelled a cactus on a damp, cool day in Arizona. 'We're *eating* now,' I said. 'That's all that we're doing for the next ten minutes. *Capiche?*'

Alison's right arm shot up.

I sighed so deeply that I accomplished the next week's dusting in two adjoining rooms. 'Yes?'

'What happens if we all finish in eight minutes?'

'Eat!'

So that's what we did. We ate, although with varying amounts of gusto. I nibbled. Gabe ate moderately, as per his usual custom. I was pleased to see that both my guests not only had hardy appetites, but they practically inhaled their desserts. As for Alison, she obviously needed extra calories to fuel her teenage rebellion. In fact, she ate more than any Amish farmer I'd ever met, even more than Morris Gindlesperger, who had a chest like a half whisky barrel, and used to strap himself inside a mule harness, and pull the plough himself after Sadie, his beloved mule, died of old age.

After my guests had virtually licked their dessert plates clean, and drained their cups of decaffeinated coffee, they tossed their napkins on the table, and pushed back their chairs. I winced, because one is supposed to support the chair seat with one's hands, whilst lifting the chair up and back. One does not simply push oneself straight back, digging such deep gouges into the floor that a train of flatcars bearing military tanks can roll through this newly created landscape completely undetected.

'We'll have breakfast at five,' Sarah Conway said.

'Suit yourself,' I said with a smile that did nothing to help global warming. 'The cereal's in the cabinet to the right of the fridge. The bowls are just below the cereal.'

'Not so fast, young lady,' Gordon Gaiters said. 'Your brochure claims that you serve a hot breakfast.'

'We do: between the hours of seven and ten.'

'But we have to drive up to Bangor, Maine tomorrow,' Sarah Conway said.

'No, you don't, dear,' I said. 'According to the itinerary that you sent me, and the number of nights that you paid for, you don't check out for another six days.'

'Harrumph,' Gordon Gaiters said. 'You realize then, that I won't be giving you a favourable write-up in our glorious autumn issue of *A Woman's Place*?'

'I thought that "harrumph" was just a word that one read in English novels,' Gabe said. 'I didn't realize people actually said it – especially Americans. But now you've said it twice. Perchance you're a British spy? Or could you be one of those secret Canadians, since you speak with a rising inflection.'

'And yet your wife thinks you're so brilliant,' Gordon Gaiters said.

Ever one to stir the pot, Alison clapped her hands. 'Hey, everyone! I just had *me* a brilliant idea. Seeing as how we ain't got us no elevator, and them stairs is more crooked than a dog's hind leg, and it's steeper than Miss Conway's nose when she sticks it in the air, why don't my dad carry the old man up the stairs?' Alison looked into her father's startled eyes. 'So whatcha think? Ya can carry Mr Alligator up them stairs, can't ya, Dad? I mean, ya did the same for me when I had the flu bug, remember?'

'That does it,' Sarah Conway huffed. 'We're leaving now. *Right* now!'

'Alison,' I said, 'you apologize now. Right now!'

'Yeah,' she mumbled. 'Hey Dad, I'm sorry. He might be an old man, but he has himself a big old man's belly. I wouldn't want ya to hurt your back or nuthin'.'

'You see?' Sarah Conway screeched. 'That child is incorrigible. She should be stripped of all her privileges and confined to her room indefinitely. No, that's not enough. Since you're so fond of quoting scripture, then here's one meant just for you: Proverbs 13:24. "He who spare his rod hates his son, but he who loves him disciplines him promptly."'

'Well done,' I said. 'Brava! Do you have any children, Miss Conwhack?'

'That's Con*way*, as you well know.'

'Sorry about that mispronouncing your name, dear. You are undoubtedly aware that we Mennonites are pacifists, and in my rush to be passive, I might have gotten a wee bit aggressive, heh, heh. But do you have any children?'

'None that I'm aware of, heh, heh,' she said.

'How very droll of you, Miss Conway,' I said. 'My point is that if you have no children, then you haven't a clue as to what sort of punishments are effective in this day and age, and most especially in regard to our daughter. In other words, butt out!'

'That's telling her, Mom!' Alison said, and then she gave Sarah Conway an anaemic, countryside version of the infamous Bronx cheer. But instead of blowing through her closed lips, she merely stuck out her lips in an exaggerated fashion, and then spoke a single syllable that sounded like 'blurp'. However, I have no doubt that, if she'd been surrounded by supportive friends, my fourteen-year-old would have made me proud and gone all the way.

'OK, that does it,' Gabe said. 'Clear the dining room. Everyone out! Get out now!'

Please don't get me wrong. My oh-so-handsome husband is not a coward; he is just not someone who can handle confrontation. This pretty much means that he can't say 'no' to anyone. This makes him an easy mark for any salesperson, even the Girl Scouts of America during their cookie campaigns, or the elementary schools when they hawk magazines for their fundraisers. We would both have become morbidly obese while reading ourselves blind a long time ago, if I hadn't stepped in and cancelled the subscriptions, and sent all the cookies to our troops serving overseas in our nation's longest war, Afghanistan. I am opposed to the taking of any human life, mind you, but I am also in favour of bringing these young women and men a bit of comfort, a taste of home.

It must be noted that Gabe, I am proud to say, was a member of Harvard's famed Hasty Pudding Club, the nation's oldest theatrical group. So even though he is not confrontational, he can *play* the part of someone wielding great authority. However, he has to be properly motivated in order to do so. In this case, Sarah Conway's parenting advice was the bridge too far. Although, if you ask me, he should have ponied up a bit earlier, like right after I referred to her as Miss Conwhack. Instead he put it on me and Alison to shoulder the burden of rebuttal. By the way, it was only my guardian angel that kept me from calling her Miss Con*whacky.*

I suppose that I shouldn't complain. The room cleared out, and the guests climbed up the stairs in the time that it takes a rumour about a cheating pastor to circulate during a packed church service. What was truly astonishing was to see that Miss Conway, who was trailing, literally lifted the old coot up by the armpits, and placed him on the landing, which is midway up. The step up (or down) to the landing is the steepest, and something really needed to be done about it. But that would have entailed reconfiguring that entire half of the stairs, which not only would have put the inn out of commission for a long time, it would also have meant that Alison would have had to share our downstairs master suite (wherein the nursery is located) a lot longer than three nights. Gabriel is a lusty man, and I don't think that would have set well with him. I'll leave it at that.

SEVENTEEN

I am convinced that mothers have an innate ability to wake more easily than fathers. No baby book, no matter how prestigious its author, can change my mind. On second thought, maybe I'm wrong, maybe it's just because many fathers abrogate their duty to be nocturnally vigilant in favour of catching a few winks. Whatever the case may be, my better half, who was on call for twenty-four-hour shifts during his medical residency, now sleeps like a stone. That is to say, he hears *nothing* for at least eight hours a night.

During the night of our dining room drama, I was awakened by noises emanating from upstairs. When I pushed the knob on my bedside clock which illuminated the time, 3:02 a.m., it occurred to me that our guests might have decided on an early departure after all. No matter. They would get no hot breakfast, and no refund for checking out early. As for a favourable write-up in *A Woman's Place*, hadn't the bombastic Gordon Gaiters already brought the axe down on my scrawny Yoder neck? That is why mere seconds after being awakened, I rolled over and went back to sleep.

At some point after I'd fallen back to sleep, I was awakened by a tapping on my shoulder. I remember sitting up in the darkened room and calling out. But it's Alison who swears by our dialogue.

'Not now, Lord,' I supposedly said, sounding quite panicked. 'Go away, Angel of Death. Don't take me to Heaven now. Little Jacob is still a baby and needs his mama! And Gabe needs me too. And I need them.'

'What about me, Mom?' Alison said. 'Don't ya need me too?'

All I am sure of is that when she said 'Mom,' Gabe turned on his bedside lamp, and I was indeed in a sitting position. Oh, and also, my dear sweet daughter was on the verge of tears. I pulled her down on the bed and held her in my bony arms.

'Of course I need you, dear. I need and love you more than you can ever possibly know.'

She wiped her eyes with the base of her thumb, and then she wiped her nose on her nightgown. 'Yeah?' she said. 'Cool.'

I nodded, my eyes filling with tears as well.

'So ya ain't gonna die on account of no death star angel?'

'Something like that – at least not tonight, it seems. But one never knows, so that's why it's important to be right with the Lord.'

'Yeah, yeah. Hey Mom, ya hear that noise upstairs a while back?'

'I did.'

'I think they was doing the rumpy-pumpy.'

'What?' I said, perhaps a wee bit irritated. I consulted the clock again. It was only 3:12 a.m.

'That's English slang,' a large lump from the other side of my bed said. 'It means the same thing as doing the two-sheet tango.'

I turned on my bedside lamp. 'Do you really think so? He's eighty years old. Won't it kill him? I mean, is it even possible?'

Gabe cleared his throat. 'Ahem. The walls have ears, if you get my drift.'

'Hey!' Alison said. 'I ain't no wall. And I ain't stupid neither. Mom, I knew ya was lying when ya said that Dad found Little Jacob growing in our cabbage patch. Them cabbages was eaten all through with caterpillar holes, and Little Jacob didn't have a single hole on him, except for them necessary ones. Besides, most of my friends live on farms, just like me, and we ain't blind; we watch them animals. But poor Emily Mischler lives in town, and her mama told her that same story that ya told me, when I asked ya where babies come from.'

'What story is that?' Gabe said.

'Oh nothing,' I said.

Alison hopped across the bed to snuggle with her dad. 'All our moms would say is that married dads gave their wives seeds when it came time for the couples to have babies. After the seeds got planted in the moms' tummies, they grew into babies. But then Emily swallowed a grapefruit seed and was so scared that a baby would start growing that she tried to kill herself.'

'No, she didn't!' I said.

'Yes, she did,' Alison said. 'You don't know her.'

'Sweetheart,' I said gently, 'that was just an expression of horror, not disbelief. Does her dad own a shoe store over in Bedford?'

'Yeah.'

'I do know Emily. She's in the Sunday school class that I teach. When did this happen, dear?'

'When we was in the sixth grade. She took some of her mom's sleeping pills, but they wasn't the kind the pharmacist hasta give ya. They just made her really sleepy and her mouth real dry.'

'Alison, honey,' Gabe said tenderly, 'I'm sorry to hear that about your classmate.' Then he turned to me. 'Mags, why didn't you give our daughter facts, instead of some stupid tale that even a nitwit wouldn't believe?'

'*Me?* She's your daughter too!'

'Hey,' Alison said. 'Don't argue. I hate it when the two of you argue. It's *my* job as a teenager to irritate both of you, because I'm beginning the process of breaking away and establishing my own identity. If the two of you continue to bicker so much, then I might end up as a maladjusted adult. Who knows? I might even mature into a psychopath, and murder someone in this very inn. Then Mother can investigate the case, and be responsible for her own, dear daughter's incarceration. Is that what the two of you want? Huh?'

'She called me "Mother",' I squealed, 'and not Mom!'

'Mags,' Gabe said, 'are you nuts? Is *that* what you noticed? How about the fact that not only did she speak correct English again, but she offered an important insight into the psychology of the teenage mind? This shows that she actually read some of the psych books that she checked out of the library. I'm curious to know why she exhibits such a wide dichotomy of behaviour.'

'OK, Gabe,' I said, 'please take it down a notch for the simple-minded peasant woman on this side of the bed.'

'You're not simple-minded,' Gabe said, with a wink. 'You're single-minded. That's why you accomplish so much. Anyway, what I meant was, I'd like to know why our darling daughter speaks like a third-grade dropout most of the time, when she's clearly very intelligent, and capable of so much more.'

'Yeah?' Alison said. 'Ya really wanna know the answer? I already told ya – because I know that it bugs the crap outta ya, that's why.'

'Fair enough,' Gabe said calmly. 'But just now, when you switched into Standard English, it seemed so effortless. Was it really that easy?'

Alison shrugged. 'I dunno, because it's not like I was thinking about it, or nothing. It just sort of happens when I'm stressed.'

'And we were causing the stress with our "bickering", as you so eloquently put it?' I said.

'Yeah.'

'Then we'll just have to bicker more,' Gabe said.

'No, please don't!' Alison said.

'Then how about a group hug,' I said, half expecting my suggestion to be soundly rejected.

'Sounds awesome,' Alison said.

The hug was brief. Gabe comes from a family of huggers, and I from a family that acts like human backs are hot potatoes. We might have compromised, except for the fact that even the Babester could tell that Alison had skipped her shower that day, and maybe the day before. During the school year peer pressure is enough to keep her toeing the line when it comes to personal hygiene. Out here on the farm she is likely to have, at the most, two face-to-face interactions with kids her age a week. The rest of the time she communicates via texting.

At any rate, almost the second our daughter hopped off the bed, we heard another thump overhead. It wasn't as loud as the previous ones, but curious, nonetheless.

Alison, who had frozen in place, turned around. 'Well, *I* think that's more bedroom bossa nova.'

Gabe laughed. 'I think it's time that your mother stopped using euphemisms.'

Oh, I wish that my daughter's suspicion had been true.

EIGHTEEN

My doctor husband claims that one sleeps better in toe-stubbing darkness. One of the wedding gifts we registered for at Lowes in Monroeville were blackout blinds. Therefore, even though morning had arrived in Hernia, and birds were singing, and our two cows lowing, as they waited to be milked, half of the Yoder-Rosen clan remained somnolent. The other half of the family was in the kitchen doing its thing: the tall skinny one was busy feeding the very short chubby one, but both of them were oblivious to the man watching them.

'Miss Yoder?'

I dropped the spoon containing cream of rice when I saw the look on Gordon Gaiters' face. He was whiter than the cereal.

'Mr Gaiters! What's wrong? You look ill. Shall I call my husband?'

'Yes, please. But it's not for me; it's for Miss Conway. I think she might be dead.'

'*What?*' Go ahead and blame me, if you will. Call me the most evil woman in the world, more wicked even than Jezebel, but the first thing that I thought of was that, if Gordon Gaiters was correct, finding another corpse in my inn was going to have an effect on my business. Even if Sarah Conway died of natural causes, it would still make a difference. Believe it or not, there are folks out there, ghost-hunters for instance, who seek out places where an unusually large number of people have died. There are even people who desire to sleep in beds where other folks have met untimely deaths! You see? The Devil is at work everywhere. And of course there comes a tipping point when any establishment comes to be seen as so cursed, that no person in their right mind would spend a night there.

'Please, Miss Yoder,' Gordon Gaiters said. He'd begun to tremble. 'Call your husband. My wife needs him.'

I rushed back into our bedroom. 'Gabe! Wake up!'

'Not now, hon, I have a headache.'

'This is important; Mr Gaiters says his wife needs you.'

'What?' Gabe sat up, pulling the sheet around him.

'He sounds confused. I think he means Miss Conway. Something must have happened to her. You need to go up and check.'

'All right. Tell him I'll be there in a minute.'

I dashed back into the kitchen to find Gordon Gaiters slumped in a chair, his head buried in his arms on the kitchen table. He was sobbing.

Meanwhile Little Jacob had taken up his spoon, the one with the fat ceramic handle, and was merrily splashing away in his oatmeal. Although my chubby cherub's pronunciation was a mite off, nonetheless, it made my shrivelled heart swell with pride.

'Winkle, Winkle, widdle stah,' he sang, 'how I wandah how ya ah?'

Of course, then was not the time to revel in the accomplishment of someone I loved, when it was quite obvious that Gordon Gaiters was distraught over Sarah Conway's condition – whatever that was. I thought about what I would want a virtual stranger to do, if she found me sobbing on her kitchen table. I'd want her to leave me *alone*. Even after well-wishers patted me on the back after Mama died and said 'there, there', I responded with 'where, where?'.

However, there was no way for me to know if Gordon Gaiters was one of those people who swallowed platitudes like vitamins and claimed to thrive on human touch. Well, there was only one way to find out, so I borrowed from the British and stiffened my upper lip. But only metaphorically, mind you, as I didn't have time to wax my lip, and leave a bit on – either the wax, or the bristles.

'There, there,' I said, after I touched his shoulder. Believe me, my contact with his shirt took less time than it takes me to test my clothes iron, to see if it's reached the setting marked 'cotton'.

When Gordon Gaiters raised his hoary head, I observed that despite all the audible sobbing that I'd heard, there didn't appear to be a trace of tears. His eyes weren't red and puffy. There were no signs that rivulets had trickled down along his nose. As for his nose, I ask you: who sobs vociferously, and then doesn't have to blow his, or her, nose?

'Would you like a cuppa?' I said, still taking a page from my British friends.

'What?'

'A cup of tea.'

'No, thank you. But I would like a beer, if you have one.'

'We don't.' Yes, I was shocked by his request, but then this was not the time to say so.

'How about some wine then.'

'Mr Gaiters, I'm a Christian. I never touch the stuff.'

Did I detect a soft snort? 'Your husband drank some last night. We all had at least a sip, except for you.'

'That's right. I refuse to even touch the bottle. It's there in the cabinet above the broom closet. But it's pushed way in the back, since I don't allow my guests to climb stepladders, so you're going to have to wait for my husband to come back to get it for you. May I offer you some coffee instead?'

The force with which he managed to bring his fist down on the kitchen table was astonishing. The salt and pepper shakers danced, extra teaspoons that I keep in a glass on the table rattled, but worst of all, my precious son screamed in terror. That did it. That ended my brief ministry to the bereaved Gordon Gaiters. I undid the latch on Little Jacob's highchair, scooped my sodden bundle of joy in my arms, and trod upstairs with him.

Lest I be judged an unfit mother for hefting a toddler up my admittedly impossibly steep stairs, I must in my own defence point out that I have lived in some version of this house (this one being an exact replica of the original in which I was born) my entire life. I have climbed those stairs a thousand times, sometimes in the dead of night without any illumination, when the house was as dark as Melvin Stoltzfus' soul. That man, by the way, besides being my biological brother, is Hernia's most notorious serial killer, one who has tried unsuccessfully to kill me on several occasions. So you see, my feet knew the way up those creaky, crooked steps, and not once did I put my precious baby at risk.

At any rate, I found the door to Miss Conway's room wide open. About six feet inside lay the body of Miss Conway, which Gabe was now covering with a sheet, one which he had stripped off the bed. Obviously, the woman was dead.

'Heart attack?' I asked.

He shook his head. 'Why did you bring him up?'

'Because Mr Gaiters wants some of your booze, and I won't get it for him. Now he's angry.'

'He's just upset. I don't blame him. This is pretty ugly; I've never seen anything like it.'

'Tell me! What is it?'

'Take Little Jacob downstairs, and then come back.'

'You take him, you're his daddy! I'm not going anywhere.'

Gabe stood. 'Mags, I'm not sure you can handle this.'

'Is that so? Well, did you ever open a barrel of sauerkraut and find a pickled woman inside?'

'Uh – no.'

'Or a man who'd been flattened into a pancake by one of those machines with the giant drum in front? They're used to smooth out asphalt.'

'No. You win. Here, give me my boy.'

After Little Jacob was safely in his arms, and they were well clear of the room, I gingerly pulled back the portion of the sheet that covered Miss Conway's face. I will admit that I felt a few butterflies in my stomach, but what I beheld wasn't anything nearly as gruesome as an inch-thick man, or a pickled woman. To the best of my recollection, and I say this with all Christian charity, Miss Conway had not sported what one might describe as a 'kind' face. In death her features were contorted to such a degree that she resembled a caricature of a snarling albino cat. I state this as one who is very fond of felines, and before I had to give mine up due to Alison's allergies, I spent a great deal of time stroking my silken pussy, Samantha.

Dread is the spawn of fear and experience. Sadly, I'd seen far too many corpses in my life not to recognize that this one was the victim of foul play. Sometimes I think swiftly on my big feet, at other times I take more time to sort through my options and consider the consequences. On this occasion, I did far too much of the latter. That was my first mistake.

'Cool beans,' a disembodied voice said.

I jumped. 'Alison! What are *you* doing here? How did your father let you up here?'

'He's changing Little Jacob's diaper. That kid's a stinker.'

'Go away! You shouldn't be seeing this.'

'Mom, I can't *un*-see what I been seeing for the last umpteen minutes. Ya know, she looks like she's wearing a Halloween horror mask.'

'Duly noted. But since, by your own admission, you've been up here for umpteen minutes, it's time for you to go back downstairs.'

'Aw, all right. Ya want me to send Dad back up here? I mean, if he's done changing Little Stinky-Pants and all?'

'No. And tell him not to make any phone calls either, and not to let Mr Gaiters make any calls either. Can I count on you to act as Temporary Assistant Mayor to do this?'

Alison grinned. 'Ya bet!'

I waited until the sound of her racing down my wickedly steep stairs confirmed she was out of earshot before I placed my call. Toy picked up on the first ring, which probably meant that he was bored. Now that we've hired a second officer to handle the more mundane things like issuing speeding tickets to horse and buggy drivers, catching raccoons in someone's attic, and neighbours squabbling over fence placements, Chief Toy gets first crack at the fun stuff.

'Madam Mayor, at your service,' Toy said cheerily.

'Chief Graham, I might just make your day if you hurry over here. But no siren or lights, please. One of my guests passed during the night, and if I was a betting woman, I'd bet the PennDutch that it was the big M.'

'Menopause?'

'No, but if you don't see the whites of your eyes in ten minutes, this menopausal Mennonite is going to fire you.'

'Be there in five,' Toy said and hung up.

Although I went back downstairs, I opened the front door and stood in it, so that I could both keep a lookout for Toy, as well as an eye on the dining room door. Twice now Alison had displayed a morbid curiosity in grisly deaths, so it was conceivable that she would try to sneak back up to the murder scene behind my back in order to get a second look at the corpse. It occurred to me that my eldest child might grow up to be a pathologist, an embalmer, or worse yet, one of those imbecilic mystery writers whose books contain improbable plots and ridiculous characters.

But Toy arrived in just three minutes, which meant that he'd risked drawing attention to himself for speeding, or else he hadn't been at the police station. Now is not the time to nit-pick, Magdalena, I told myself. *You* used to break the speed limit yourself, until your baby was born; now you've convinced yourself that it's a sin.

'Hey, Magdalena,' Toy said as he bounded up the front steps. 'Lead the way.'

'Shh,' I said. 'The others are in the kitchen. I want to keep it that way.'

'Yes, ma'am. Sure thing.'

'I'm warning you, Toy. She's not a pretty sight. Alison said that her face looks like a Halloween horror mask.'

'Alison saw her?'

'I'm afraid so.'

'And Gabe?'

'Yes. He was the first one to go up after Mr Gaiters came down asking for help.'

'What was his demeanour?'

'At first he seemed genuinely distraught. He sounded like he was crying buckets of tears, but the funny thing is, Toy, he didn't shed a single one. Is it possible to have a good, old-fashioned, boo-hoo session, without turning on the waterworks? A "dry cry", if you will?'

'Hmm,' Toy said. 'I guess that all depends on who's interpreting the sounds and – what the hel*met*!'

'Good save, dear,' I said, as I closed the door to the murder room behind us. 'I told you it was gruesome. You see that her expression seems as if it was frozen. Her hands too. Some poisons do that.'

'And you know this, how?' Toy asked.

'Studied up on a few of the more commonly available lethal substances for self-preservation.'

'Magdalena, if you're afraid for your life, or for your family, then you should shut this business down. It's not like you need the money.'

'That last bit is true,' I said. 'I have been very blessed. But I wasn't afraid that I, or my family, was in danger of being poisoned – until *now*, thank you very much. Hithertofore, I was concerned that a guest's untimely demise might get pinned on me. I thought that if I had a thorough knowledge of lethal poisons, I might be able to exonerate myself by finding the real culprit. In that same vein, I've also been studying ballistics.'

'Magdalena,' Toy said, shaking his head, 'you're amazing.'

'I know. Now dear, there is something really important about this case that you should know.'

'I'm sure that there is, Magdalena,' Toy said. 'But there is something even more important that I need to tell you.'

'Why, I never!' I said. 'I am your boss, young man, and I am older. It could be that my information is more urgent than yours.'

'Well, I doubt that,' Toy said. 'You're going to want to hear what I have to say first. I promise.'

'OK, hit me. Just not literally, of course.'

Toy looked at his feet. 'When you called, I was already in the cruiser, and that's where I took your call.'

'So?'

'Sheriff Stodgewiggle was in the car with me when you called. We were comparing notes on a hit-and-run involving a loose cow along Solomon's Creek, since it marks the border of our jurisdictions. Anyway, when he heard the report of this case, he hopped out of my squad car, and more than likely he followed me back. I was just three minutes away. Or thereabouts.'

'Three minutes, exactly,' I said, as I ran to the window. Sure enough, there was the sheriff's car. I gathered my skirts and leaped over Sarah Conway's prone body in my haste to get to the bedroom door. When I opened the door, it was quite obvious that the potbellied lawman was already inside The PennDutch Inn and hard at work.

It is no secret in these parts that I am no fan of Sheriff Stodgewiggle, and that the sheriff looks down his bulbous red nose – he is extraordinarily fond of rum – at me for being a female amateur sleuth. Although, it's possible that what truly sticks in his craw is that I refused to contribute to his political campaign when he attempted unsuccessfully to run for state senator. Yes, I am quite aware that my description of him might seem a tad unkind, but I ask my critics this: is it my fault for stating the truth, or Sheriff Stodgewiggle's fault for having 'distillery breath'?

I closed the bedroom door as quietly as was humanly possible. 'Toy, do you believe me to be a truthful woman?'

'No,' he said.

'*What?*'

Toy winced. 'I don't mean that you lie – exactly. But you definitely exaggerate at times to the point that it may as well be a – well, an untruth.'

'A lie. That's what you're saying, isn't it?'

'On the other hand, Magdalena, when it comes to self-honesty, you're miles ahead of everyone else whom I know. Sometimes you don't even know when to draw the line.'

I looked away for a second so that I could wipe tears from my eyes. By gumdrops, no one was going to see Magdalena Portulacca Yoder cry, especially not a whippersnapper of a male police chief who was just barely half her age.

'So, Toy,' I said, 'would you believe me if I said that I murdered someone?'

That focused Toy's attention. 'No, I would not.'

'What if there were two credible witnesses who claimed to have heard me say: "I'm going to kill you both"?'

'I might believe that they heard you say that, but I still would not believe that you murdered anyone.' He sighed. 'Did you say that, Magdalena? Is that what this is about?'

I sat heavily on the bed. 'Yes. Last night at dinner. But I didn't even say it to Sarah Conway – this woman. I screamed it at her boss, the editor of *A Woman's Place*.'

'That rag? No kidding? He's here? My grandma down in Charlestown loves *A Woman's Place*.'

'Hey, isn't your grandmother Episcopalian?' I said. 'I thought they were liberal. Didn't they have a woman bishop once?'

'There are two kinds of Episcopalians, Magdalena: High Church, and Low Church. Here in the States, the High Church ones, like Grandma, tend to disapprove of women clergy and gay marriage, and they love their incense and the little bell that rings during mass at consecration. That's why the Low Church folks – that's me – call the High Church folks the Smells and Bells Church.'

While it might seem odd to some that I spent time conversing about Toy's grandmother and her church, there was a method to my apparent madness. I was strengthening our bond before I confessed my biggest transgression. Think of it, if you will, in the same way that hostage negotiators try to establish a personal rapport with kidnappers.

'Toy,' I said, 'what if I said that I thought that the editor, who is eighty, by the way, was trying to get me to have sex in the old elevator alcove, *and* let Alison watch, and that I hauled off and slapped the baby Moses out of him?'

'Whoa,' Toy said. 'Give me a moment to let me unpack that question.'

'You better hurry, dear, because I think I hear voices getting closer. As in people coming up the stairs.'

Toy grinned. 'Personally, I'd say that the old coot had it coming. But what does slapping the "baby Moses" out of someone mean?'

'It's just an expression Gabe says, instead of saying "slapping the b'Je" – I won't say it because it's sacrilegious.'

'I got it.'

The door opened, and Sheriff Stodgewiggle entered, preceded by two of his three chins. 'Well, well,' he said, in his usual pompous tone, 'another delightful chapter of *Death Dines at The PennDutch Inn?*'

'No, sir,' I said, and without a trace of sarcasm.

The sheriff took two steps back so that he had enough room to view the corpse without having to bend at the waist, which was now virtually a physical impossibility. I could tell by Gabe's bright red face, now framed by the door, that my beloved had been coerced into pushing the sheriff up my wickedly steep stairs. It was a wonder that the two of them had survived. How were the two of them to get down safely? More to the point, how was Gabe to get down safely?

And where was Alison? Had she been left behind on the stairs, after being turned into a teenage pancake? As one can imagine, my mind, supposedly given to exaggeration, was reeling with tragic possibilities. At least I was no longer thinking of myself, which must prove to *someone* that I'm not all bad.

'Hmm,' I heard the sheriff say. 'Aha! Yes, I see. It's exactly like those twin cases over in Lancaster last year, and the year before down in Frostburg, Maryland.'

'What is, Sheriff Stodgewiggle?' Toy said. I could hear tension in his voice.

'The type of poison. Of course, we'll have to wait for the lab report to get back to the specifics on that to make it one hundred percent. Right now, I'd put it at ninety-nine percent probability.'

'You're that certain?' Toy said incredulously.

Instead of answering, Sheriff Stodgewiggle pivoted slowly in my direction. 'Magdalena Yoder, you're under arrest for the murder of Sarah Conway. You have the right to remain silent . . .'

I didn't need to listen to my Miranda Rights being read. I knew them by heart. Instead I stared in disbelief over the sheriff's shoulder, at the man who had betrayed me.

NINETEEN

I f I have the face of a horse, as I so often claim, then it's possible that my entire head is sculpted from stone. Mama always said that I was hard-headed, and more than one teacher called me 'dense'. Perhaps more than anything it was spite that motivated me to turn a deaf ear to Gabe's insistence that we spare no expense and hire the best attorneys in Pennsylvania, even the nation. *Or*, it could have been hubris.

As a mild-*mannered* Mennonite woman, one who was raised to be proud of her humility, I have found the sin of pride one of the hardest to conquer. I won't elaborate on my other failings, lest I come across as a truly horrible person. Anyway, I'm not artistic, musical, or athletic, but I was born with a head for business and what some would call a 'gift for gab'. That is to say, I have, upon a number of occasions, displayed a talent for talking myself out of some pretty sticky wickets. Therefore, I declined any sort of representation other than Yours Truly. After all, I had done nothing wrong.

Judge Evelyn Stehly, who presided over my arraignment the day after my night in the pokey, shook her well-coiffed head when informed of my decision to defend myself. She shuffled papers for a minute before responding.

'I usually don't recommend that, Miss Yoder.'

'Yes, ma'am, Your Honour.'

'Nevertheless, I will allow it.' She then addressed the state prosecutor, Attorney Mike Avey. 'What are the charges?'

Mike Avey is known locally as 'El Zappo', because of the number of people he has managed to put on death row, where the electric chair is the means of execution. I will admit that Mr Avey is an exceedingly handsome man with piercing blue eyes. They might have sent a surge of electricity through me, menopause notwithstanding, had my life not been on the line.

'Magdalena Portulacca Yoder is charged with murder in the first degree, in the death of Sarah Ruth Conway,' Mike Avey, a.k.a. El Zappo, said.

'How do you plea, Miss Yoder?' Judge Evelyn Stehly said.

'Not guilty, Your Honour.'

'So noted. Your bail is set at one dollar.'

The courtroom rocked with laughter. Surely the judge had been joking, they must have thought. Handsome Mike Avey just stood there with his mouth open, uncertain how to make sense of her statement. After allowing a moment of merry mayhem, Judge Stehly brought her gavel down on the podium with the rapidity of a manic woodpecker.

'Order,' she shouted. 'Order, or I shall instruct my bailiff to clear the room.'

Since not a soul wanted to miss what was to come, the room became so still that one could have heard frog flatulence fifty furlongs away, had the space been that large. I realize that this will sound like hubris again, but I already knew what the judge was going to say. Not only that, but *why* she was going to say it.

'I will say this again just one more time. Bail for the defendant is set at *one* dollar.'

The spectators gasped in unison as Mike Avey jumped to his feet. 'Your Honour, this is outrageous! The defendant is a very wealthy woman, capable of flying anywhere at a moment's notice. Rio, Tahiti, London, Amsterdam – you name it. She's the very definition of a flight risk.'

Judge Stehly brought her gavel down again. Twice. 'Miss Yoder is also the Mayor of Hernia, Pennsylvania, as well as a deacon at Beechy Grove Mennonite Church. She was born and raised in Bedford County, unlike you, Mr Avey. Her roots here go back for over two hundred and fifty years, unlike yours, Mr Avey.'

The crowd in the packed courtroom tittered in a controlled sort of way, and I could sense that they were supporting me. I smiled graciously, as was expected of someone whose standing in the community and lineage was known to even a magistrate in Bedford, population 26,732.

'But you see,' Judge Stehly said, raising her voice to make others lower theirs, 'I am quite confident that Miss Yoder won't fly, drive, or even run away, because she is as stubborn as a team of mules, and she has more pride than any peacock God ever created.' She waited for the inevitable laughter to subside, which was well before my cheeks cooled.

'Miss Yoder has a compulsive personality, with a need to always prove that she's right,' Judge Stehly continued. 'You might ask me "how do you know this this?".' Well, I know this because we were best friends in middle school.'

Then it was my turn to gasp. It has been said that with every breath of air we breathe, we inhale at least one molecule of every person who has ever lived in the past, going back many centuries. I'm not sure if I believe that, but if it's true, then I inhaled molecules of Jezebel, Nero, and Attila the Hun. On the other hand, my overactive imagination may have been stimulated by what Mr Mike Avey had ingested for breakfast that morning.

I popped to my boat-size feet. 'Is that *really* you, Bug Eyes?' I inquired of the judge.

'Yes, it is, Horse Face. Now sit down, before I hold you in contempt of court. Magdalena, I got contact lenses in high school, but that was after we moved to Bedford, so you wouldn't have known. By the way, I must say, you have outgrown your horse face. You are quite a stunning woman.'

'Your Honour, I most strenuously object. This courtroom banter between the bench and the accused is unethical to say the least.'

'Objection noted,' said Judge Stehly. 'In that case Magdalena and I will have to visit on our own time. Court dismissed.' She gave the podium two more whacks with the gavel and I was free to go.

The courtroom erupted in cheers, whoops and hollers. At least two people whinnied, but I took their teasing in good stride. One of the horse-imitators was Alison, and the other just had to be Judge Evelyn Stehly, a.k.a. Bug Eyes. The judge did it while exiting the courtroom, and from the relative obscurity of her robes. There might have been a third person, but hey, all's well that ends well, as some English guy once said, and the morning had ended very well for me indeed.

My mood was so expansive that I forgave Gabe and Alison repeatedly on the way home, although it wasn't easy. Jesus said in Matthew 18:22 that we are supposed to forgive those who wrong us seventy times seven. Pastor Diffledorf, who's been to seminary, said once that this was an ancient expression which really meant 'boundless'. But even if Jesus had said we should forgive only a million times instead of boundless, it's not easy to forgive someone whose loose lips got you sent to the pokey, no matter how short one's stay.

For me, what is even harder than forgiving is *forgetting*. I realize that it's not Christian of me, but I can hold a grudge like linen holds an ink stain. When I heard that it was Gabe who had cracked first, and spilled the so-called, incriminating 'beans' to Sheriff Stodgewiggle, I was dismayed, but somehow not surprised. Alison spent her early years fending for herself, and thus grew up with a modicum of what some folks call 'street smarts'. Gabriel grew up with two overly indulgent parents, and at no single point in time wants to be disliked by anyone in the room. In other words, as soon as the sheriff started to lean on him, so to speak, my devoted husband caved. Instead of obfuscating, or clamming up, like a loyal husband should have, Gabe blabbed in order to keep himself in the sheriff's good graces. No doubt once the big nut had been cracked, it was easy for Sheriff Stodgewiggle to pulverize Alison with threats against her parents.

The one person whom I most wanted to see since being arrested did not show up for my arraignment, and thus was not with us after I'd been released on bail. When I didn't see him waiting for me in the hallway outside the courtroom, my blood began to simmer. I'll just wait, I told myself, and see how long it takes Gabe to tell me where the little guy is.

Allow me to say this. Had I been a hybrid – part Magdalena, part radiator – my blood would have boiled to the extent that the safety vent on my radiator cap would have popped open, my eardrums would have burst, and steam would have billowed out of my ears, nose and mouth, before the intuitive Alison piped up.

'Look at it this way, Mom, at least Dad made Grandma take Little Jacob across the road over ta her fake convent. That means she can't be snooping through your drawers or nothing or trying on your sturdy Christian underwear. Anyways, Grandma had herself a baby boy, so it ain't like it's something new ta her.'

'That's true,' I said, 'but just look at how your dad turned out!'

'Hey, I resent that,' Gabe said.

Ever the peacemaker, Alison ploughed on. 'Besides, ain't they always saying on TV that it takes a village ta raise a baby? Well, that's what they is over there, a whole village full of nuns, even if they is all fakes.'

'They're not only fakes, dear,' I said, 'but their creed is that they are apathetic about everything. That means that they don't care. If they don't care about anything, why would they care about changing Little Jacob's diaper?'

'Mom, that ain't no problem! Grandma said she weren't gonna change no poopy diaper, so she was gonna let him run free like God intended in the first place. See? Ya don't have ta worry.'

'Land o' Goshen!' I cried, clutching my chest. 'That woman is driving me to an early grave. As Mayor of this town – and yes, that fake convent lies just inside the village limits – I am going to shut that place down. But first I am going to retrieve my precious bundle of joy, my late-life gift from God when once I was as barren as the Gobi Desert, from the clutches of that heathen mad woman and her lunatic followers.'

TWENTY

The Babester, the second most important male in my life, was a bit upset with me. He pushed the pedal to the metal, as the saying goes, until we screeched to a stop in the middle of Hertzler Road, in front of the drive that led to the convent which was, conveniently for him, directly across from The PennDutch Inn.

'Get out!' he said.

'You can't be serious,' I said.

'I am.'

'If you want to act like a spoiled little boy instead of a mature man, then at least do it after I've retrieved our son.'

'Fine!'

He stomped on the gas pedal and made such a sharp left turn that he left parallel tyre marks in black arcs. But when we stopped, even though he got out of the car, he refused to go in with Alison and me. Instead he thrust the car keys at me.

'Here, take them. I'm walking home.'

'Why?' Alison said.

'I've got packing to do,' he said.

'What?' I said, in disbelief. 'Where are you going?'

He shrugged dramatically. 'I don't know. Maybe fishing.'

'Don't be silly, Gabe,' I said. 'You don't fish.'

'How do you know? Maybe I used to fish before I came to Pine Valley.'

'This isn't Pine Valley,' Alison said. 'This Hernia, Pennsylvania. Dad-Daddy – if you go somewhere, then you aren't going alone. I forbid it!'

'Honey,' he said, 'I appreciate the sentiment, but I think that your mother and I need a little space right now.'

'Fine then,' she said, as she grabbed his hand. 'You can sleep in my bedroom upstairs, and I'll sleep downstairs with Mother.'

'No honey,' Gabe said tenderly. 'I need to get a little farther than upstairs. You stay here and take care of your mother and little brother, but you may call me anytime you need me. Or anytime you want to.' Then my husband looked at me with narrowed eyes. 'And you, Magdalena, if you need anything, you can reach me through Ma. Or through your precious boy, Toy.'

Even the words of a childish husband can sting like a swarm of bees, or a field of nettles. I'd eat my hat without ketchup before I went through the heathen huckster he called 'Ma', if I needed anything. And I'm not so naïve that I missed his double entendre when referencing our Chief of Police as 'boy, Toy'.

Although the Devil immediately supplied me with a quiver full of nasty rejoinders, even worse than the one that had just punctured my thin skin, I opted not to use them. It would only hurt Alison if Gabe and I continued to fight. But neither would I apologize to the man who had fathered my child. I had merely spoken the truth: his mother *was* a lunatic heathen.

I mean, one can't just make up their own religion, co-opt another faith's religious dress and terminology, and then recruit your adherents from among the emotionally-challenged segment of society. At least not here in White, Anglo-Saxon America where everything is supposed to be picture-book normal – Amish horses and buggies, and eighteenth-century clothing aside.

So Dr Gabriel Rosen walked back to The PennDutch Inn, leaving a weeping Alison and me behind. As I didn't want to leave Alison alone for a minute, nor did I want to run into 'Ma', I gently suggested that my daughter be the one to go in and retrieve her little brother. I reasoned that she would be focused enough on her errand to be temporarily distracted, and she surely would not be alone, once she stepped inside the massive oak doors just beyond the gates.

It is a myth that Jewish and Catholic mothers have the monopoly on feeling guilty. The truth is that Mennonite mothers have the market cornered on this emotion, but since we are far outnumbered by either of those two religions, and we Mennonites are too humble to brag about our spiritual defects, how is the general public to know? So there you have it, we poor Mennonite mothers just limp along, the most guilt-ridden mothers on the planet, and without a shred of well-deserved notoriety. What a crying shame!

This is to say that of course I felt terrible about sending Alison into a den of heathens alone. But I didn't even have time to wallow in my guilt before Alison came streaking out, with my baby bouncing on her hip.

'Boil my eyes!' she screamed. 'Boil my eyes!'

I grabbed my naked progeny and buckled him into his car seat before attempting to have a conversation with my hysterical teenager. Like her mother, she can be given to hyperbole at times. Even so, a good mother owes it to her child to be informative.

'Alison, dear, if I were to boil your eyes, I would have to scoop them out first with the gadget that we use on melons to scoop out fancy little melon balls, which in itself would be terribly painful. Or else I'd have to hold your head under water and scoop them out with a teaspoon, and you know how much you hate getting water up your nose.'

By that time my dear daughter was laughing and thinking of other grotesque ways how she might remove her eyes before boiling them. 'Ba-ya ma ah-ees,' Little Jacob chanted, clapping his chubby hands. 'Ba-ya ma ah-ees.'

Thus far we were still in the parking lot in front of the convent, because I was loath to drive the several hundred metres it took to get us home. Just as long as I didn't cross Hertzler Road, and drive up to my inn, it was theoretically possible that the Babester was still there. Perhaps he was back in the sitting area of our master bedroom, ensconced in his leather reclining chair, watching a ball game. On the other hand, putting off the inevitable sometimes just compounds the problem, so I put the car into gear and turned toward home.

'Tell me, Alison,' I said, as I inched the car back down the drive, 'what did you see that was so awful?'

'What I seen was that all them pretend nuns was naked, every last one of them. Even Grandma Ida. The only people wearing clothes were them two men nuns – ya know – them uncles of your friend, Agnes.'

'Now that's a switch. Her uncles are long time nudists.'

'Yeah? Anyway, remember the other day when I burst in on ya taking a shower?'

'Unfortunately, yes.'

'Ya ain't gonna believe this, Mom, but them ladies is saggier and wrinklier than you. Every last one of them!'

'Is that a fact?'

'Yeah. They was like elephants, with everything flapping and swinging in the breeze. Mom, I ain't never gonna grow old, and I ain't never gonna join no convent that has nudist days.'

Alison was sitting in the front passenger seat, so I reached over and patted her arm. 'First, count yourself fortunate if you *do* get to grow old. Second, if you do, you won't have to worry that you'll outlive your finances. And lastly, whether or not you join a convent is up to you. Now let's go home, shall we?'

'Uh – stop!' Alison ordered in a shockingly adult voice. We had just reached Hertzler Road. Straight across it was our more modest driveway leading to a circular parking area, with the inn on the right, and the barn and corrals on the left.

'What do you mean "stop"?' I said.

'There's one more thing that you should know; it's something that Daddy was afraid to tell you.'

My heart pounded. 'Afraid? Why would Daddy be afraid to tell me?' I'd tried to sound upbeat, but it's hard to do when one's voice is quavering.

'Because ya get too hysterical sometimes, Mom. Ya know that.'

'I do?'

'Yeah. Like just then your voice went so high that it cracked, and ya was saying only two words.'

'All right. I get the point. So give me his message already.'

'Strictly speaking it ain't a message. It's more of an update, I guess ya'd call it. Sheriff Stromboli, or Stoogewillow, or whatever his name is, didn't want that creepy old man ta leave town for a while – least not until after your raining-mint, so Daddy said that the old geezer could keep on staying at the inn.'

'Slap me up the side of the head and butter my bread on both sides!' Yes, I am fully aware that is a hybrid oath, but it was either that, or sit there and be speechless. Magdalena Portulacca Yoder is seldom rendered mute.

Alison giggled. 'Mom, if your bread was buttered on both sides, and ya'd dropped it on the floor, then ya'd have a hundred percent chance of it falling face down.'

I grinned. 'True. But in the olden days, if you could afford to butter your bread on both sides, it meant that you were rich.'

'Yeah, I can see that,' Alison said. 'But who would want to get slapped up the side of the head?'

'Well, I didn't mean it literally,' I said. 'But before we get back to the inn I need to know where Mr Gaiters will be sleeping. Still upstairs?'

'Right, but because I'm as strong as a pack mule – that's what he said – it's my job ta make sure that he gets up and down them dangerous stairs of yours that is just begging for a lawsuit. Them was his words, not mine.'

'Understood.'

TWENTY-ONE

One can rest assured that first thing that I did upon returning to The PennDutch Inn, after attending to my children's physical and emotional needs, was to fall into the warm, welcoming embrace of Big Bertha. Before I married the Babester, and discovered true marital bliss, my extra-deep bathtub, with her thirty-two jet sprays, capable of massaging every millimetre of my body in ways both ordinary, and shameful, was my greatest source of earthly pleasure. There was nothing that I could put in my mouth, no savoury morsel of meat, no delectable sweet, and no garment, no matter how soft and smooth its fabric, that could come close to offering the sensual pleasure of that offered by time spent within the white porcelain embrace of Big Bertha.

However, when I married Dr Gabriel Rosen, I had taken a vow to be a faithful wife in mind, body and soul. Spending half an hour in the arms of Big Bertha, as it were, with the jet func-tions activated, would certainly be a betrayal of at least one of those promises. Perhaps if I merely *soaked* in mountains of gardenia-scented bubbles, I reasoned, I would remain a faithful wife.

Mind you, the odour of this particular bubble bath was guar-anteed to dissipate rapidly after one finished bathing. Believe me, there is nothing more off-putting than to be pushing one's trolley through a supermarket in the wake of someone whose scent of lavender is so intense that one could trail them throughout the store if one were blindfolded.

So there I was, with snow-covered mountain ranges of bubbles running the length of the tub, but I was still not enjoying myself. How could I be? My marriage was rocky, to say the least; I had a delightful, but nonetheless rebellious teenage daughter; I still had the mother-in-law from you-know-where to face; and I'd been indicted for murder. Could it get *any* worse? Oh yes, the vindictive editor of *A Woman's Place* had been given a week's free lodging. In a scrawled note, that looked like a drunken spider wrote it, Gabe explained his decision: *This guy's had a traumatic experience. You don't want him to sue!*

Gabe was right, I couldn't argue about that. The first thing that I needed to do, and so often neglect to do until I've dug my slough of despond even deeper, was to pray. When praying one should always close one's eyes tightly and fold one's hands. I don't care that Gabe says Jews are allowed to get away without doing those things. Mama and Papa both claimed that closed eyes kept one's mind from getting distracted, and Pastor Diffledorf backs them up on that. But to be perfectly honest, the second I close my eyes, the Devil plays a movie on the blank canvas of my eyelids. Nonetheless, I adhere to the teachings of my youth.

The other thing that was impressed on me at a young age, is that somewhere in every prayer, one should confess one's sins and ask to be forgiven. After all, one can never be certain when the Lord will choose to take one Home. Ergo, it's a wise person who is ready to meet one's Maker. As I had approximately ten minutes before the water cooled too much for my liking, I began to pray aloud. While I know that God can hear all the way up in Heaven (straight up from Hernia, *not* up from Australia, those poor people!), it has been said time and again that I have an exceptionally thick skull, so I saw nothing wrong in giving him a little assistance with sound.

'It's me again,' I said. 'But in case you don't recognize my voice, it's exceedingly sinful Magdalena. Sin, sin, sin, that's all I ever seem to do. Anyway, I'm sorry about all that sinning, really I am, and I hope that you forgive me.'

'Of course I forgive you,' said the Lord in an oddly feminine voice, 'but you need to list your sins.'

'I do?'

'You betcha.'

'Well, I've been selfish.'

'Go on.'

'And judgmental. I'm terribly judgmental when it comes to my husband's mother, who is a real pain in the patooty, if I can speak frankly without getting zapped. I'm sure there's no need to remind you, Lord, but getting zapped whilst in the bathtub would cut short my confession, and you wouldn't get to hear my laundry list of misdeeds. Just a suggestion, Lord, but since you have eternity on your hands, which is an awful long period of time, and which could eventually become a trifle boring, might I suggest that you spare me until I've had a chance to enumerate, and bewail, all my manifold sins?'

'I shall keep that as an option,' said the Lord's gender-neutral voice.

'Thank you, Your Grace. By the way, I just want to add that Ida Rosen – a.k.a. Mother Malaise – happens to be one of your people, you know, of the Chosen Persuasion. Maybe you know her family up there – *if* they're even allowed. A lot of folks down here say that they won't get in, and there is scripture to back them up. Even some very famous TV preachers claim that you won't let her people in. But I say, what about Abraham, and the Prophet Samuel? Oh well, there I go digressing again, when all I meant to do was confess my contempt for that woman who calls herself Mother Malaise.'

'Uh-huh. Whom else do you judge harshly?'

'Oh, lots of people. Too many to name before my bath water gets cold.'

'Then that is a sin. Just tell me though, what do you think of your lifelong friend Agnes Miller?'

'Do you want an honest answer, Lord?'

'Absolutely. "Thou shalt not lie" is one of the Big Ten, right?'

'Well, in that case, I think that Agnes Miller is a busybody snoop, a social climbing blabbermouth who is twenty IQ points shy of being half as clever as a brook trout.'

'Magdalena, how could you?' Agnes shrieked and then burst into gales of laughter. 'Mags, at what point did you know that it was me talking to you, and not a direct line from above?'

'The second you walked into my bathroom – *behind* your lavender bath salts, which far overpowered my gentle Gardenia Garden.'

'A bit much, eh?'

I nodded. 'So what brings you here, and who is managing Amish Sinsations? Don't tell me that Sheriff Stodgewiggle closed it down!'

'No, in fact, after he booked you he circled back and expected me to give him a table for lunch.'

'Why the nerve of that man! What did you do?'

'I told him I'd be happy to seat him for lunch six weeks from now, at the second seating, because that was the earliest possible reservation I had available.'

'What did he say?'

Agnes giggled. 'He cursed and stormed out.'

'Really! Do tell, Agnes, how bad a curse word was it?'

'Too bad for your Conservative Mennonite ears, Mags.'

'Oh, come on. We've been best friends since we were babies. You can tell me anything.'

'Yeah, but you can't hear everything.'

'That's what you think. You forget that now I'm a married lady, and my husband is a New Yorker. They say everything in New York. You can't shock me.'

'Maybe, but your ears might shrivel up, and you could spiral straight down into you-know-where.'

'That's mocking my faith, and you know it. Go ahead and try me; I dare you to.'

At that Agnes leaned down so that she could whisper into my ear. Even though it was just the two of us in my bathroom, so strict was my upbringing that my dear friend felt the need to whisper the obscenity behind a cupped hand.

'Oh, my word!' I said, feigning shock.

'Stop it,' she said. 'You don't even know what it means, do you?'

'No, but it's pretty bad, right?'

'Some would think so.'

'In that case I'm absolutely indignant! Morally outraged.'

'Good. So anyway, not one person cancelled their reservation, even after the news broke on TV. In fact, I had to disconnect the phone because it kept ringing so much with all the calls from people begging for reservations run by the famous murderess, Magdalena Yoder.' She paused. 'You don't look surprised.'

'According to a note that Gabe left taped to my computer, Sarah Conway's body arrived at Bedford County morgue at half past nine yesterday morning. By three in the afternoon, the inn's website had racked up over two thousand requests for reservations. We call these people "ghoul hounds". We get this kind of internet traffic every time there is a murder in Hernia. Although yesterday we – I – received some hate emails as well. That's also normal.'

Agnes reached out to pat my bare shoulder, but just in time to spare both of us a great deal of embarrassment, she retreated from my personal space. 'Well, at least you've got your husband to keep you safe.'

'Ha! Not hardly. When the going gets tough, my mouth gets going, and sometimes – well, sometimes my mouth brings his mother into the fray. Long story short, it appears that Gabe has bailed on me.'

'I'm sorry, Mags, I really am.' After an appropriate pause, she spoke again. 'Speaking of his mother, yesterday she came barrelling into the restaurant, practically tripping over her habit, demanding that I shut down the place. And you *did* shut it down.'

'I'm afraid that I had to.'

'Because of her?'

'It wasn't Ida's place to demand that we shut down the restaurant, but it did need to be done. This is important; tell me exactly what Ida said.'

I had yet to drain Big Bertha. Before she answered, Agnes invaded my space again to sit on the tub's edge and pick at the lingering foam. Doubtless she hoped that as the bubbles diminished, the suspense would build. I, however, would not have it.

'Agnes,' I growled, 'get on with it, or I'll splash.'

'OK,' she said. 'Your mother-in-law practically shouted that the dinner which Sarah Conway had eaten here, at The PennDutch Inn, had been cooked at Amish Sinsations.'

'No, she didn't!'

'I wish you'd been there,' Agnes said. 'Everyone immediately dropped their eating utensils, and then they immediately picked them up again and burst out laughing. It was almost as if it had been choreographed. I'm telling you, Mags, people are becoming so blasé now because of cable television. It's like no one can separate reality from what they see on their flat screen high definition TVs anymore.'

My little round friend was waving her hand vigorously in my bath water, whilst teetering dangerously on the edge of Big Bertha. The childish part of Magdalena was tempted to give her a gentle tug. The mature part considered the danger to her physically and, of course, her feelings. Fortunately for both of us, the adult Magdalena ruled the day.

'Agnes, this is going to sound harsh, but those people were idiots.'

'Excuse me?'

'I'm not blaming you – so please don't get me wrong – but Mother Malaise had a good point. The substance that poisoned Sarah Conway came out of our kitchen at Amish Sinsations. So far there's been no lab report, so neither Toy nor I have any idea how long it took for the poison to act. It may have been cooked into her food that evening, or it may have even been in our kitchen for some time. That's why the restaurant had to be closed down.'

Agnes stood, thank heavens. 'That's impossible. We make everything fresh. From scratch. Every day.'

'Not everything,' I said. 'Some of our sauces and salad dressings are made in large batches and stored in the fridge.'

'So what are you saying?' Agnes said. 'That one of our staff is responsible?'

'Maybe,' I said. 'Maybe not.'

'But Mags, that's ridiculous. How would any of them know the assistant to the editor of *A Woman's Place*?'

'Maybe the poison was meant for him,' I said. Don't ever gasp in abject horror whilst in a tub of dwindling bubbles. The result was a mouth full of suds, not to mention that I exposed parts of me that even the Babester was no longer permitted to see. 'Ack! What's wrong with my big thick head? Any one of us could have been poisoned that night!'

'Why Magdalena, I'm surprised to hear you say that. You're a woman of unshakable faith. Surely you don't believe that things happen by chance, do you?'

'Agnes, now is not the time to compare and contrast my current statements with any of my past rhetoric. After all, inconsistency is part of the human condition.'

Agnes calmly tossed me a Turkish bath towel. Meanwhile I grabbed my thick terry robe from the stool adjacent to Big Bertha and used it as a shield while I rose like a Mennonite Venus from a sea of lightly scented froth (for the bubbles by then were much depleted).

'Turn around, dear,' I ordered her. 'I wish to save you from the sin of lust.'

'Oh, puh-*leeze*! Trust me, thoughts of you have never crossed my mind.'

'*Never?*' I said.

'Never. Magdalena, you sound disappointed.'

'Don't be silly,' I said. Of course, I was a smidge disappointed. But only a smidge.

Agnes proved that she could turn around quite hastily for someone who was horizontally-enhanced. 'Oh gross! It sounds like you're running for public office. Maybe even for President.'

Before I could think of a clever comeback, my landline rang. Unfortunately for the caller, by then the needle on my crabbiness meter had dipped slightly to the left of centre. In my defence I must state that virtually everyone in the area had, for months, been subjected to a variety of telemarketer scams that could often be traced back to anonymous callers in Mumbai. I lunged for the phone, snatching up the receiver after the first ring.

'This is Mrs Patel,' I said irritably. 'Tell my husband to come home *now*. His *tikka masala* is getting cold.'

TWENTY-TWO

'Wife, darling, are you vexed with me yet again?'

'Vexed?'

'I hope so, darling, because there is nothing quite like the sight of a mature, well-seasoned woman such as yourself, to keep the juices flowing in the loins of the studliest stallion east of the Ganges.'

'Sam Yoder, eeuw! Yuck, and double yuck!'

For the record, Sam Yoder used to be my first cousin, until I discovered that I was adopted. Then he became my biological double second cousin, which was no surprise, given our denomination's intersected family trees. But because Sam and I are the exact same age, I am fairly sure I won't someday discover that Sam Yoder is my father, or my son. Then again, I've lived long enough to know that just about anything is possible.

What I have never understood is why Sam developed a crush on me in the second grade and never outgrew it. When we were in elementary school, he made his affection for me known by dipping my braids in his ink well, sitting on my paper lunch sack, putting a frog in my desk, and even belching loudly in my face.

By the time we were in high school my braids were up and coiled around my head like every other proper Conservative Mennonite girl, but Sam was still sitting on my lunch (or squashing it into his armpit) and belching in my face. One might think that I eventually grew to dislike Sam, but then one would be wrong. Truth be told, I gave as good as I got, for it doesn't take much to distract a teenage boy in love.

Instead of lettuce leaves in with his tomato sandwich, Sam got a mouthful of poison ivy that made his face swell up like a puffer fish. Instead of drinking chocolate milk from his thermos, Sam chugged down chocolate flavoured laxative dissolved into milk. Eventually Sam called a truce and we became pals. Good friends. However, never, not once in my most wild Big Bertha moment of physical release, did I ever conjure up Sam Yoder's face, nor did I cry out his name. But I will admit that when Sam broke from tradition and married that Methodist girl, Dorothy, right out of college, I was stunned. Possibly even hurt. But enough about that.

'Sam Yoder,' I said, as I tried with no avail to wrap the Turkish towel even tighter around me with just one hand. 'Why are you interrupting me?'

'Interrupting you?' he said. 'Why, what are you doing?'

'I just got out of my bathtub,' I said, 'and my towel is slipping, if you must know.'

'Let it slip,' he said. 'You're on the phone, not TV. Besides, I've seen everything there is to see, remember?'

'Don't remind me!' When I was pregnant with Little Jacob, I was alone with Sam in his store, Yoder's Corner Market when my waters broke. Even though mine was considered a 'geriatric pregnancy' because I was forty-nine, the Good Lord did indeed look out for me that day. My bundle of joy came sliding out like a greased pig down a Teflon-coated chute, right into the hands of Sam, who calmly cut the cord. This all happened so fast that Gabe, even though he is a heart surgeon, and not an obstetrician, felt cheated, because he couldn't get there in time.

I will forever be grateful to Sam for being there and acting as my midwife, and I realize that we now share a special bond. What astonishes me is that Sam was not only thrilled to watch me give birth, but that the experience actually revived his romantic interest in me. Furthermore, he views the experience as somehow advancing his bid for my affections.

'Hear me out, Magdalena,' Cousin Sam said. 'The Amish grapevine is abuzz like never before, and you can guess who they're talking about.'

'Ouch,' I said, but it was my cheeks that were burning, not my ears. I hate being the object of gossip just as much as anyone does.

'Yeah but get this: there are at least three theories floating around about who is actually responsible for doing the deed, and you're not the villain in any of them.'

'Get out of town and back!' I cried. How I love those secular, Southern expressions.

'Easy, girl. I only have two eardrums, and I think you broke one of them the last time we talked. Anyway, hustle your bustle, and let's meet up, but not here at the store. If the Amish who shop there see you, they might clam up.'

'Where then?'

'Your place?'

'Stucky Ridge. We'll get the most privacy there.'

'I get it, Magdalena. There's trouble in paradise again.'

'Don't get your hopes up, Sam. What I mistook for my first sexual impulse in the fifth grade, when we went swimming at Miller's Pond, in retrospect was more than likely just a grain of sand that managed to get inside my bathing suit. I haven't felt a spark of desire for a blood relative since, especially one so closely related that you could yet turn out to be my twin.'

'Hmm, if you're positive.'

'Meet me by the picnic benches in ten minutes. Tootles.' I hung up.

'Mags,' Agnes said, 'I'm coming with you.'

'No, you're not.'

'But I'm your BFF.'

'Of course you are, dear,' I said, as I scurried to fetch clean clothes. 'And doesn't BFF stand for Best Forensic Friend?'

'No,' Agnes said, her voice rising, which made her sound like a Canadian. Not that there is anything wrong with that, mind you, but I have been hearing so many rising inflections lately, that I am concerned that we might sorely need a wall along our northern border.

'Now keep your head averted, dear,' I said, as I struggled into the bottom half of my sturdy Christian underwear. 'Mark my words, Agnes, you have a keen eye, and you would have made a wonderful forensic detective.'

'Really?' Agnes said.

'Absolutely,' I said. Believe me, if flattery will get one just about anywhere with me, it will certainly get Agnes over the finish line. 'What I need you to do is take a complete inventory of the contents of my refrigerator, and list those items that might be leftovers from the meal that might possibly have been fatal.'

'Really? Is that *it*? Is that all you want to use my keen eye for? And how do you expect me to recognize yesterday's leftovers when you're always taking home so-called "free food" from the restaurant that you don't even own in its entirety?'

'Why, I never!' I said indignantly. My ears burned as if held to a flame, because as we all know, the truth hurts.

'Really? You're always taking food home. You can't possibly deny that.'

'Agnes, that was just an expression of annoyance because you called me out on something that I shouldn't be doing. And speaking of which, if you don't stop saying "really", I'm going to scream. Now then, there's an actual pad of paper on my nightstand and a pen, so you can take copious notes on your keen observations on what you observe in the fridge. Also, please write down everything that you remember hearing at work dealing with this case – like who said what, and about whom. Try to recall their tone of voice, and did anyone attempt a rebuttal, that kind of thing.'

'Do you mean I should be a stoolie?' Agnes said.

'The word is a stooge, dear, but that comes next. Fold your notes into a wad and stuff them into the mouth of the concrete dragon on the back steps. You know, the thing that you told Alison that I would absolutely adore, when you took her to a flea market to shop for my birthday.'

'Really?'

'Eeeeeee-aaaahg!'

It was actually fortuitous that Agnes said 'really' again, and that I shrieked. Even at its finest moments my voice has been known to put the hens off laying, and birds to fall from the sky (although they land gently in the nearest trees). But my less than melodious outburst roused Alison from whatever she was doing and brought her running. As for Little Jacob, the voice of his mother is always soothing, whether being expressed off-key, or on.

'Your mother has to go out,' I said to my teenager. 'Auntie Agnes will be here for a while doing a little snooping – I mean sleuthing – on my behalf. When she's gone, lock the doors behind her, and don't let anyone in. *Anyone*, and that means you-know-who.'

Alison's lip protruded far enough to be a helipad. 'You mean Daddy, don't you?'

'No, dear. Besides, Daddy has his own key.'

'Oh,' said Alison, as she nodded slowly and with great emphasis. 'You mean *her*. You mean the woman who can't stand you.'

I jiggled pinkies in both ears, in case I'd heard it wrong. I was expecting her to say, 'the woman who *you* can't stand', but then she'd flipped the sentence around.

'Alison, dear,' I said, 'please repeat what you just said.'

'Ah, it's nothing, Mom. Just go do what you gotta do, and don't worry about me taking good care of Little Jacob. Ya know that I love that rug rat like there's no tomorrow.'

'It's not you whom I'm worried about,' I wanted to say. Instead, I clammed up like a mollusc at low tide, and that's the way I intended to behave from that minute on. There had already been enough alienation and strife in my family, and so help me, Magdalena Portulacca Yoder was not going to contribute further to the fraying of our family's ties.

'I love you, dear,' I said, as I turned tail and ran from the house before my tongue could betray me. It's been said that 'loose lips sink ships'. The serpent in the Garden of Eden most certainly didn't have lips; however, he did possess a tongue.

TWENTY-THREE

I f one were to rent Room 6 at The PennDutch Inn (the price of which had just been doubled, thanks to the recent murder of Sarah Conway), and lean dangerously far out the window on a clear, late autumn day, one might possibly get a glimpse of Lovers' Leap on the north face of Stucky Ridge. This landmark is of great importance to local Anglophiles in that it is exactly as high as Scafell Pike, the loftiest spot in England. That is to say, Stucky Ridge soars up to a dizzying 978 meters (3208 ft.), which is respectable for the northeastern states, but downright pitiful to citizens west of the Mississippi River. Don't be misled though, because the height of Stucky Ridge (named after an ancestor, of course) is measured against sea level, not the valley floor. The Delaware Indian maiden and her warrior lover who supposedly threw themselves off Lovers' Leap sometime pre-conquest by the Europeans, fell to their death only nine-hundred feet or so.

It is five miles as the crow flies to Stucky Ridge, but as Magdalena the Shrew drives it is just a wee bit longer because Hertzler Road follows meandering Slave Creek. Four miles from my house one gets to the bridge where a right turn takes one into the village of Hernia proper. Continuing past the bridge for another mile, one drives along the well-tended fields belonging to Rudy Swinefister, Hernia's only openly gay man.

At the farthest edge of Rudy's farm, the abrupt north face of Stucky Ridge begins. At that point, one can elect to continue on Hertzler Road, now County Road 96, until one reaches the wild and woolly State of Maryland, or turn off on the narrow dirt track that winds up the eastern flank of the ridge until, after many heart-stopping moments, one has reached the summit. If one elects to visit Maryland, my advice is to take along one's own provisions – I'm just saying. Now I shan't say another word about that fair state.

The surprisingly flat summit of Stucky Ridge is divided into three sections that cover roughly equal areas. The most popular portion is a patch of dense woods at the north end behind Lovers' Leap. This where the young people in our community, Mennonites and Amish included, come on the weekends to – it disgusts me to say this – 'make out'. The Brits call it snogging. Because the Amish are permitted to rebel in their late teens in a sanctioned practise called *rumschpringe*, they even go so far as to drive cars up to the ridge.

The picnic area with its panoramic western view is the second most popular spot, especially with families. The third area, called Settler's Cemetery, has many permanent residents. In order to be buried in Settler's Cemetery, one must be descended from one of the ten founding families. I am descended from five of those. Spouses of descendants, as well as adopted children of descendants, are also given the privilege of being planted for eternity in this small plot of land.

When I asked Mama why the settlers would go to all the trouble of lugging their dead up to the top of the ridge just to stick them in the ground, she said that the answer was as clear as the Yoder nose on my horsey face. It was so that on the day of resurrection, the dead would have a head start at meeting Jesus in the sky. Then I said that I knew that Heaven was up in the sky, but what if that part of the sky was on the opposite side of the globe? Like over Australia. In that case, I said, our relatives would go floating off into space in the wrong direction, and they would miss Jesus's return entirely. Mama was so mad that she washed out my mouth with soap and made me stay home from church that day.

At any rate, I didn't find Cousin Sam at the picnic area as per our agreement. Nevertheless, I knew exactly where to go. He was sitting on a folding chair next to his sister's grave. Sam, age six, and Evangeline, age three, had been frolicking about in a huge pile of leaves one fine day in late autumn, when a neighbour's German shepherd from across the street leaped over a low picket fence and joined them. The dog become agitated watching the children play and didn't stop to consider that this was a game. Instead, the German shepherd went straight for Evangeline's throat, biting through her jugular vein.

The tragic sequence of events took only a few seconds and

Evangeline died almost immediately. Sam's mother observed helplessly from behind the kitchen window. Sam, terrified and bewildered, made a beeline into the nearby woods and remained hidden in a dense thicket for two days.

Although Sam had not run far, he managed to avoid discovery because those searching for him refrained from using dogs, on account of his traumatic experience. No sane adult would have blamed a six-year-old boy for not being able to protect his sister from a dog attack that happened in a split second. However, that didn't stop Sam's father from blaming him. After all, Sam was supposed to be the 'man of the house' when his father was at work. In time Sam internalized the blame and vowed never to have children, as he saw himself incapable of being a responsible father. Unfortunately, his decision to remain childless was unilateral, and not communicated to Dorothy before they tied the knot.

'Hey cousin,' I said when I was within speaking distance. As is common knowledge, one should not shout whilst in a cemetery. The dead may no longer have ears (at least if they've been dead long enough), but a few of them can hear, nonetheless, and are capable of getting very feisty when annoyed. Take Nina Petersheim, for instance, who will literally growl at anyone who walks across the burial plot that she occupies. Miss Petersheim died in 1932, and this strange and frightening phenomenon has been happening regularly since at least 1934, when it was first mentioned in the now defunct *Hernia Village Gazette*. But I have again digressed shamefully.

'Hey, Magdalena,' Sam said. He rose and collapsed the folding chair, tucking it under one arm. 'Let's go sit at a picnic table.'

'I hear you,' I said. 'It's getting hard to walk in here anymore, much less sit down. You're lucky that you still have an empty plot.'

'Yeah, it's earmarked for me personally. Even though Dorothy will likely be the one to go first, given her many health issues, she doesn't want to be buried up here among a bunch of Amish and Mennonites.'

'And you? You're a Methodist now, right?'

'I haven't been to any church in ages. Dorothy can't get out, and I don't like sitting alone. Besides, Dorothy and I have hit a new low point in our marriage.'

'I'm sorry to hear that,' I said.

We walked in silence until we reached the first picnic table and then sat opposite sides on fixed benches. After we'd admired the view that we'd seen our entire lives, ever since our eyes could focus on distant shapes, Sam cleared his throat.

'Well, you know what it means if Dorothy and I split up?'

'Sam, stop it! This isn't a good time.'

'But does this mean that you and Gabe—?'

'*Shut Up, She Said Kindly* – that would be the name of my autobiography,' I said, 'if I were to write one. Beginning now. Mull that over.'

Sam nodded. 'New topic, then. Let's talk about the rumours that might well be helpful to your case, and how I came to hear them. But – and it's a big but – you have to pinkie swear that you're not going to rat me out to the Feds after you find out what I've done.'

I felt my hopes lifted, and then dashed in the space of two seconds. 'Sam, have you broken the law? Did you suddenly get elected to the state legislature? What did you do?'

My double-first cousin howled with glee. 'That's why I adore you, Magdalena. Only you would come right out and suggest that I might do something utterly nefarious. Rest assured, if I was going to be a corrupt politician, I'd go for the gold. I'd run for President of the United States, or at the very least, the nation's senate. However, while I am pretty sure that what I did *is* unethical, and it might be illegal, I pay every penny of federal income taxes, and I have never slept with a woman other than Dorothy.'

'Shut the front door!' I said.

Sam nodded. 'Aha, Magdalena, I knew that would impress you, because even you have known more than one man – in the biblical sense.'

'But I was an *inadvertent* adulteress! I didn't know that Aaron Miller was a bigamist; no one in Hernia knew that, including you, and you know everything that goes on in this village.'

'True. But let's get down to brass tacks now, because I need to hit the "information highway" again on your behalf – plus I need to get back to minding the store. Melon is a competent enough sales clerk, and appears to be honest, but really, how far can one trust an Episcopalian named Melon?'

I waved a hand impatiently. 'Get down to those tacks, dear. Even brass can tarnish if left in the elements too long.'

'Right. As you know, Toy was standing right there when Sheriff Stodgewiggle arrested you. He called me immediately so that his trusty C.I. could put his ear to the Amish grapevine and give a listen.'

I waved my hand again, but this time to ward off a fly the size of a helicopter. The good citizens of Hernia are supposed to carry home their own trash, but I'm afraid that not all of us behave like Girl Scouts. And it has only gotten worse in recent years, when world events seem to be pointing to Armageddon, and the subsequent end of this world as we know it. As Clarabelle Livingood said to me just last Sunday, 'What's the point in fixing my roof if the Good Lord's coming back before winter?'

'Remember, Sam,' I said, 'I've only ever been an amateur sleuth, so bear with me. What is a C.I.?'

'Oh,' Sam said, taking care not to smile too broadly, as he folded his hands on the beginnings of a paunch. 'It's a confidential informant. Sometimes police departments pay them a little, in order to keep them coming back with new information, but I do it because I'm a concerned citizen.'

'So you're a snitch? I mean that in the best possible way, of course.'

Sam frowned. 'Seriously, Magdalena, Toy recruited me; it wasn't the other way around. He's used me on a number of cases now. Small things. Disputes between the Amish and their Englisher neighbours, because as you know, the Amish try to avoid court as much as possible, and thus folks often take advantage of them.'

'And why did he ask *you* to be his spy,' my voice rising with every word, 'and not me?' Now I had a new worry to add to my ever-expanding list: besides being an inadvertent adulteress, what if I was an inadvertent Canadian?

'Really?' Sam said. 'Do you need to ask? It's because I speak the local dialect of Pennsylvania Dutch. If you'll recall, when I was six years old, my mother sent me to live with her Amish parents, who refused to speak English. So, I started school in a one-room Amish school house. By the time I returned to Hernia the next summer, I'd forgotten how to play in English. That's why I latched on to you in the second grade. You were easily the friendliest face on the playground.' He paused for a nano-second. 'Now look what's happened to you.'

I stuck my tongue out at him. 'Tell me about your high crimes and misdemeanours, dear. *Tempus fugit.*'

'Right,' he said. 'Anyway, as soon as I heard that you'd been arrested for murder, I hung a sign that read "out of order" on the Amish phone booth in front of my store. Yes, I know, strictly speaking, anyone may use it, but we all know it's there for the Amish, because they're forbidden the ownership of private telephones.'

I grunted in exasperation at another of Sam's well-meaning, but hare-brained, schemes. 'How does that help anything?'

'Easy, girl. The sign also instructed them to go around to the rear of my store and enter though the freight entrance. They have to be buzzed in. Because of my recent expansion, you may recall, my office is now just a corner of the storeroom, and the walls are only movable screens. They're really just to keep my work space separate from my inventory. Anyway, I set a landline phone on a little table on the inventory side of one screen, within inches of my desk on the other side. A sign next to the phone says that all local calls were free. Every time the door buzzed, I let someone in, and then went to my desk and pretended to work. Instead I eavesdropped.'

'Why, you snake!' I cried happily. 'Why, you evil dog!' Then I slapped my mouth for having uttered such terrible expressions, but I slapped it gently. After all, it behoves no one if the punishment exceeds the crime.

Sam grinned. 'You know, either these women forgot that I speak the dialect – which I speak on a daily basis with some of them in the store – or else they didn't care. Magdalena, you've never seen a gossipier group of ladies. Or more convincing arguments about who Miss Conway's killer is.'

I swatted away another fly. 'And that would be me, of course.'

'Don't be ridiculous, Mags. There's only one person who's accusing you of this dastardly deed. Even her myopic minions aren't spewing her poisonous rhetoric.'

I swatted at that ding-dang fly again, missing him by just a wing length. 'You're undoubtedly referring to Mother Malaise. So who else are we talking about?'

'Whom do you think?'

'Not Barbara!' It came out more as a loud whinge, than a wail. 'Why must poor Barbara always be the butt of everyone's suspicion, everyone's joke, just because she came from somewhere else? You know, Sam, I don't think that most of us Christians realize this, but the most repeated commandment in the Bible is to love and care for the stranger in our midst, for we were once strangers ourselves. Gabe says that this commandment occurs thirty-nine times in the Torah, which is the first five books of our Old Testament.'

'Huh. Well, I don't think that applies to illegal immigrants.'

'I didn't bring that up to start a political debate, Sam; I'm speaking only about Barbara. It seems that she constantly rubs people the wrong way, but I just don't see it. I don't find her abrasive at all. Do you, Sam?'

Sam cleared his throat, and suddenly appeared interested in the beginnings of some liver spots that were forming on his ruddy hands. Even though he was a shopkeeper, he was also a ginger, who spent Sunday afternoons soaking up the sun.

'Let's just say that she's more direct than the local Amish.' He cleared his throat again and began pushing the cuticle back from his left index finger. 'Rather like you – but that's not a bad thing. You're my favourite relative, you know.'

I swallowed my irritation yet again. Incidentally, it is a scientific fact that irritation contains not a single calorie. Given that I am forced to swallow so much irritation on a daily basis (hence I never feel hungry), perhaps that is the reason my physique is somewhat on the bony side.

'Sam, *dear*, through our ancestor Jacob Hochstetler who arrived on the *Charming Nancy* in 1738, we are related to approximately eighty percent of the Amish and Mennonite families in Pennsylvania. Tell me, have you seen Barbara's so-called doppelgänger?'

Sam stood, and stretched, holding his hands up as if cradling the sun before sitting again. 'You mean Barbara's mother?'

'She is *not*!' I said.

'That's what the buzz on the Amish phone line says.'

'That's crazy,' I said. 'They haven't even seen her – have they?'

'No, but you have two cooks with Amish connections other than Barbara,' Sam said.

'Chef Marigold Flanagan, and assistant chef, Lydia Burkholder,' I said.

'Well, you know how I hate to gossip,' Sam said, 'but it was Flanagan who started the rumour that the deceased Miss Conway was Barbara Hostetler's mother. Really, Mags, you can't trust a woman who is born into a decent God-fearing Amish family, and then runs off to India and prays to elephants.'

'They don't pray to elephants,' I snapped. 'Sam, don't you ever read?'

'I read *TV Guide*,' he said. 'My point is that she took up Hinduism when she discovered an age spot on her forehead, then went back to being Presbyterian when the spot vanished after she started using a lightening cream. That woman is as flaky as one of Freni's pie crusts.'

I reached over and patted his heavily freckled arm. 'Yes, you do hate to gossip, dear. That's always been one of your worst faults.'

Sam moved his arm just out of reach. 'You're mocking me, but that's all right, because I know how you hate to mock, and how uttering your hurtful words to me right now hurt you even more than they did me.' He winked. 'So, shall I continue, or shall I take my toys and go home?'

'Stay and play!' I said quickly. 'I'll be nice-*er*. I promise.'

'OK then,' Sam said, 'let's talk about Agnes.'

I recoiled in genuine surprise. '*Agnes?* What has she been saying?'

'I don't mean what she's been saying; I mean *her*. I mean Agnes as our murder suspect.'

I leaned over and gave Sam a light push. After unloading food trucks for thirty years, Sam doesn't budge easily.

'Sam, this isn't a time for joking.'

'I'm not joking, Mags.'

I might be nonviolent, but I gave his arm a somewhat playful smack. 'Agnes is my best friend, for crying out loud. What are you saying? That she somehow set me up to take a murder – uh – rap? By sneaking poison into the same food that Gabe just happened to bring home from the restaurant?'

'Yup. Where did Gabe go to pick up the food when he got there? I presume that he called the order in first, so that he didn't have to wait. Am I right?'

'Yes, of course. Agnes had it all packaged up and waiting for him behind the hostess stand – no, wait! That doesn't mean anything. Marigold or Lydia could just as easily have poisoned the food, or even Barbara, for that matter. The toxicology report isn't even back in yet. All we know is that Sarah Conway was poisoned, and that she died at The PennDutch Inn. But we still don't know what the poison was, or how fast it acted, or in what form it was delivered. This is all premature speculation.'

'My thoughts exactly,' Sam said. 'Except that you, my cousin, my very dear, *dear* friend – and I am hurt that you didn't say that I was your best friend – have to keep your eyes open and consider all possibilities. *Everyone* in your life has to be a suspect.'

I snorted nervously. 'Even Little Jacob?'

'No, not wee Little Jacob, and not Alison either. Tell me, how is she coping with this? With the prospect of her mother being behind bars? Having a girlfriend in jail named Brunhilde, etc.'

'Brunhilde was taken by another inmate, Sam. I had to go it alone. But Alison's a trooper. She's more upset about the rift her grandmother is causing between her father and me.'

'Ah,' Sam said, 'so again I ask, if Dorothy and I were ever to—'

'Shut up, Sam,' I said with a smile.

'Don't flirt with me, Mags. Tell me, where do you plan to go from here?'

'To get Freni. I need a reliable childminder if I'm going to do some serious sleuthing.'

Sam laughed. '*Childminder?* Have you suddenly turned into a Brit?'

'Alison is fourteen, for goodness' sake. Somehow referring to Freni as a babysitter just doesn't seem right, even though she's going to be there for both of my children.'

'Fair enough,' Sam said. 'What makes you think she'll make herself available? Didn't you ruffle her feathers a bit when you hired Barbara as your chef?'

'That's true,' I said. 'But I'm counting on the fact that Freni will find it easier to forgive me than the thought of spending more time with Barbara, now that the restaurant has to stay closed for the duration of the investigation.'

'Hey,' Sam said, 'you're going to think I'm crazy, but remember what I said about keeping an open mind about *everyone*.'

'Even you?' It was meant to be a joke, but I sounded like a startled blue jay. That's because I knew where he was going with the conversation, and I didn't like it.

'On that high note,' Sam said, 'I bid you *adieu*.'

TWENTY-FOUR

'**A**ch,' said Freni, 'it's you.'

'It's you, too, dear,' I said sweetly. 'And you look fit as a fiddle, Freni. Although why fiddles should look fit, or a healthy person look like a fiddle, is beyond me. Legend has it that Nero fiddled while Rome burned, but Nero wasn't very fit, even if his fiddle was, and since that's neither here nor there, I won't fiddle around anymore, but get right down to the point. May we please continue our conversation on the porch? Your plethora of progeny are provoking my penchant to prevaricate.'

'Always with the riddles, Magdalena.' Freni virtually pushed me over the threshold and back on to the front doormat. 'But my answer is "yah".'

'Excuse me?' I said.

'You came to ask me back? Good. Now we go, yah?'

'Just like that?' I said.

'So,' Freni said, 'what shall we wait for? Christmas?'

I've always been afraid to look a gift horse in the mouth, lest I find myself gazing fondly in my bathroom mirror. Ergo I was quite happy to hoof it down the walk with Freni and hustle her into my car before we got struck by lightning, or the earth opened up and swallowed us like it did sinners in Old Testament days.

I reckoned the calamity zone to have about a mile radius, with Barbara's house being the epicentre, and once we were free of that, I pulled to the side of the road alongside a field of corn. That's when I noticed a small sign advertising that this crop had been genetically modified, which as everyone hereabouts knows is a sin, on the grounds that modification is akin to evolution. Therefore, I had no choice but to drive on a bit until we reached an area where cow pastures flanked both sides of the country lane.

'Is your car making trouble?' Freni said, as we stopped the second time.

'No,' I said, 'but I wanted to talk to you about something important before we got home, and this seems like a better place.'

No sooner did the words come out of my mouth than a small herd of Jersey cows rounded the top of the rise to my left. Don't get me wrong, I think that Jersey cows are the most beautiful dairy breed there is, and their high yields of milk are exceptionally rich in butterfat. My beef with them is that they most certainly are not biblical. I started moving the car again.

'Ach,' said Freni, 'we stop, or I get the whiplash.'

'But they're Jerseys!'

'So, this matters how?'

'Freni, when God created the world, what kind of cow did he create? Holsteins, or Jerseys?'

Freni stared at me through her bottle thick lenses. 'This is a serious question?'

'Come on, Freni, answer. Don't think about it. He only created one kind, so it had to be either Holstein cows, or Jersey cows.'

Freni stuck her left index finger under her black travelling bonnet, at a spot near her temple, and scratched vigorously for a few seconds. 'Well,' she said, 'when you were a little girl, I read to you from a children's Bible story book with pictures. This story is about Creation, and Adam and Eve are naming the animals. In the picture Eve has her arms around a Holstein calf, so that is my answer.'

'Excellent,' I said. 'My point, exactly. Both hybrid corn and Jersey cows—'

'I think that now you are knitting with only one needle, Magdalena.'

'What?' I demanded.

'Maybe you are a few eggs less than a dozen, yah?'

'Are you saying that I'm—?'

'In a rowboat with only one oar in the water.'

'Why, I never!'

'Then maybe now you should, yah?'

'Should do *what*? I'm perfectly fine, thank you very much!'

'Maybe now you ask for professional help, yah?'

'That's ridiculous.'

That's when Freni, my double second cousin once removed, overcame five centuries of inbred Amish and Mennonite reserve, to reach across the seat and gently pat my arm. In order to deviate a similar distance from her comfort zone, an English woman would have to chat up strangers in an American accent, whilst wearing a clown suit, and riding the tube during rush hour.

'Magdalena,' she said, 'I think maybe you have the nervous disease like your mama.' Freni tried to pat me again, but I pulled away. Her effusive display of affection was making my head spin.

'Freni, yes, Mama had a nervous *breakdown*, but I'm adopted. Remember?'

'Yah,' Freni said, 'but your other mama had the nervous breaks too. There are many in our family with this disease.'

'Freni I did *not* kill that woman; I did not kill Sarah Conway. Do you believe me?'

She stared at me, wordlessly inscrutable behind her thick glass lenses. Outside the gorgeous Jersey cows were now crowding the fence, craning their tawny necks to get a good look at me. Was this the Devil's way of mocking me? Or was I really having a nervous breakdown? Maybe it was just the mega-amount of stress I'd been under, what with being arrested and thrown into the slammer, and having my Dearly Beloved driving off angrily. Not to mention having to come to grips with my teenage daughter's fascination with magic. What is the difference between a so-called 'break-down', and a stress overload?

'Freni dear, I asked you a question. Do you think I'm a murderer?'

I honestly don't think that I'm a paranoid person. But Freni continued to stare at me on one side, and the Jersey cows on the other. As far as I can tell, not one of the cows was wearing glasses. Their big black eyes seemed to say, *You have judged us harshly. That children's book with the picture of Eve's arms around a Holstein calf was just some artist's opinion. You are a judgmental woman, Magdalena.*

'But I'm not!' I said vehemently.

Finally, Freni spoke. 'Yah, you cannot kill a person, Magdalena. This I truly believe, because you cannot kill a chicken. Always Mose or I must kill the hen for the stewing pot, for to make the dumplings.'

'Then why didn't you say so sooner, instead of just staring at me?'

'Because I cannot believe that you ask me such a question,' Freni said. 'Even if you are having the nervous breaks, I do not think you can kill a person. Not even a very bad person.'

I put the car into gear. 'In that case my "nervous breaks" is over – well, at least halfway over. The sooner we get to The PennDutch, so you can watch the kids, the sooner I can put the screws to a few more suspects.'

'Hmm,' Freni said. Since it was a word that wasn't part of her lexicon, I felt compelled to follow up on it.

'Hmm, what?'

'What about Thelma Bontrager?'

'Oops.' I'd completely forgotten that Thelma, who'd been hired to cook for me after Freni had quit in a snit, was scheduled to work today.

'No prob, Bob,' I said, repeating one of Gabe's worn-out phrases. 'Thelma can do the cooking and cleaning, and all you need to do is enjoy the children. You know how much they love their Cousin Freni.'

Freni did her best to nod in agreement. With little neck to speak of, she tried to engage her torso in the action, but found her shoulder harness constraining. It looked more like she was attempting to scratch her back – then again, maybe she was.

Nevertheless, by the time I got back to The PennDutch Inn Thelma was already making lunch for Gordon Gaiters and Alison. To my astonishment the two of them were in the dining room bonding over a game of Scrabble. I wasn't surprised, however, to see that my daughter – she of the horrible grammar – was beating the pants off the old geezer. When she was in fifth grade, Alison came fourth in the Bedford County Spelling Bee. As for my bouncing bundle of joy, he'd already been fed, and was in his high chair happily singing to himself. Never mind that he was wearing a plastic bowl on his head, and had apple sauce oozing down into his eyes.

'Ach,' said Freni and immediately bustled over to her second cousin *twice* removed and gathered him up in her grandmotherly arms. Little Jacob squealed with delight, and it's a fact that Freni squealed with delight right back at him.

Quite satisfied that my children were in good hands, and that my beloved Freni was happy to be where she was for the moment,

I felt my confidence returning. With the help of the Good Lord, of course, I was going to put the brakes on the 'nervous breaks'. And I certainly wasn't going to feel sorry for myself, just because my handsome husband was who knows where, and I still had to prove that I was not a murderess.

Yes, I know it is not politically correct to use that 'ess' ending anymore on nouns, as it is considered sexist. However, if I was going to be convicted of that heinous crime, and had to spend a life behind bars, perhaps with some girlfriend named Heather or Courtney, I would at least want to be referred to as a murderess, not a murderer. At least not the way we Americans say it by pronouncing the final 'r'. But if being a murder*ess* is no longer possible, and if I ever *did* kill someone, which I would never, ever do, I'd do it in Great Britain, where I would be a murder-*uh*. Of course, I would never take the life of another human being – only God has that right – I'm just saying.

At any rate, as I walked from my kitchen to my car, I suddenly felt like I was moving under water. It took effort just to open the car door and close it again. All I wanted to do was lie down on the back seat and go to sleep, but in order to do that, I'd have to get out of the car, and then climb back in. That was way too much trouble. Or, I could clamber over the console, and sort of launch myself into the rear seat. That was way more effort than I was willing to expend.

But the thing is, when one has the 'nervous breaks' one doesn't necessarily have control over one's emotions. One minute I was sitting in my car, feeling so defeated by life that I could barely breathe, and the next minute I was bawling like Little Jacob when Alison takes his binky away because she decides that he's too old for it. Soon I couldn't breathe through my nose, unless I blew it. Although I keep a box of tissues in the car, who wants to be seen with a bright red nose, and have people think that you've been drinking? Especially when one has spent her life being a teetotaller?

So after about five minutes of boo-hooing, I managed to talk myself into calling it quits. After all, the tissue box was beginning to run low, and I was getting a sore spot at the base of my nose from wiping it so much. Besides, what good is it to throw yourself a pity party, if no one comes?

Get a grip on it just long enough to drive out to Agnes's, I told myself. She's your best friend, but she's also on your list of suspects. Agnes is the perfect person to see right now. She will either comfort you with her loving words of friendship, or become so indignant at your leading questions that you'll become angry, maybe even suspicious in return. Love, anger, suspicion – feeling any one of those three emotions was a sight better than despair and self-recrimination. One thing was for certain: Agnes was not going to blame me for taking a stand against Ida's interference in my marriage.

Although Agnes had never had a mother-in-law, due to Doc's advanced age when they married, she had never been a fan of Mother Malaise. When Agnes's two dotty, elderly uncles sold their neighbouring farm and joined the Convent of Perpetual Apathy as its only male postulants, Agnes was horrified. When she learned that her uncles had signed their assets over to the convent, she was livid and attempted to sue on her uncles' behalf. Most unfortunately, thanks to a court-appointed psychiatrist, the dotty nudists were deemed merely eccentric, still quite capable of making their decisions.

As soon as I pulled on to the lane that leads to Agnes's farm, I stopped and called Freni to let her know where I was. Heaven forfend that I should cause her the worry that Gabe was causing me. Trust me, one can be furious with a husband, whilst still loving him with a passion.

Having made that important call, I kept a sharp eye out for the billy goat and was quite relieved when I saw that he was back in his pasture. Then came a complete surprise; there was a vehicle other than Agnes's parked up by the house. Moreover, it had a logo stencilled on the side that read: *Armageddonland, Inc.* The van was black, but the letters, which were bright red and composed of tongues of flames, were painted on a pale-yellow background in the shape of a long, narrow oval. My first thought was that this was yet another sick joke foisted on us, the community of believers, by some of those more militant, left-leaning liberals. You know, like the ones who affix the Christian symbol of a fish to the rear of their car, except that their fish sports legs, which indicates that they believe in evolution.

Imagine, then, that when I got inside her house, I found my

dear friend engaged in a serious conversation with a young man named Lawrence, who really did work for a company called Armageddonland Inc. Lawrence's mission was to purchase forty thousand acres of farmland in Bedford County for use as the future home of the greatest and most important theme park that the world had ever seen.

TWENTY-FIVE

'OK, I'll bite,' Agnes said. 'What is going to make yours the greatest and most important theme park in the world? But first tell me, have you ever been to Disneyworld?'

'Yes, I have,' the young man said. 'To be perfectly honest, I found it very entertaining. But I was a child then, and I thought like a child.'

'How old are you now, Larry?' I said.

'My name is *Law*rence,' he said, with a flip of his blond bangs. 'Only my parents call me Larry.'

'Gotcha, dear,' I said, borrowing from teenagers' lingo. 'So then, how old *are* you, Lawrence, now that you are no longer a child?'

'How old are you, ma'am?'

Agnes chortled. 'He's gotcha there, Magdalena.'

'I'm seventeen, Lawrence,' I said.

Lawrence snorted. 'I don't think so.'

'I might prevaricate from time to time, but I don't tell boldface lies. I am indeed seventeen years old, as well as eighteen, and thirty, all the way up to fifty-one. That's my upper limit. What's your upper limit, Lawrence?'

Lawrence tossed his head again, but not a hair moved out of place. 'Frankly, Magdalena, that's none of your business.'

'Ooh,' Agnes said, 'this is going to be interesting.'

'Tut, tut, *Law*rence,' I said calmly, 'only my friends call me Magdalena. Everyone else addresses me as Miss Yoder.'

'Or Mrs Rosen,' Agnes said, who never shied from poking the bear.

So far, we'd all been standing in Agnes's large country kitchen, which was good, because young Lawrence had room to recoil without causing any damage. There's not much harm one can do by stepping back against a refrigerator, except for knocking a handful of magnets askew, and sending some recipes and newspaper clippings fluttering to the floor.

'By any chance are you *that* Magdalena Yoder?' Lawrence finally managed to say.

'As big as life, and twice as ugly,' I said.

'I beg your pardon?' he said.

'Nothing,' I said. 'One of my guests said it once, and I thought it rather suited me. It's an affirmative answer to your question, dear.'

'Forgive me, ma'am,' Lawrence said. 'I didn't mean to be so rude. I thought you were just – well, just a regular somebody.' He held out his hand for me to shake. On the outside of his wrist was the tattoo of a tiny blue flower with a bright yellow centre. It was incongruously sweet, given the vibe that I was picking up from this young man. Somehow I could tell that he could be one of those guys who would break practically every bone in my long slim fingers, and then shake my damaged digits until my arm separated from my bony shoulder. Seeing as how my fingers were my most attractive physical attribute, I was not about to let Lawrence have his way with them.

'Sorry, Lawrence, but I don't shake hands. Given that I still don't know your age, for all I know you still might be in elementary school. Who knows, you might have cooties or something. So thanks, but no thanks.'

Lawrence smiled. 'Gotcha. But for the record, I'm twenty-two.'

'Are you single?' Agnes said. 'Would you like something to drink? I only have soft drinks, but I also have three kinds of juice. And coffee. I could put on a pot real quick. And tea. The kettle's right here.'

'Down girl,' I said to Agnes, who in turn shot me an underserved dirty look. Lawrence was twenty-nine years younger than her, for crying out loud.

Lawrence didn't respond to Agnes's beverage offer. 'Miss Yoder, you're the owner of Amish Sinsations, yes?'

'I own sixty percent. Why?'

'Because I'm about to make you an offer you can't refuse.'

Agnes giggled. 'She doesn't watch movies. She's certainly never seen *The Godfather*.'

Lawrence cocked his head. He was clearly amused. 'Is that so?'

'Yes, I'm a rube and a country bumpkin,' I said. 'A cultural philistine. I wouldn't know the Louvre from a loo. What of it?'

'Mags, this is serious,' Agnes said. 'You wouldn't believe what he just offered me for my forty acres.'

'What?' I said. I have nothing against acquiring information.

'A quarter of a million,' Agnes said.

'Rubles?' I said. I wasn't being serious, of course.

'Is she always like this?' Lawrence asked.

'Yes, unfortunately she is,' Agnes said. 'Go ahead and tell her what your company is doing. It's right up her alley, so I'm sure she'll hop right up on board.'

Given my prominent, probing, Yoder proboscis, I can smell a conman a mile away, and although young Lawrence didn't reek of deception, I already knew that I would hate his proposal. I would have bolted for the door, had I not so desperately needed to speak to Agnes privately after the cheeky youth's departure.

'Please make your spiel quick,' I said to Lawrence, 'or else we need to go somewhere so that I might sit. As it is, I'm too tired to hop on board anything. The best that you can hope for is that Agnes pushes from behind, and you pull to get me on board. But by no means do you get to push my behind. Capiche?'

'OK, Miss Yoder,' Lawrence began, speaking agreeably fast, 'Armageddonland, which is scheduled to open in the next five years, will be the largest amusement park in the world. But more importantly, it will be entirely Bible based, primarily on the Book of Revelation, of course. You see, so many young people these days are drifting away from the Church. Generations ago, church services were your Sunday entertainment. Now it's your phones, social networking, video games, and movies, anything but church.

'Not only that, many people find Christ's promise to return quickly disheartening after more than two millennia. Telling them that "God's time" is different from our time just doesn't ring true anymore. But we at Armageddonland have thought of how to make people excited about the *end times* once more.

'Our park will include terrifying, and glorifying, passages from the Book of Revelation brought to life inside the largest covered dome anywhere on the planet. Our state-of-the-art holograms are so realistic, for instance, that they're guaranteed to give you nightmares unless you've been saved. Take for instance, the horse-size locusts described in Revelation 9:7, with women's hair and lion's teeth. Their awesome wings sounded like chariots being pulled into battle by many horses. And they had giant scorpion tails which, if they stung you, hurt for five months.'

'I see,' I said.

But Lawrence wasn't through with his pitch. 'You get to role play too. You know, slay demons, and watch sinners die by the tens of thousands while God's holy wrath gets poured down upon them. And there will be plenty of rides, like an unbelievably real lake of fire your train will pass over, and you get to hear the unrepentant screaming in perpetual agony which, of course, they will have deserved by then.'

'Will it be called Lake Schadenfreude?' I said.

'What?' Lawrence said.

'She's being facetious,' Agnes said.

'What does that even mean?' Lawrence said. 'Is that Pennsylvania Dutch as well?'

'It means that I think Armageddonland is a horrible idea. Do you know that many Christians believe that the Book of Revelation was either John's dream, or allegorical?'

'Then they're not true Christians,' Lawrence said.

'Tread carefully,' Agnes said, 'or you might not get what you came for. Remember that she holds the lynchpin.'

'I beg your pardon?' I said to Agnes. 'What's this about a lynchpin?'

Lawrence literally stepped in front of Agnes. 'Miss Yoder, it's safe to say that as an eating establishment, your restaurant is history. No one is going to feel safe dining at a place where the food killed someone.'

'She didn't die *there*,' I said. 'She died at my inn.'

'Po-tay-to, po-tah-to,' the young squirt said. 'The food came from there, all the same. No matter how thoroughly you clean that joint of yours, you're never going to convince people that you've gotten every speck of ricin out of every nook and crack.'

'Cranny,' Agnes said.

'What?' Lawrence said.

'The phrase is "nook and cranny", not "nook and crack".'

'*Ricin?*' I said. 'What makes you think it was ricin?'

'Because that's the substance the previous owner put in her

pie when she murdered that famous author two years ago. It astounds me that your restaurant did remarkably well after all that, but then again, your genius is legendary. But let's be realistic, Miss Yoder, the public has a strong will to live, so I doubt if they're going to want to take their chances a second time. That's why I'm here to offer you a fair market price for a cramped lot on a busy highway, so close to the Turnpike that the roar of traffic practically has diners holding their hands over their ears, rather than clutching their eating utensils.'

'Oh, those poor dears,' I said. 'And to think that all this time I was abusing their ears, as well as their wallets, completely unaware of the torture that I was inflicting on them. I was, in fact, double-tasking.'

'Stop it, Mags,' Agnes snapped. She turned to Lawrence and wrung her hands. Figuratively. 'What you've just witnessed is Miss Yoder's unique brand of sarcastic humour. Trust me, she can be quite amusing at times once you get to know her – or so I've been told. Anyway, it's probably time for you to cut straight to the chase and tell her how much she plans to profit by selling that worthless pile of bricks and mortar formerly known as Amish Sinsations.'

'Is that supposed to be a joke?' Lawrence said.

'Excuse me?' Agnes said.

Lawrence scowled. 'It's common knowledge that women are incapable of being funny. As for sarcasm, that's not in their nature; that's not the way God created them.'

Agnes slapped her forehead. 'Oh my gracious! And to think that all these years my best friend might have been besting me with her beastly sense of non-existent humour.'

'And now I know that you're joking,' Lawrence said. 'And at my expense.'

'That's impossible,' I said. 'As a woman, she's incapable of joking.'

'Ineffectual attempts at humour, and actually being funny are not the same thing,' Lawrence said. He showed himself to the door. 'The two of you are going to be sorry, mark my words.'

TWENTY-SIX

'Geez Louise,' Agnes moaned before the door was finished slamming behind him. 'I sure could have used that quarter million dollars.'

'Agnes, setting aside that hideous venture for a moment, Armageddonland was taking advantage of you. Sure, that's a lot of money for just forty acres, but you're not factoring in this historic farmhouse, a large barn in tip-top shape, and the building that Old Doc used for his veterinary practice. If your goal was simply to buy a cosy cottage in town, I'm sure that you could find a young, horse-loving couple, with a growing family, who would gladly pay you that same quarter mil. They'd be winners, and you'd be a winner, knowing that your town wasn't destroyed by millions of stampeding tourists.'

'Really?'

'Really. And if I wasn't the emotionally stunted woman whom you know me to be, I'd throw my long gangly arms around you in a warm embrace as added assurance.'

Agnes laughed. 'If you did, you'd have to pat me on the back like you were burping a baby. That's the way we were raised, as if human backs were too hot to touch for more than a millisecond.'

'It's too bad we weren't born English,' I said. 'At least then we wouldn't be so repressed.'

Agnes laughed harder, which was my goal because I had a few very important, dicey questions to ask. But first I steered her into the living room and got her seated in Doc's comfortable old recliner. Then I smiled pleasantly which, alas, may not have been the right move.

'Mags,' Agnes said, 'do you think that you can hold it in until you get home? I haven't had the energy to clean any of the bathrooms since Doc died and, well – they're in a sorry state.'

'I'm fine, dear. Agnes, tell me, did you think that Sarah Conway was a dead ringer for Barbara Hostetler?'

Agnes' plump little mouth formed a perfect 'o'. 'What kind

of macabre joke was that? Frankly, Mags, that kind of humour is beneath you.'

'What?' I said. 'I wasn't joking. Did they look alike? That's all I want to know.'

'Oops, sorry. I thought the "dead ringer" part was intentional. But no, I didn't see a resemblance. Did you?'

I scratched my head. 'Not just a resemblance, but Sarah was Barbara's doppelgänger. She was like a carbon copy – no, a Xerox copy, or copy on a 3D printer. Same face, same hair, same body, same height, same everything.'

'Same height? Mags, no way! Sarah Conway was at least four inches shorter than Barbara. Maybe six.'

'Well,' I said, 'that's not possible. I stood right next to her, and she towered over me, just like Barbara does.'

'Was she wearing heels?'

'Heels?' I said.

'High heels,' Agnes said. 'Stiletto shoes. Of the sort you like to make fun of.'

'Harrumph,' I said. 'That's embarrassing. I don't suppose that you have any cracks large enough for me to crawl into.'

'Oh, I'm sure this old house has plenty of cracks that will need patching before I put it on the market, but none which can accommodate a giantess like you. However, I can't believe you didn't notice her shoes. The minute she walked into the restaurant, I was worried that she might fall off those things, and then we would have a huge lawsuit on our hands.'

'Ding, dang, dong,' I said.

'Magdalena, you potty mouth!'

'Sorry dear for getting carried away with my swearing. I can't believe I missed that. I mean, I saw her shoes – I just didn't figure them into her height. I must be losing it. So nothing else about her made you think of Barbara?'

'Nope,' Agnes said.

I took a deep breath as I prayed for guidance. 'Agnes, do you ever find it difficult to be my friend?'

I was pleased to see that my question startled Agnes. However, I immediately wished that I hadn't asked it.

'Yes,' Agnes said without a second's hesitation.

'You do? Why? How?'

'The same reasons that everybody else does, of course.'

'*What?* I can't think of anyone else who might be so envious of my success that they might want to sabotage one of my businesses, even if I do own just a sixty percent share.'

It is plum amazing just how fast a sphere-shaped woman can pop to her teeny-weeny tootsies and stick a landing like the Olympic gymnasts I've seen on Gabe's massive flat-screen television. My right foot is the size of England, and my left foot the size of Scotland, and I have the body mass of a bean pole, yet I would pitch forward and land on my significant Yoder nose if I tried a move like that.

'Out, Magdalena,' Agnes shouted. 'Get out now.'

'Whatever for, dear? I thought we were making progress?'

'*Progress?* On what? You came here for the express purpose of interrogating me, didn't you? I'm one of your suspects, and don't you deny it. I can tell when you're lying, Magdalena. We've been friends our entire lives, best friends even – until now.'

I teetered to my feet. Incidentally, folks who are envious of tall persons would do well to watch nature films of baby giraffes attempting to stand.

'But we're still best friends,' I cried. 'We're bosom buddies without the bosom part, because that would be a sin. Besides, I'm a carpenter's dream: I'm flat as a board.'

'Just shut up, Magdalena. There are times when I find your inane prattle amusing, but not now. I can't believe that you would think, even for a second, that I would be capable of killing someone. I just need enough money to survive, that's all. I'm not some money-grubbing woman who enjoys fleecing the pretentious elite just because they're too stupid to realize that they're being conned.'

'You're ninety percent right,' I said through clenched teeth. 'Everything that you just said was true, except for one thing.'

'What was that?' Agnes snapped.

'I'm not telling you!' I shouted. Then like an oversized toddler I stomped from the house.

'Magdalena, come back now,' Agnes called.

I didn't as much as turn my head.

'I order you to come back!' she screamed. 'I want to know what that one thing is. Come back!'

TWENTY-SEVEN

kept walking to my car. After I got in, I roared away in a spray of gravel, although I'm quite sure that none of it hit Agnes, because in my rear-view mirror I could see that she had already gone inside. Most probably she'd even slammed the door behind her.

Before I got to the end of Agnes's long drive, I knew that I would be returning to throw myself at her feet to beg her forgiveness. I couldn't blame her for being furious with me. But I wasn't ready to grovel just yet. The truth hurts, and at the moment I felt like I'd been attacked by a nest of hornets. Hornets of my own making, to be sure, but that didn't mean that their stingers were any less painful. It's been said that time 'heals all wounds'. Or was it 'kills all wounds'? Either way, we were both wounded animals who both needed a little time to lick our wounds before reconnecting.

Obviously, I needed to talk to someone about what had just happened, but I needed it to be someone who was both a friend, and who would be impartial. That ruled out Sam. Agnes and Sam had always been cordial in my presence – post-puberty, that is – but only out of their mutual love for me. What I didn't want at the moment was for Sam to see my fight with Agnes as an excuse to start badmouthing her.

It occurred to me that the friend who was most likely to remain neutral on the subject of Agnes would be Police Chief Toy Graham. The police station is located in the heart of beautiful downtown Hernia, across the street from Yoder's Corner Market. In recent years, due to our village's notoriety as a community chock-a-block with corpses (thanks to my inn), the downtown has exploded in growth. Besides the first Mennonite Church and the First Baptist Church on opposite corners of Main Street, between the police station and Miller's Feed Store, one can find two antique stores. The first one (going west) is called Amish Quilts and Treasures and is owned and staffed by Miss Belinda

Thornapple. In the same building is Pennsylvania Dutch Antiques owned and operated by Miss Virginia Thornapple, who is Belinda's identical twin sister. The women are in their mid-sixties and it is said that they have not spoken to each other since they were in their twenties. There is a red line painted down the centre of their building, and which extends all the way to the curb.

The south side of Main Street gives off a friendlier vibe. Two related, but non-competing businesses set up shop recently. Across from the antique shops we now have Timothy's Auto Repair, and right next door to it is Stucky Brothers' Blacksmith Shed. On any given day, folks getting their cars tuned up can wander next door and watch a horse getting shod by one of their distant cousins who still keeps the faith of his forefathers, and who preserves the old-time traditions.

But back to Toy, our disconcertingly handsome, young, Chief of Police. I'd called him soon after exiting Agnes's long driveway and accessing Hertzler Road, and I was relieved to find him at his desk. I was even more relieved when I learned that Sherry Baumgartner, his gal Friday, was off that day. I'm ashamed to admit that Sherry had gotten under my skin like a bad vaccine. It had little to do with the fact that she was a Lutheran, and much to do with the fact that she was named after an alcoholic drink. Plus, she laughed like an asthmatic hyena – not that I've ever heard one, mind you.

'Hey there,' Toy said brightly, when I knocked on the doorjamb. 'Come in and have a seat. What's up?'

Because Toy asked, I gave him an earful. However, because I am my own harshest critic, I tried to present both sides of everyone who'd had dealings with me ever since I'd received that first phone call from the now deceased Sarah Conway at *A Woman's Place*. I even tried to find excuses for Ida's hostility. Granted, I can be an emotional woman, but I try to be fair at all times, even when faced with obnoxious and unreasonable people.

Toy listened attentively, his masculine chin resting on his folded hands. If only I was a quarter of a century younger, and not married, I thought – then: 'Get behind me, Satan!' I said aloud.

'Excuse me,' Toy said.

'I didn't say anything,' I said.

'Yes, you did. Something about you and Satan's behind.'

'Oh, you mean *that*?' I said.

'Yes, that,' Toy said. His cornflower blue eyes were twinkling like the tanzanite earrings a guest once wore.

'Well, if I told you what "that" was about, then I'd have to kill you, and since I'm not a killer, that's a nonstarter.'

Toy smiled and stretched. 'OK, Magdalena, you came in to unload, and for a little feedback. Am I right?'

'Right as rain.'

'Then hang on, because the ride is going to be a little bumpy for you at first,' Toy said.

'I can hardly wait,' I mumbled.

'You were dead wrong to confront Agnes the way you did. Or even at all. Yes, until Miss Conway's killer is caught, theoretically anyone could be guilty of her murder. But Agnes? Come on, Magdalena, what were you thinking?'

I hung my head in shame. 'I wasn't. Thinking that is. Now I've probably ruined fifty-one years of friendship, and over what? My ego? And all because I wanted my best friend to finally express even a little bit of envy over something in my life.'

Toy smacked the top of his desk with palms of both hands. 'Gee golly whiz, Magdalena! I can't believe you. So that's what it was about, huh? You risked alienating your best friend just so you could see if she was jealous of your success? What are you? Stuck back in high school?'

'Sixth grade,' I said. 'I'm not trying to be funny. Because I was five feet, eight inches tall when I was eleven, I had to do everything else perfectly if I wanted to get any respect. Or so I thought. Anyway, I sort of went overboard on that. By the way, I was five feet, ten inches in the ninth grade, but rumours that I topped out at six feet are patently untrue.'

Toy's blue eyes lost their sparkle. He shocked me then as he leaned back in his high-end office chair and propped his feet up on the hideously expensive desk which I had paid for out of my own pocket.

'This may come as a surprise, Magdalena, but you're not the only one to have had a difficult childhood. Some of us never even made it to five feet, eight inches. *Ever*. Toy is not my given name, if you'll recall. It's Terrence. However, when I went away to prep school, I was bullied for being named Terrence. It so happened that nicknames, like Toy, were considered cool. That's why I stuck with it. Since we're not going to get anywhere debating who's had it worse, the world's shortest giantess, or the world's tallest male toy, then I suggest we move on to topic number two.'

I gasped in indignation. 'Giantess?'

'*Shortest* giantess,' Toy said. This time he at least winked.

'In that case,' I said, 'I could see you as a Ken Doll. But not a GI-Joe figurine. Since we're a pacifist family that would have to be a GI-No.'

Toy nodded. 'Item two is the reason you caught me in my office. Sheriff Stodgewiggle just called to say that he was faxing me the toxicology report on Sarah Conway.' Then he slowly shook his head.

'Don't leave me in suspenders!' I cried. 'What does it say?'

Toy smiled ruefully. 'Suspenders? Our Magdalena, Hernia's unique gift to mankind. Forever cracking jokes, even at the most solemn moments.'

'Solemn my *butt*erscotch! This isn't Sarah Conway's funeral, Terrence, but it just might be a clue to helping me clear my name. I think you'd be a mite more understanding if you had to wear an orange jumpsuit for the rest of your life and perform your bodily functions in front of a cellmate named Bertha.'

'Terrence, huh? I certainly didn't expect that from you, Magdalena. Until now, you've been my best friend in Hernia, in Pennsylvania, in all of the north, as a matter of fact.'

Take it from me, the bottom is as low as one can get. Unless Little Jacob, my bouncing ball of joy, the fruit of my once barren womb, refused my embraces, I couldn't fall any lower. My first impulse was to blame Toy for the depth of my despondency, because I *hadn't* said anything inappropriate, and his sarcasm when calling me a 'unique gift to mankind' had been extremely hurtful.

I sat across Toy's desk from him, trying in vain to blink the tears back into my faded blue eyes. Nobody, except Little Jacob, gets to see Magdalena Portulacca cry. The first time that child comments on this very rare sight will be the last time he gets to witness it – unless we cry at the same time, and I can tell him that those are his tears, not mine. As for Toy, the good Southern boy, he was aghast at what he'd done. To bring a woman as old as your mama to tears in the South is tantamount to spitting on the graves of your ancestors and swearing allegiance to General Sherman, post-mortem.

Whether it was real, or I'd just imagined it, I couldn't stand to see the agony on the poor boy's face for very long. Therefore, it was me who capitulated.

'I'm sorry,' I said. 'I'm sorry for hurting you, and I'm sorry for being so flippant.'

'No, no,' Toy said. 'It's me who should be sorry; I was harder on you than you were on me. It's just that you're in a real pickle here, Magdalena, and it worries me.'

'What kind of pickle? Kosher dill, or sweet gherkin? Oops, hush my mouth.' I slapped my pie-hole, and none too gently, either.

Toy managed a grin. 'It's all right. You wouldn't be Magdalena without your flip lips. Like I said, I'm just tense right now.' He reached behind him, plucked a sheet of paper from the fax machine and handed it to me.

I scanned the report, and then reread it slowly. '*Aconite?*' I said after my third pass. 'From monkshood?'

'That's the problem,' Toy said. 'Monkshood grows wild everywhere in this part of the country. I'd be surprised if there wasn't some growing on your property. Or a dozen other places you could just as easily have gotten your hands on the stuff.'

'But then so could anyone else,' I said. 'Besides, I don't even know what the plant looks like. I have no idea which parts of the plant are poisonous. I don't know anything about it!'

Toy rubbed his jaw. 'Those are all good points. Unfortunately, the internet will be your enemy in this case. The prosecution can claim you researched poisonous plants and got the info from a website.' He turned to his computer and typed in a few words. 'It says here that the leaves, which are poisonous, have been used on salads to commit murder. The roots are even deadlier. They can be dried into a powder resembling powdered sugar. Then they can be put into medicine capsules, baked into cakes and pies, or just sprinkled on top of desserts.'

'Barbara!'

'Oh, come on, Magdalena, not you too. Don't tell me you're another of the Barbara Hostetler bashers.'

'What? No! I'm actually getting to be quite fond of her. The more gossip I hear against her, the more I like her. It's lonely being the only black sheep.

'My concern with Barbara is that when folks find out that monkshood can be so easily used in making desserts, then that will not only confirm their suspicions, but now she'll be arrested without further ado. Sheriff Stodgewiggle is a mite impulsive, as we both know. After all, you said that monkshood grows just about everywhere in the wild around here, and the Hostetler farm has a lot more acreage than my place.'

Toy shook his head. 'Man oh man, I can't figure you out. One minute you're worried about having to wear orange and using the crapper in public – pardon my crassness – and the next minute, you worry about the possibility of having someone else taking the fall. How many personalities reside in that beautiful head of yours, Magdalena?'

'What?' Had I just experienced a so-called mini-stroke? Had I hallucinated the 'b' word?

'Nothing,' Toy. 'I didn't say anything.'

'But you did,' I wanted to say. I almost said it. After all I was tired, and frightened, and lonely, and had less self-esteem than a piece of old roadkill. I wanted to be desired, to be flirted with, even if it was someone outside the bonds of marriage. But just flirtation, mind you. Why at that point, if the needle on my emotional compass went any lower, I might even appreciate the attentions of my potential cellmate Bertha.

As I sat there, in front of Toy's desk, pondering the depths of my moral depravity, the door to the police station burst open, and in flew my worst enemy.

TWENTY-EIGHT

'You!' she said, pointing a stubby finger so close to my right eye, it grazed my lashes. 'Vere veer you vhen your murder-in-law eez looking everyvere?'

'Somevere else?' I said.

Meanwhile, Toy had leaped to his feet and pulled up a third chair, which he placed a satisfactory distance from me. Ida, who'd used up a fair amount of energy on her grand entrance, plopped into the arms of the proffered chair, where she panted like a sheep dog on a hot summer's day. Clearly, it had been a mistake to line the burlap robes of her order with synthetic fabric that didn't breathe.

'Now this is an interesting development,' Toy said, as he regained his seat behind his desk. 'Is your murder-in-law one of your murder suspects?'

I stole a glance at the woman in question, who was still breathing so hard that she couldn't possibly hear our conversation.

'Well, I wouldn't put it past her. Nothing would make her happier than to have me permanently out of her son's life.'

Toy frowned. 'There's something about that old woman that reminds me of my grandma. And Ida Rosen – a.k.a. Mother Malaise – she's definitely eccentric, but a cold-blooded killer?'

Ida stopped panting. 'Old voman? Who you call old voman?'

'I love my grandma,' Toy said.

'Good,' Ida said. She'd no doubt been placated by his twinkling tanzanite eyes and was beginning to lose her accent. If I wanted to take advantage of her lapse into Standard English, I needed to hustle.

'Ida, dear,' I said, 'why have you been looking for me?'

'It's about that magazine,' she said. 'A Woman's Place.'

'I know that magazine,' Toy said. 'My grandmother used to read that. She was really upset when they stopped publishing it.'

'No, they didn't,' I said. 'Sarah Conway worked for A Woman's Place. She and the editor, Gordon Gaiters, were here to do a feature on Asian Sensations. That's why they were staying at my inn.'

'Yah, *und* no,' Ida said.

'What?' Toy and I said in unison.

Ida plucked imaginary strands of hair from the edges of her hood in what I took to be a triumphant gesture. She finally had a rapt audience besides her postulants and her adoring son.

'Yah to vhat dis vomen says about dem staying at my son's inn. But no to da magazine making feature story on dis one. Da magazine go kaput now for ten years, mebbe more.'

'It's my inn,' I said, 'not Gabe's. I built it from scratch twenty years ago with the money my parents left me after they were squished to death in the Allegheny Tunnel!'

'Mebbe,' Ida said. 'Or mebbe eets fake news.'

'There's no "mebbe" about it,' I said furiously. 'It's a fact!'

'Ladies, please,' Toy said. 'Now is not the time to argue about something that happened so long ago.'

I could hardly believe my ears. I wasn't 'arguing', I was 'declaring' a fact: one verifiable by obituaries, wills, and operating licenses. Anyone with an ounce of sense could see that Toy's foolish comment had the power of giving Ida's idiotic claim validity of a sort. A wise, mature woman would have just dropped the mature and moved on, whereas a woman with a need to set the record straight, and perhaps even up the ante, might have struck back.

'Check the county records,' I said. 'It's all there. And by the way, maybe Gabe isn't your son after all. I haven't seen his birth certificate. When we got married, he wouldn't show it to me, only to the marriage registrar. Why was that, do you think? Maybe he's the one who was born in Kenya. Gabriel Hussein Obama, maybe that's his real name.'

Ida turned the colour of beet borscht and began sputtering like an overfilled kettle on a hot stove. Toy, on the other hand, turned away from her in order to hide the battle that his facial muscles were fighting. To grin, or not to grin, that was the question. In the end, professionalism won out.

'Magdalena,' Toy said, 'when this pair checked into the inn, what sort of identification did they provide?'

'Uh – well – not much, I guess.'

'Are you saying that you didn't ask them for *any* identification?' Toy asked.

'Why should I have?' I said. 'They were driving a fancy-schmancy car with Missouri license plates. *A Woman's Place* is – was – published in Springfield, Missouri. Everybody knew that. So when they said who they were, should I have drawn their blood? Swabbed their cheeks for DNA samples?'

'Yah,' said Ida, her normal colour returning. 'I vould have.'

Toy winked at me. 'Don't you normally put a credit card number on file against possible damages, or maybe further expenses? I would imagine that you at least write down driver's license numbers.'

Now it was my turn to have flaming cheeks. 'Yes, to both things. Unfortunately, I was too focused on getting their stamp of approval for the restaurant. A lot of my wanting their approval was truly on behalf of Hortense Hemphopple, who is co-owner of Amish Sinsations. You see, Wanda's daughter has also been an innocent victim of her mother's crimes.

'Yet when I search the deepest recesses of my heart, for my purest motive, I have to confess that I have been driven to make a success of Asian Sinsations, in order to show Wanda Hemphopple that I could do it. That I could take the shambles of an inheritance that she left for her daughter and turn it into a so-called "cash cow". A veritable gold mine.'

'She make long sermon, yah?' said Ida. 'Like crazy woman.'

Toy stroked his chin. 'More like a passionate woman with a strong sense of justice. The kind of woman whom I admire.'

'*Oy gevalt*,' Ida said, as she squirmed her way off the chair. When she reached the door, she paused. 'Now I give Yiddish blessing to both you *meshuggah* peoples: *May you grow like an onion, with your head in the ground, and your feet in the air*.'

Toy waited until the door closed behind Ida. 'Didn't that seem more like a curse than a blessing?'

'Absolutely,' I said, 'unless one were a carrot, or a red beet. Possibly even a potato. So now what, Toy? What are we to think of these two characters who suckered me into thinking that they were doing a story on Asian Sensations? What could their motive have been in doing that?'

He thought a minute. 'Well, how flattered were you? Did you

give them a discounted rate on your astronomically overpriced, but very fine, establishment?'

My cheeks burned again. 'Actually, the moment Sarah Conway – may she rest in peace – told me the nature of their visit, I gushed all over them like Niagara Falls. Not only did I comp their stay at the inn, I instructed Agnes to comp their meals at Asian Sensations. So in the vernacular of my sister Susannah who, as you know, is wasting her life in our state prison system, these supposed guests from *A Women's Place* "made out like bandits".'

'They were freeloaders,' Toy said. 'I've heard about these sorts of con games before. They didn't ask for any money, did they? Like maybe investment in their magazine?'

'No,' I said emphatically.

'Or in that mammoth, watch-the-sinners-fry amusement park?'

'No, and you shouldn't judge. The sinners have their chance to repent and believe. Right now. It's on them if they don't.' Toy is one of those liberal Christians who buzzes right past the parts in the Bible that detail the excruciatingly painful consequences that will be in store for those folks who don't accept their free gift of salvation.

'Well,' Toy said, 'I'm not going to argue theology with a Mennonite woman who is twice my age. In any case, that theme park would be a nightmare for Hernia. It would irrevocably change its character.'

'I can't believe you said that, Toy.'

'I know it for a fact, Magdalena. My Aunt Billie Rae married a fellow from Pigeon Forge, Tennessee. They said it was hardly a blip on the highway until Dollywood came along—'

'No, Toy, I can't believe your reference to my age. That was rude!'

He looked confused. 'I was just stating a fact. It was more like a compliment, really. You're twice my age, so you know twice as much.'

I closed my eyes and clapped my hands over my ears. 'Lah, lah, lah, lah, lah, lah.'

When I finally grew up, and started acting my age again, I could see Toy shuffling papers on his desk. 'Hey, I've got to run,' he said. 'Dorcas Moser just whacked her husband over the head with a croquet mallet.'

'Not that I'm judging,' I said, 'but Fred Moser could use an extra whack, if you ask me. Sam says that Dorcas has come into Yoder's Corner Market twice with black eyes, and numerous times with bruises.'

'I am aware of that,' Toy said. 'And I have gone out there numerous times. For a small, dainty woman who moves like a cat, Dorcas Moser has got to be the clumsiest woman there is. But until Dorcas pressed charges, there was nothing that I could do.'

We stepped out onto the sidewalk where I let out a loud groan. '*Oy, gevalt!* Now it's going to be that *no-goodnik* husband of hers, Fred, who will be pressing charges.'

'We'll see, Magdalena. Maybe it was self-defence. Or just maybe Fred ran backwards into an upraised croquet mallet. Now go home. Relax. Climb into Big Bertha and take a long, hot soak. You'll feel better, I promise. My mother always does after she uses her tub – if you get my drift.'

Just as Toy opened the door to the police cruiser, which I paid for, by the way, something horrifying dawned on me. My knees started to buckle, and I had to grab a light post to keep from falling.

'You know about Big Bertha, with her thirty-two adjustable jets of water, that when you press against them, they begin to pulsate and throb—'

'Everyone in Hernia knows about her by now. Later.' The car door slammed and off he sped.

That left me at my wits' end. I take that back; given my current emotional condition, it was more like my half-wit's end.

TWENTY-NINE

S omeone with a whole wit might have taken Toy's advice and driven straight home. That is not what I did.

Instead, halfwit that I am, I got a bee in my bonnet, as the old saying goes, and decided that I had to talk to Hernia's biggest source of gossip in person. It was one thing to get it filtered through Cousin Sam, but when it came straight from the horse's mouth, then one could observe the slandering party's shifty eyes and shifting limbs. That's because gossipers invariably embellish their tales, which is a form of lying, and liars can be detected by their body language. I know that to be true because, alas, whilst I'm no good at embroidering cloth, I'm quite talented at embroidering the truth.

I was relieved to find my recent employee, Marigold Flanagan, hanging wet sheets on the clothesline out behind the cottage that she shares with her brother Isaiah. The siblings are in their mid-sixties. Isaiah is a retired postal worker. He has never been married and is what we locals call a 'confirmed bachelor'. Both Gabe and Toy, who hail from urban areas, have tried to convince me that this term is an old-fashioned way of saying gay. If that's true, then gay men have been around for generations, and are not the result of prayer having been taken out of our schools, as Pastor Diffledorf would have us believe.

One thing that could be said about Marigold Flanagan's sexuality, is that she doesn't seem to have any. She's not unattractive by any means. Nor is she pretty; she's merely pleasant to look at – then again, so is a Holstein cow. She lacks spark, if you get my point. I'm not into kinky bedroom stuff of any kind, believe you me, but even my refrigerator would make a more electrifying date (were I not married, of course).

'Mar-whaap,' I said, unable to avoid the corner of the soppy wet sheet she'd thrown over the line in my direction.

'Hey boss,' she said. 'What brings you out to the far side of town?' Are you looking for a place to lie low? There's a cute little Cape Cod number on Songbird Drive that's just been listed. Southern exposure, white picket fence, grape arbour, rose garden, and you wouldn't believe the price. But you probably didn't come here to talk to me about houses, so what gives?'

'Marigold. Do you suppose that we could go inside and have our little chat?'

'Our little chat? What did I do *now* to displease you?'

'Nothing, dear. May we go in?'

Marigold glanced around. I'm not a mind-reader, a pastime akin to fortune-telling, which everyone knows is a sin, but I was one hundred percent sure that Marigold was hoping that someone, anyone, would spot me talking to her before we went inside. If there is one thing that I've learned during my half century on this earth, it's that gossips enjoy being the victim of someone else's gossip. That's why they write gossip columns; the mean things they write give them a notoriety that they wouldn't have otherwise. Well, I knew a cure for her.

'Now that's a fine how-do-you-do,' I said, in a voice loud enough to put the hens off laying in three counties in either direction. 'Whatever happened to good manners in this town? The hospitality gene must have skipped a generation in your case. One would think that a world traveller such as Marigold Flanagan, who ran off to—'

'OK, you win,' she growled.

Marigold led me inside her two-story, Victorian house, with the gingerbread wooden trim on the wraparound porch, and I trotted behind expectantly. Very few Hernia natives have travelled abroad, and Marigold is the only one whom I know of who has lived on the subcontinent of India. I didn't have any definitive ideas of what I might see – but I did rather hope to see a stuffed Bengal tiger and either a mural, or a model, of the Taj Mahal. And of course, there simply must be the smell of exotic incense, preferably sandalwood. Oh, yes, I almost forgot, somewhere there needed to be a yellow silk umbrella with tiny tassels all around it, and a pair of white ceramic elephants. I really didn't care about the floor covering, but everyone knows that Kashmiri silk carpets are exquisite, and that just the right shades of blue and orange would really set off the stuffed tiger and white ceramic elephants. That's all I have to say about my expectations.

Imagine my disappointment when I followed Marigold into a living room that had bare walls, painted white, and the floor was covered in a cheap brown carpet that most builders would be ashamed to install in starter homes. There was no chandelier, not even a light fixture, just a single light bulb dangling from a chord in the middle of the room. Being vertically-enhanced, as I am, I was able to read the wattage, and was not surprised to see that it read sixty.

As for the furniture, at least I can say that all the pieces matched. All three aluminium folding lawn chairs appeared to be relatively new. Perhaps there was a fourth chair somewhere that had the extension that supported one's legs, and which could be made to lie flat. It occurred to me that Marigold was using it as a bed in another part of the two-story house.

'Don't judge me,' Marigold said.

'I'm not,' I said, 'I'm merely observing.'

'Ha. Everyone knows that Magdalena Yoder does nothing but judge and criticize. Just last week, Heidi Bachman's sister told me about the time you criticized Heidi's skirt to her face. You said it was so short and such a bright shade of red, that somewhere a clown wanted his nose back.'

'But that was thirty-five years ago! I was a sophomore in high school.'

'That just proves that people never change. By the way, neither has Heidi Bachman, according to Prudence Gabbard. You know that Heidi moved to Pittsburgh years ago, but Prudence ran into her last week at a mall there. Prudence says that Heidi still dresses like a slut, but now those legs have so many spider veins that they're a virtual road map. You don't need a GPS to find your way to San Jose, just take Heidi – or one of her legs – with you.'

'That's mean,' I said.

'Oh, if you think that's mean, you should hear what Griselda Bowman said about Holly Jansen. If Holly didn't shave both of her—'

'I'm sure that you have to shave both of yours as well, dear,' I said, although I had no idea what she was about to say. Could it have been her arms? Her big toes? Because I'd made it part of my spiritual discipline not to listen to gossip, I would never find out what it was that poor Holly Jansen felt compelled to shave – in pairs – and wondering about it might just keep me up at nights.

'Marigold,' I said, 'may I finally sit. My legs are certainly not getting any younger.'

Marigold snorted softly. 'Sure, why not? Would you like something to drink?'

I briefly considered the wisdom of a positive response, given her decorating scheme. 'A glass of sky juice would be lovely. But skip the addition of frozen precipitation.'

'One glass of water, without ice, coming up,' she said. She was back in two shakes of a lamb's tail with the beverage. To my astonishment, the glass was sparkling clean.

'Thank you, dear,' I said, as I turned the glass, unable to get over how clean it was.

'You think that you're so clever, don't you?' Marigold said. 'Sky juice, indeed.'

'I try not to think that, because "pride goes before destruction, and a haughty spirit before a fall". Proverbs 16:18.'

'Touché,' Marigold said.

'Whatever,' I said, quoting Alison that time. 'One thing I do think is that you are a very observant woman. You have a keen eye for detail, and an exceptional memory. Why, if I had any sort of imagination, I might even speculate that you were with the C.I.A., and that's the real reason you dropped everything and took off for India.'

'Ha, now that's a laugh.'

'Is it? Maybe you didn't even go to India; maybe you went to Moscow instead. That would certainly explain the lack of exotic furnishings in your house.'

Marigold popped to her feet. 'You are amazingly rude! Magdalena, you need to leave. Now!'

'No, I need to hush my mouth and get down to brass tacks. Did you think that Sarah Conway was Barbara Hostetler's mother?'

Marigold resumed sitting. 'Do you have mad cow disease?'

'What?' I cried in disbelief. 'No!'

'Who the heck is Sarah Conway? And how should I know what Barbara Hostetler's mother looks like? Doesn't she live somewhere in the Midwest?'

I rolled my inner set of eyeballs. 'Sarah Conway was a giantess of a woman, who clomped about on mile-high heels in the company of an old man who claimed to be the editor of a monthly magazine called *A Woman's Place*. Miss Conway was murdered the day before yesterday. She was poisoned. Anyway, *that's* who she was.'

'Oh, *her.*'

I wanted to grab her with my invisible set of hands and shake her. 'Yes, her. So, did you see a resemblance? Do you think that she could possibly have been Barbara's mother?'

Marigold laughed. 'Why in the world would an Amish woman be hanging out with Wanda Hemphopple's uncle? That man is a real sleaze-bag, from what I've heard. Did you know he's already run through the fortunes of three women, and somehow found ways to dump them all? Penniless too! And for the record, Magdalena, the woman who came in with Wanda's Uncle Stanislaus looked nothing like Barbara. That woman wasn't any taller than I am, and I'm five feet eight. She was wearing a pair of killer heels, though – no pun intended.'

'I'm sure there wasn't.'

'And no matter what people say about Barbara being pushy and overbearing, she's not half as obnoxious as you are.'

'Why, I never!' I leaped to my feet. 'This interrogation is over.'

'I knew it,' Marigold growled. 'Out, out, out!'

'Well done,' I said. 'Brava! Three "outs". A landscaper once told me that one should always plant trees and shrubs in group-ings of threes. Supposedly, it's more pleasant to the eye. I see that you've applied that same theory in using just three chairs in your captivating, minimalist decorating scheme.'

'Wait a minute,' Marigold said. 'Do you really like it, or are you just being snarky?'

'On a scale of one to ten, which number of truth would you like, with ten being the one God would approve of?'

Marigold thought for a moment. 'Hmm. Seven.'

'I believe that your approach to decorating could be used as a metaphor for the judicious use of the earth's raw materials, of good stewardship. Why spend our resources on useless knick-knacks, trinkets, and thingamajigs?'

'Magdalena,' Marigold said, her eyes wide with surprise, 'you're not as mean-spirited as I thought.'

'Oh, then think harder, dear. I won't disappoint.' I stepped outside but turned right around. 'Wait a minute. You're positive that the old man who accompanied the deceased – a.k.a. Sarah Conway – is Wanda Hemphopple's uncle?'

'I'd stake my life on the fact that he's Stanislaus Sissleswitzer. Uncle Stan, that's what we kids called him then. He lived next door to us, and of course after Wanda's parents died, he took them in. I remember that my dad, Uncle Stan and the man across the street all played golf together on Sundays over by Bedford, which really ticked my mom off. Then one day the man across the street caught his wife and Uncle Stan in flagrante delicto, in the garage of all places. That guy grabbed one of Uncle Stan's putters and really let Uncle Stan have it. He smashed his cheek bone, and nearly blinded him in the left eye.'

'What about the wife?'

'He didn't do anything to her – in public. Except yell at her to get on home. Where she stayed. And I mean *stayed*, because we almost never saw her outside again.'

'I'm not trying to be argumentative, Marigold,' I said, choosing my words carefully, 'but I've lived in Hernia my entire life, and I've never heard that story. I'm not saying that it didn't happen. I'm just saying that it's odd that no one has talked about it.'

Marigold's smile barely registered. 'Maybe's that because my dad drove Uncle Stanislaus all the way into Pittsburgh himself that night, to one of the big hospitals there to keep the affair quiet. We kids were told that if we breathed a word to anyone we'd be spanked so hard that we wouldn't have butts to sit on, and that Santa Claus would lose our address.'

'What about Wanda and her brothers? Why did they stay quiet?'

'Well, for one thing, they were all grown up by then, except for Wanda, who'd just started college. That's where she was that night. Uncle Stan never came home from Pittsburgh, so wherever he ended up, I guess that's where Wanda went on school vacations. Anyway, you saw the divot in his face, didn't you?'

'I did. Thank you, Marigold, you've been very illuminating.'

'You're welcome.'

There is a saying that goes: my mama didn't raise no fool. Unfortunately, I have acted in a foolhardy manner too many times to count. After I was safely ensconced within the protective shell of my automobile, I dialled Hortense Hemphopple, Wanda's daughter. The dear girl answered on the first ring.

'Miss Yoder! I've been on pins and needles, waiting for you to call. I haven't been able to leave my dorm for two days because the press is camped outside. Every time I open the door someone shouts a question about what it's like to be in business with a cold-blooded killer. Don't worry, Miss Yoder, I know that you're not a murderer, not with a face like yours. But now I've been holed up in here so long that they're starting to think that I have something to hide – you know, like guilt by assassination.'

'That's guilt by *association*, dear. Hortense, I realize that you're in a pickle, but I need you to answer a very important question for me. Do you have an Uncle Stan?'

'I'm sorry, Miss Yoder, I don't mean to be disrespectful to an adult, but I'm stuck here in my dorm, reporters are insinuating that I'm at least covering for you in that woman's murder, and I want to know what's going to happen to the restaurant. I don't see what my Uncle Stan has to do with this at all.'

'So you *do* have an Uncle Stan?'

'Yes, but—'

'Who looks like he was kicked by a horse?' I said.

'It was a golf club that got him,' Hortense said.

'Excuse me, dear,' I said, as I dashed back to the privacy of my car to call the family landline back at The PennDutch Inn. While Freni's Amish faith forbids her from owning her own telephone, it permits her to use her employer's. In my absence, I require that she answers it if at all possible. The times when she can't are usually when Alison is hogging the line.

This time I got the answering machine, which pointed the finger at Alison again. I wasn't about to leave a message, however, for fear that Gordon Gaiters might overhear it. Perhaps I should have called Toy, but he had needlessly embarrassed me by mentioning Big Bertha, and I wasn't in the mood to see him just then. Besides, I had twice as much life experience, which should be roughly equivalent to a gun – at least in my current state of mind. So, I said a short prayer and shifted into foolhardy mode.

THIRTY

There's an old joke that goes something like this: what goes 'clop, clop, clop – bang – clop, clop, clop?' The answer: an Amish drive-by shooting. Due to the frequent presence of horse drawn buggies along Main Street, the speed limit is just ten miles per hour. Due to my elevated stress level, folks with keen hearing may have heard my worst swear words escape my lips, as I tried to take the shortest route home. If so, they would have heard: clop, clop, clop – 'Ding, dang, dong!' – clop, cop, clop.

It was as if a representative of every Amish family in the community had chosen that morning to mosey along Main Street, and in an organized fashion as well. Their nineteenth-century conveyances were blocking the street in either direction. Tooting the horn at horses is forbidden and trust me when I say that it would have been a rather foolish thing to do in any case. Therefore, I was forced to weave at a crawl around quite a few creatures, including the horses. When I was finally out of town, and across the narrow bridge that spanned Slave Creek, I sinned grievously by pressing the pedal to the metal and drove twice the legal speed limit of forty-five miles per hour.

Drivers who text, or even just talk, on their phones are my pet peeve. How dare they risk the lives of my children? That said, the lives of my children now lay in the hands of Wanda's murderer of an Uncle Stanislaus. In for a penny, in for a pound – of sin, that is. Theoretically, or so I've been told, each human life is as valuable as the next. At least in the sight of God. President, king, pope, or murderer, He loves us all the same. Well, try selling that argument to a mother at a time like this.

Finally, Alison picked up our landline on the first ring. 'Don't eat anything!' I screamed. 'Gordon Gaiters poisoned Sarah Conway.'

'*What?*'

'Tell Freni. And call the sheriff.'

'Mom—'

'Just do what I say, dear. Now!'

'Mom, shut up and listen!'

I listened.

'Mr Gaiters took Little Jacob with him.'

I screeched to a rocking, thumping halt in the nearest unpaved driveway. 'Why? Where?'

Alison's next words were interspersed with sobs. 'When he . . . came down stairs . . . he . . . seemed like ner . . . vous that you . . . were gone so long, and when Freni told him that you had . . . gone to see Auntie Agnes, that's when he took Little Jacob. Mom, he said he had your permission.'

I had to will my heart out of my throat in order to speak. 'When was that?'

'Just a few minutes ago. Mom, I tried to call you, but your phone was busy.'

'Right. Alison, call the sheriff. The number's by the phone. Remember, nobody eats.' I hung up.

Whereas previously I'd been merely driving at breakneck speeds, this time I literally flew the back roads to Agnes's place. Then again, as I've stated before, I am prone to bouts of enhanced imagination. Whatever the case may be, I hurtled to a stop less than a meter from the back of Gordon Gaiters' luxury sedan.

The evil man was already halfway to the house with my precious son tucked under one arm like a squealing piglet. Like a piglet, Little Jacob was stark naked. Before my mind could jump to the worst conclusion possible, I discovered the reason for my baby's bare bottom. On the ground, just in front of the car, lay the fullest nappy I'd ever seen. Apparently, Gordon Gaiters had decided that his hostage's dirty *tushie* was the lesser of two evils.

Wanda's monstrous uncle was not surprised to see me. If anything, he was relieved to have me at his mercy. He set my squirming son on the ground, but he kept a tight grip on one of the child's wrists. In the other hand he held a pistol which he pointed directly at Jacob's head.

'So,' he said, 'by now you've figured it all out.'

'But maybe I haven't,' I said, stalling for time. 'What is it that I supposedly know?'

'Don't give me that,' he said, his eyes flashing. 'You know that I'm Wanda's uncle.'

'That's preposterous,' I said. 'How am I supposed to know that?'

'Because you gave Hernia's biggest gossip the third degree, and when she told you that she recognized me as Wanda's uncle, you immediately called my grand-niece Hortense to crosscheck her story.'

'Well, fiddle-dee-dee,' I said. 'That Marigold ought to get a medal. Not only is she Hernia's biggest gossip, but she's the fastest gossip this side of the mighty Mississippi. So, I guess both Marigold and Hortense were in on your murderous scheme too, huh?'

'What? No! You leave my precious niece out of it. Hortense didn't know anything about the revenge scheme Wanda cooked up.'

'Well, it didn't work, did it, you nincompoop? You murdered the wrong person; you killed your wife instead.'

That startled him enough to make his gun hand shake. I had to be more careful.

'How did you know that Karen was my wife?'

'I heard you say so the morning after she died.'

'She wasn't supposed to be the victim,' he said. 'But . . . she was stubborn – like you. She had certain principles.'

'Those are terrible qualities for a woman to have,' I said. I strained to hear the sound of police sirens in the distance, but *nada*. Other than our two voices, and the perceived pounding of my pulse in my ears, the earth was quiet. Even Little Jacob was uncharacteristically mute, staring at me with eyes the size of dinner plates. Trusting eyes. While he waited for his mama to finish gabbing with this strange man, he was doing due diligence on his thumb.

'I'm not some capricious, run-of-the-mill hitman,' Gordon Gaiters said. 'I don't knock people off on a whim, or because Wanda bears you a grudge. What you don't know is that she's promised me a fortune if I ruined your life.'

'Ruined my life *how*?' I said. Even the hairs on my toes started to curl.

Gordon Gaiters chuckled. 'Hmm, let me see. How about if I killed someone near and dear to you?'

'You harm one hair on my baby's head,' I spat, 'and I'll tear you limb from limb!' Believe me, no truer words were ever spoken by a pacifist Mennonite woman.

'Ha! Wanda said you were a first-class idiot. I wouldn't hurt a child; I have five kids, and ten grandchildren of my own. I only took your son with me as a hostage, in order to keep them other two back at the inn from calling the police.'

'Then who *was* your intended victim?' I said.

'Your husband. Your so-called Babester. Wanda says that it's sickening the way the two of you love each other.'

'Is that so?' I said. 'Well then, maybe she can tell me where to find him, because right now I don't have a clue.'

Stanislaus Sissleswitzer grinned triumphantly. 'Bingo! That's what I thought. Since I'm not into killing kiddies, why not go for the bestie. You and Agnes Miller are as tight as ticks, Wanda says.'

'Tell Wanda to eat a bowl of stewed ticks for lunch,' I said. 'I despise Agnes Miller. Go ahead and perform your dastardly deed for all I care, but kindly return the fruit of my loins to my loving arms post haste.'

'Magdalena Yoder, has anyone ever told you that you're nuts?'

'Is that a "no" then?'

'If I were you, Magdalena, I would shut up now, before this little fellow loses his mommy.'

By then I was quite positive that Gordon Gaiters was not the praying man that he had originally posed as. He was about as dastardly as they came. I was also quite positive that he had the upper hand, and that if I expected to get out of yet another jam, I needed to pray for guidance, to pray that the Lord would open my eyes to the agencies of help, and the tools of assistance around me.

'Ask, and you shall receive,' it says in the Bible, and that is so true. Why, once I asked for help in defeating a murderess who was a veritable giantess, and the Lord directed me to use my brassiere as a slingshot. I managed to take down that big broad with a single stone. Anyway, as I cast about for divine answers, I noticed that Agnes's goat, Gruff, had finally broken out of his enclosure again, and was standing stock-still, a mere ten feet from Gordon Gaiters, and was staring intently at him. I had originally been sceptical when Agnes claimed that Gruff had been neutered, and now by the way that Gruff regarded Gordon Gaiters, I was almost certain that he was not. That old goat had sniffed out Gordon Gaiters' maleness and regarded him as a rival. All he needed was a little provocation to deliver this monstrous man into my hands.

By its all-pervasive odour, I was also quite aware of my little tyke's loaded nappy lying virtually at my feet. Believe me, I am not an uncouth woman, given to fighting dirty. I would never consider flinging a filthy diaper at another human being. No siree, and Bob's your uncle. Not when the Good Lord had provided a rogue goat with three-foot curved horns. Not to mention – and I say this with all modesty – Yours Truly, had been a pretty ding, dang, dong good softball pitcher, both in high school, and in college. 'Goad the goat,' a voice in my head said.

'Stanislaus Sissleswitzer,' I hissed, 'you city-slicker sissy. Let go of that child and fight like a man.' In addition to sounding like a bag of angry snakes, I presented my fists, as I supposed a boxer might, and shuffled my feet a couple of times.

Gordon Gaiters – a.k.a. Stanislaus – was so taken aback by my behaviour, that he actually did let go of Little Jacob's chubby hand. The sudden release of his hand startled my son, who had not yet mastered the skill of walking indoors on a smooth surface, much less on stony ground. Little Jacob sat abruptly with a yelp, before toppling backward and just barely striking his head on the ground. My poor boy screamed, but I knew instinctively that it wasn't physical pain that caused him to cry out; it was fear that brought on this outburst. On the plus side, my son's reaction distracted Stanislaus Sissleswitzer long enough for me to scoop up the soiled diaper, and throw it underhand, like I'd thrown many a softball.

Again, I don't mean to toot my own horn excessively, but I have been blessed with a wicked aim. The diaper landed right where I had intended, which was directly between Billy Goat Gruff's eyes. Yes, I pitied the poor, innocent animal, for he had done nothing to deserve such shabby treatment. But let us focus on the pluses. Gruff was instantly enraged by the incident. He lowered his head and charged Stanislaus Sissleswitzer with so much force that the old man went sailing into a tangle of black-berry vines and rose bushes. Meanwhile Little Jacob had righted himself and was chortling.

'Guff, guff,' he said. Gruff, who knew my son quite well, ambled over, and even allowed Little Jacob to pull himself up by tugging on the goat's beard.

Or so I imagine, because I was too busy locating Stanislaus Sissleswitzer's gun. When I had his firearm gripped tightly in my right hand, and my body was shielding Little Jacob, I tried calling Toy again. Before his phone rang the first time, I heard two sets of sirens approaching down Agnes's long lane.

THIRTY-ONE

I interviewed Wanda Hemphopple at the women's penitentiary three months after her uncle was arrested. Ironically, it was the same prison where my sister Susannah was serving time for aiding and abetting the convicted mass murderer, Melvin Stoltzfus. Incidentally, somehow the superbly inept Melvin managed to escape, and ever since then he has devoted his life to thinking of ways to kill me.

There were things that I needed to say to the woman who hated me so much that she would try to kill me and my daughter, and then after being sent to prison, she arranged to have my husband murdered. In order to get Wanda to agree to my visit, I had to appeal to her vanity. It was actually the Babester who came up with the idea for how to pull that off. Yes, if you must know, the two of us were back together by then, but put a pin in that for now, as the saying goes these days.

Gabe told me that one of his favourite television programs had been a series titled *Breaking Bad*, in which a teacher turned to a life of crime to pay for his medical bills. The astonishing thing to me is that the teacher, who manufactured drugs, was not portrayed as a villain, but as a quasi-sympathetic, multi-dimensional man. Apparently, this show was very popular, and it and its actors won many awards. The ways of this world are often beyond my ken, nonetheless this bizarre plot, as I understood it, gave me the idea that eventually got me to interview Wanda.

To make a long story short, a nationally syndicated, hour-long television show that airs in prime time pounced on the polished idea I finally presented to them. When I got a message through to Wanda that the show would be called *Breaking Even More Bad*, she pounced on my offer like a chicken on a June bug. There would be a guest host, a somewhat reluctant man named Bradley Heist (the regular host declined the assignment), but he would be restricted to introducing us, and jump into our conversation only if we found ourselves at a loss for words. But fat chance of that happening.

I refused to be made over for television. Why put on yet another false face? I am who I am: big pores, busted capillaries, crow's feet and all. But when Wanda shuffled into the room, accompanied by two armed guards, I was stunned by her appearance. It wasn't just that she was minus her signature French roll hair style (into which I had once dropped the hotdog), but she was now sporting a man's buzz cut. Plus, she'd gone completely grey. But what made the biggest difference was that the once skinny Wanda Hemphopple had put on at least thirty pounds. Although I must say that the colour orange did not flatter her in the least, because she looked more like a scowling pumpkin than the Wanda that I once knew.

It is now my opinion that TV hosts love the sound of their own voices. I have no doubt that Bradley would have been happy to fill the entire hour talking about himself, and how he had overcome his fear of conducting the interview in a penitentiary housing dangerous female psychopaths. Unfortunately for Bradley, one of those dangerous female psychopaths was not about to have her screen time squandered on someone other than herself, or the object of her loathing.

'Yada, yada, yada,' she said to Bradley, cutting him off in mid-sentence. 'Wrap it up, will you? I thought the name of this show was *Breaking Even More Bad*, not *Bedtime with Bradley*.'

Although we were surrounded by camera crew and guards, Bradley shrank back in his chair and nodded to me as if to say that it was my turn to speak. Being quite familiar with Wanda's personality, I knew that her bite was worse than her bark, murder plotting aside. If I wanted to say my piece, and perchance ask a few questions, I needed to jump right in without a second's delay.

'Wanda, dear,' I said, 'you look absolutely stunning.'

'Oh, cut the bull-bleep,' she said.

I feel that I must state here that, sadly, prison had coarsened even Wanda's language, if one can imagine such a thing. Therefore, although I have attempted to provide a careful transcription of a portion of that video, I took the liberty of omitting obscene words and references to bodily functions.

'I mean it,' I said. 'I was stunned when you walked into the room.'

'Because I'm fat now?'

'Pshaw, I say. A nice full face fills out all the wrinkles. Just look at skinny old me. I've been thinking of tucking business cards into all my creases. Then I won't lose them, and I just might start a new fashion trend.'

'You've never been funny, Magdalena – just pathetic.'

'Very true,' I said, although I disagreed strongly. 'You, however, have been mean and angry for as long as I've known you, which is my entire life. Why is that?'

'Why do you think?' Wanda pounded on the metal table that separated us, her handcuffs clanking loudly. It made for good TV, I'm sure, because the camera moved in closer.

'Don't tell me it's because you've had a hard life,' I said. 'I've had a hard life too, but I've never killed anyone.'

'You don't have the nerve!'

'Wanda, the Bible says that I'm supposed to forgive you for trying to kill Alison and me. Maybe even Gabriel. But I just can't. I pray and pray, but my thoughts hit a wall. A wall of hate. I'm supposed to love you, but instead, I hate you. I don't want to hate you, Wanda. I sincerely believe that I could break through this wall if you asked for my forgiveness.'

Wanda snorted with derision. '*Me?* Ask forgiveness from *you*? No bleeping way!'

'Please, dear. I need to move on.'

'Ha. Look at you – begging for something from me. That's ironic as heck, considering you always had everything, and I never had anything.'

'What did I have that you never had?' As soon as those words left my mouth, I wanted to catch them and stuff them back in.

'For starters, Miss Money Bags, while I was working my butt off running a grease pit, married to a broken-down, flat-footed lush who could take out half of North Korea with his morning breath, you were married to a handsome Jewish doctor who was so fertile that he knocked you up when your womb was as dry as the Gobi Desert. Those were your words, by the way, not mine.'

'So, you wanted Gabe?'

'What woman in her right mind wouldn't? That man's a hunk.'

'But you tried to kill him!'

Wanda smiled wickedly. 'Precisely. Stan was supposed to make sure that Gabe got the dessert with the poison on it, but at the last moment he decided he hated his shrew of a wife more than he loved his niece. Can you imagine that?'

'Frankly, yes.'

'Hmph! Anyway, if I can't have Gabe, then you shouldn't have him either.'

My mouth opened so wide, that if I'd been wearing dentures, they'd have clattered out onto the metal table that separated us. What *chutzpah*! Wanda was like the man who killed his parents, and then begged the court for mercy because he was an orphan.

'Let me remind you, *dear*,' I said, 'that you are still married to that broken-down, flat-footed lush.'

She shrugged. 'If he's still alive. No one's seen hide nor hair of him since I tried to put you six feet under. By the way, I heard from a new inmate that right after you were cleared of the charges of murdering Uncle Stanislaus's wife, Aunt Sissy Sue Sissleswitzer, your hunky husband went missing for a while. Is that true?'

'Heavens to Betsey,' I said in a moment of unguarded admiration for my own forthcoming cleverness. 'Does Sissy Sue Sissleswitzer sometimes sip seltzer thru a straw?'

'What?'

'Never mind. Yes, my hunky studmuffin did take a few days off to – uh – sightsee. As you know full well, he's not from this part of the country, and there is a lot more for him to see. Anyway, shortly after he returned, I arranged for his older sister, Cheryl, a retired psychiatrist who was living in Connecticut, to pay us a visit, and you'll never guess what she did.'

Wanda grinned maliciously. 'She arranged to have you committed to an insane asylum. Am I right?'

I grinned back – in the Cheshire cat sort of way. 'Cheryl and I actually get along well. We see eye to eye on most of the big issues, like closing down the Convent of Perpetual Apathy, and integrating their mother back into a normal civilian life. To that end, Cheryl, who instantly fell in love with Hernia, bought an Arts and Crafts bungalow on Primrose Lane for herself and Ida

– now the *former* Mother Malaise. Oh, by the way, I snapped up a cute little Cape Cod on Songbird Drive and gave it to Agnes, because she was feeling really lonely out there on Doc's old farm.'

'And how did she take that?' Wanda said.

'Not well at first,' I said. 'I don't understand why it's so much easier to give, than to receive.'

'You're so dense, Magdalena,' Wanda said. 'Don't you see that some people are actually embarrassed by charity? There are even some crackpots who'd rather not get expensive gifts, because they don't want to feel beholden. But not me. I'd always be happy to take your money.'

'I have no doubt that you would. Anyway, as the elder child, you wouldn't believe the power that Cheryl Rosen wields in that family. The convent property has already been sold, and the former nuns have, for the most part, been happily resituated. As for the Babester and I – well, he and his precious ma are in therapy, courtesy of Cheryl, and in time I am sure that Gabe and I shall be swinging from the chandeliers once more. Metaphorically, of course. Once, in the literal sense, was enough.'

'Boring,' Wanda said, and made a show of yawning into the camera.

'Oh, stop that,' I said. 'If you keep being mean to me, who's going to speak up on your behalf, should you ever be eligible for parole?'

Wanda appeared gobsmacked. 'You would do that for me?'

'No, of course not. Not the way things stand now. But in twenty years, when I've mellowed so much that my heart starts to ooze out though my pores, well then who knows? But in the meantime, you would do well to treat me, and my family, a tad nicer.'

Wanda clanked her handcuffs on the table again, much to the distress of the TV sound man. 'Magdalena, did you come here just to lecture me?'

'No. I wanted answers, and you have been surprisingly forth-coming. But I do have one more question. What was in it for your uncle? That was a huge risk for him, and now he's going to be spending the rest of his life behind bars.'

'Hold your horses, Magdalena. Uncle Stanislaus still hasn't gone to trial.'

As I have a strong team of horses, I had to pull back hard on the reins. 'That's true. But he has been charged with murder and kidnapping.'

'Yeah, kidnapping your kid's nappy,' a crew member interjected.

Laughter erupted in the room. Even Wanda smiled.

'How is Hortense?' she said, her tone remarkably softer.

I was startled. 'What do you mean? Has something happened to her?'

'How should I know?' Wanda said, churlish again. 'That ungrateful child hasn't come to see me since my uncle paid you that little visit.'

Keep holding those horses, I reminded myself. 'Hortense is doing fine, Wanda. We had to sell the restaurant—'

'I see the news, dummy. You guys sold the restaurant to a developer who's having it torn down, supposedly because no one in their right mind would ever eat at a place where there could still be traces of poison lurking in crevices. How stupid is that? And I heard what a big hero you were by giving my daughter every penny of your share in that place so that she can continue with her studies. What are you trying to do, supplant yourself as her mother?'

'Absolutely not. I care about her, that's all. She's been given a lot to deal with—'

Wanda leaped to her feet with great force, obviously forgetting that her cuffs encircled a steel bar bolted to the table. I heard her grunt with pain even as two guards lunged at her, and a third guard hustled me out of the interview room.

Although that was the end of my participation in *Breaking Even More Bad,* and it had lasted only minutes, Bradley and his crew managed to flesh it out with commentary and commercials to fill up an entire hour. It aired six months after it was filmed and garnered ridiculously high ratings.

By then I'd worried myself into a tizzy over Gabe's possible reaction to telling America that his big sister could control him and had him in therapy. Although worrying is never just a waste of energy, because it consumes calories, this time I needn't have worried, because it seemed that Gabe heard only two words from the interview: hunky and studmuffin. Everyone in the United States who sank to the level of watching *Breaking Even More Bad* now knew that Gabriel Rosen of Hernia, Pennsylvania was a hunky studmuffin.

EPILOGUE

A year and two days after Agnes's billy goat, Gruff, foiled my baby's kidnapping, we citizens of Hernia celebrated a new holiday. As mayor of our village, I unilaterally declared that the third Saturday in August would henceforth be known as Billy Goat Gruff Day. The holiday would be celebrated by games for both children and adults, kite flying, a public concert, a ventriloquist show, a picnic up on Stucky Ridge, and especially, the Billy Goat Gruff parade.

The parade, to my knowledge, was the only one of its kind in the country – maybe the world, and we have maintained that tradition. Gruff, who now lives on my farm now that Agnes lives in town, is the star of the parade. For three years in a row he has pulled a cart carrying Miss Hernia across the bridge that spans Slave Creek. On the village side of the creek perhaps a hundred little children dressed as trolls eagerly await Miss Hernia's arrival. When Gruff crosses a chalk finishing line, I bring down a chequered flag and adults hand out sweets and treats of many sorts to any child who asks them to bleat like a goat.

Of course, this festival has a handful of detractors, but critical people will be with us always, just like poor. One minister claims that male goats are used in satanic rituals, and that our end-of-summer party is evocative of one. Who knew? A few have blamed their children's poor dental hygiene on me personally. The overwhelming majority of residents who dwell within the village itself have voiced their support, and participation has grown each year.

This last Billy Goat Gruff Day, boy, oh boy, did I mess up! In an effort to be more politically correct, I substituted Hernia Citizen of the Year for Miss Hernia, as our parade honouree. As in the case of the former title winner, the latter was to be chosen by popular vote.

Tell me, how was I to know that my mother-in-law's former

cult members were still so devoted to her that they would campaign so mightily on her behalf? What did these ladies (and Agnes's two nude uncles) expect us to celebrate about Ida, one might ask? The measly fact that Billy Goat Gruff Day was her eighty-fifth birthday! What a pitiful excuse, if you ask me, considering the fact that thanks to clean living (no smoking, drinking, or sex – while standing), many folks in Hernia have lived to surpass the century mark. But rules are rules, and I had to abide by the ones that I had come up with in hopes that someday I too might be pulled in a goat cart to face a throng of cheering people – albeit most of them children eager for a 'sugar fix'.

As mayor of Hernia it fell to me to count the votes that put my mother-in-law in the goat cart. Let it be known that for much of the time I executed my duties in a mature manner. Meanwhile, as Ida Rosen gloated, I bit my tongue so hard and so many times that it resembled a spoon for straining soup. Honestly, only a handful of disparaging comments made it all the way past the gateway of my lips. If that still sounds like an awful lot of sin to issue forth from the mouth of a good Christian woman, you must understand the amount of stress that I was under.

Bar none, that was the worst weekend of my life, and I have lived through some real doozies. Not only did my entire family come within a hair's breadth of pushing up daisies, so to speak, but several of Hernia's most venerable citizens perished at the hands of a serial killer. Maybe by next year I will have recovered enough to where I can piece together my thoughts, and even share details of that day, in a book entitled *Mean and Shellfish*.

BARBARA HOSTETLER'S DEATH BY CHOCOLATE

(A flourless favourite at Amish Sinsations)

List of ingredients

9 ounces of 70% (or higher) dark chocolate, finely chopped
9 ounces of unsalted butter
1 ½ cups of granulated sugar
7 large eggs
1 teaspoon pure vanilla extract
¼ teaspoon pure almond extract
Powdered sugar

Directions

1. Grease and line a 9 inch spring-form pan with parchment paper. Then grease the parchment paper.
2. Melt the chocolate and butter together in a microwave-safe bowl until the chocolate is almost completely melted. Stir until smooth. Stir in the sugar, then let the mixture cool a few minutes. Now with your pinkie take one little swipe of batter off the stirring utensil and lick it. You know you wanted to.
3. After the mixture has cooled slightly, add the eggs one at a time, fully incorporating each before adding the next, until all have been added. By now the batter should be thick and glossy. It is time to thoroughly stir in both extracts.
4. Pour the batter into the prepared pan and bake for 30–35 minutes until the torte still jiggles slightly in the middle. Remove from the oven before it is completely set. Begin checking at 30 minutes to make sure that the torte does

not overbake. Let it cool in the pan for ten minutes and then unmould. Dust with powdered sugar.

WARNING: This torte is large enough to provide six generous servings to polite guests. However, for some mysterious reason, when one eats it alone, the number of servings shrinks to 'one'.